FOR CYNTHIA

Moss

M.P. KEANE

Moss

Stories from the Edge of Nature

Marc Peter Keane

marc peter keane • mpk books
isbn: 978-0692411797
illustrations by author

Many thanks to

Cary Joseph and Mimi Millard

for their careful readings

and many insights

A
WORD
TO
BEGIN

A Word to Begin

John called out to Linda who was still rummaging in the tent.

A night to remember, sweets. God, look at all those stars. Just look at them all.

He turned in a slow circle, arms spread to catch the starlight falling like soft rain, and goggled at infinity. In all his years in New York City, the city that never sleeps, he had never really seen a night sky. But here, a couple hundred miles from New Delhi where the closest thing to humanity was the ruins of an ancient fort, the air was crystalline and the sky riddled with points of light. A host of stars, a plague of galaxies and, lurking in the darkness between them, more stars and galaxies. A universe endlessly embroidered with itself.

John's heart raced, suddenly overwhelmed by the immensity of it all. By the measureless unknown. By his own miniscule presence. And, at the same time, by a sense of somehow being a part of it all. The distant galaxies, the sandy ground beneath his feet, in some way connected to him. Or through him. He took a deep breath. His skin crackled. Heartbeats flecked the hairs in his inner ear. The fatty smell of grilled meat on his moustache reminded him, inexplicably, of the all-consuming sex he and Linda had had not ten minutes before. They had eaten. They had screwed.

A tiny red light, high high up in the night sky, winked its way into view.

Oh no. That's not right, he muttered as if being woken from an exquisite dream, the airplane an intolerable intrusion on his private epiphany.

Five minutes Linda, he shouted. We'll start in five.

A piece of sappy wood in the campfire exploded like a firecracker, sending a plume of sparks heavenward, a wave of red-hot motes rising to join the winking plane.

Three hundred yards downwind, a male tiger lay slung in the branches of an acacia tree. It woke at the sound of the crackling fire, lifted its enormous head, and sniffed at the air. With a marvelously expansive yawn, it extended the claws of one paw and scratched slowly at nothing, then set its head back down and closed its eyes. A moment passed. A pink tongue slinked like a cobra from its lips, licked across its nose and retreated.

Using his cellphone as a flashlight, John looked over his notes one more time. He had a keynote speech to give at a conference when he got back stateside and Linda had agreed to sit through a trial run. Be his guinea pig. He had procrastinated writing it, but he was flying out the next day and time had run out. Linda stepped out of the tent, buttoning her shorts. Her hair was insanely tousled. She glanced at him and broke into a broad grin, yanked her shirt down and ducked back into the tent. A moment later she came back out with her Browning in hand and a leather cartridge belt slung across her chest. She dragged a canvas folding chair over to where John was waiting and dropped herself into it, legs splayed, amused at the theater of it all. He looked her over – sunburnt, grinning, shirt half open, rifle laid across her thighs. He rolled up his notes and pointed at the gun.

Is that for me?

Better be good mate, she retorted in a thick Australian accent. I gotta thing for gazelle and academic wankers.

She stroked the wooden gunstock like it was a cat on her lap. John grinned back.

OK. That's good. Build a little tension. I like that.

He thought of the plush auditorium in Harrison Hall at his college, where he would be delivering the speech in a week. Of the university audience that would undoubtedly want to eat him alive for what he had to say. He thought he'd take the girl with the gun any day.

The tiger woke again and slipped to the ground with the fluidity of poured water. Five hundred pounds dropping without a sound and flowing through the kair trees, head slung low as it passed beneath the crazy tangle of their leafless branches.

There were no infinite galaxies no distant cities no intrusion by winking airplanes no thoughts of what fate would hold for next week. Only the scent of burnt meat.

John stuffed his notes in his back pocket and began his speech, taking a sideways step as if he were moving out from behind the podium. He liked to speak without notes, free-thinking, free-moving. Prowling the stage like a cat.

I've been asked to say a word to begin.

He paused. Looked over at Linda the way he would glance at his audience.

So here's the word… Nature.

Another pause.

What, in fact, does that word mean?

He shrugged, palms up in the classic pantomime of a question.

Nature? Well, OK, there are two ways to look at it. Let's call them Nature with a capital N, he drew a large N in the air with his index finger, and nature with a lower-case n, again drawing a letter in the air to clarify the point. The first one is easy. The definition of Nature, he drew a capital N again, which is the true and correct and all-encompassing meaning of the word, is in fact very simple. Here it is. Nature… is everything.

He turned around, throwing a grin back over his shoulder. On the back of his T-shirt were printed the words, Everything is Natural. Linda thought it somehow lewd but couldn't quite put her finger on why. John turned back to face her. The fire trickled its restless light across his face. Linda took in his slim frame and trim blonde beard and thought him handsome, if a little urbane. Everything is natural? she wondered. The bullet she had put through a gazelle's heart that morning, the jeep that had brought her there, the GPS that had guided the jeep, the satellite that guided the GPS, the Atlas rocket that had launched the satellite? She looked at him doubtfully. He looked at her dolefully. Skin bronzed, legs scratched, armpits unshaved, stroking her rifle. He wished that somehow he could be the kind of man she would want. Forever. He smiled at the thought and continued with his talk.

All things that exist are either in the process of building up out of some component parts or breaking back down into those component parts. Or, more likely, doing both at the same time. The sum-total of all those infinitesimal and nearly infinite interactions is what we call Nature. So what are these interactions? Well they can be chemical and de-structive, like a sheet of iron breaking down as it oxidizes into rust. Or they can be chemical and con-structive, like stalactites and stalagmites growing in a cave from minerals that leach out of dripping groundwater. The interactions can also be physical, the way riverwater carves a canyon out of solid rock, or the way that same river deposits what it carved further downstream to form a delta and, eventually, more solid rock. Chemical, physical, he reiterated, his fingers counting one two. Or, they can be electromagnetic, like the way plants absorb sunlight and cool the day or desert rocks release absorbed sunlight and warm the night. His hand swept to suggest the rocks around them. And… the interactions can be between various life forms, or between non-living things, or some complex combination of the two. Imagine sunlight falling on an old pine tree, energizing it over the centuries as its roots slowly split open fissures in a granite cliff, allowing rain water to enter and ice to form, which weathers the stone into mineral powder that in turn is absorbed by the old pine. The sun, the pine, the rain, the rock, all inextricably interconnected. If you add up every single one of these processes and interactions, the totality of that unfathomably large and complexly interrelated system is Nature.

John paused and looked at Linda. He knew he would pause at this point in his talk to make sure that his next point was heard, the point for which he was sure he would be torn to shreds. He continued.

And, since Nature is everything, in truth, there isn't anything that is un-natural.

And once more to drive home the point.

There isn't *anything* that is unnatural. He swiveled to show off the back of his T-shirt again. Everything is Natural.

Fifty yards from the camp, the tiger slowed, sniffed the air and lay down. Along with the scent of burnt meat and human sweat was a trace of some other burning. It was a smell that gave pause. Deep in the recesses of the tiger's brain was a sound like thunder and a sudden fiery pain. What manner of animal smelled that way had never become known to the tiger but it had stung him once, on a clear day, out of nowhere on the open grassland. Whatever it was, it was a small and speedy creature and had a bite to reckon with. The tiger waited, panting, unsure of its next move.

Typically we think of Nature as being something that exists only on our planet. You have the flora and fauna, all the oceans and the mountains, clouds and wind, all of that, but surely Nature is more of a universal condition. Something that goes well beyond the boundaries of the Earth. Consider this. He looked at Linda as he would at the audience in a week, picking out one or two people and engaging them as if he were sitting in their living room.

Surely everyone will agree that the sun is part of Earth's Nature. After all, what would Nature here be like without it? Can you imagine Earth's Nature without the sun? No. Of course not. John began to pace like a caged tiger back and forth across his sandy stage. And, clearly the moon is part of Earth's Nature as well, its gravity being the source of the tides and thus the tidelands and all the vast complexities of Nature found there. And, he said pointing a finger skyward as an exclamation point, just to suggest another possibility, certainly the meteors that have collided with this planet over the eons, and by doing so have utterly reshaped life on this planet – I'm thinking of course of the Chicxulub impact among others – surely those meteors are also part of Earth's Nature. So, even if you find the connection between Nature on the Earth and what is happening on the other side of the universe too tenuous to be treated seriously, if the relationship between a butterfly fluttering through this clear night air and the orbit of a comet in a solar system 50 billion light-years away seems too slim to be contemplated seriously – although even those minute connections and many smaller still are, in fact, real, as my esteemed colleagues well know – surely you will agree that Earth's Nature involves more than what is earth-bound. Nature…the real Nature… is everything.

Within the tiger, the weight of hunger pushed from its mind the sharp smell of the little biter, and it raised itself to a crouch, shoulders rolling as it stalked forward in slow motion. It was tracking the sound of an animal, the distinct looping chirp of a human. The sound merged with the scent of sweat. Through the fine braches of the kair trees a small fire glimmered, silhouetting an erect figure. A solitary male. Nothing to fear. The human's eyes could not be seen. It could be taken by surprise.

Linda watched John pace as he spoke, the quintessential East Coast scholar. She had been in his habitat. The dim-lit watering holes crowded with students, the wood-paneled rooms in weathered stone halls that spoke of entitlement, the shelves heavy with books in his home library, snifters of brandy swirled before a pleasantly tidy fire. It was nice for a week, tedious for two. Never did it stir her like hearing a distant guttural roar shiver the air as night closed in on Rajasthan. She knew she would never take him up on his well-meant offer to come to the States and live together. It wasn't in her genes. The campfire flared and illuminated a few of the high branches behind John. There was an unexpected prickling on her neck. She sniffed the air, sat up in her chair, suddenly intent, and slipped a finger alongside the trigger guard.

The other way to look at nature, nature written with a small n, he said finger-painting the letter, is different in that it is conceptual not actual. A human concept. This way of thinking about what nature is begins with a newborn baby feeling its way into the world, tasting and touching everything to make sense of what it finds. In the process of all its poking and sucking and sniffing and listening, at some point it becomes aware of not only the world around it, but of itself, and in the moment it realizes I am Me, it also realizes I am not That. I am *not* That. Long before this baby can be struck with the realization that it is actually made up of the stuff of the world, and is in fact only a small and integral part of the world, long before that concept can be realized, if ever it is, the idea that it is independent from the world takes hold.

The tiger inched forward to the point where three hard bounds would take it to its prey. Striking distance. Bats clicked and fluttered above it, snagging insects out of the air. They went unnoticed. There was a soft hiss as a rat snake eased itself out of the way. That too was nothing. The entirety of the tiger's being was focused on what stood directly in front of it, not thirty feet away. Rump muscles twitched. Great paws kneaded holes in the soft ground.

After that, the baby's worldview is all about degrees of separation. I am Me, not You. I am part of this Family, not that one. I am of this tribe, this village, this nation, this creed, and not of those. I am human, not anything else. And it is within this last divisive thought – the difference between human and non-human – that nature with a little n is born. When you think that way, nature is defined as that which is untouched by humans, and what humans create is, conversely, considered to be artificial or un-natural.

The tiger sprang. Bound one. The tips of the kair trees above it shivered. Linda saw the movement and jumped to her feet, planting the butt of the rifle into her shoulder, head falling to sight down the barrel. It was pointed straight toward John. His face went blank. Is this a joke? Was I that bad?

The branches behind him cracked as the tiger exploded out of them. 20 feet away. Bound two. John was directly between Linda and the tiger. She stepped to the right to sight past him, tracking the tiger's forehead. 10 feet away. Bound three. The tiger's body lifted, forelegs spreading wide, claws fully extended, rising up above John like a dark wave. Linda sighted over John's shoulder. A huge pink tongue in a wide-open mouth. Firelit fangs. She pulled the trigger. Click! The impotent gasp of an empty chamber.

Bloody hell! An instant memory of cleaning the gun, unexpected sex, not reloading.

The tiger's mouth closed around the back of John's neck, 500 pounds hurtling into him at 30 miles an hour. They slammed to the ground as one. Linda yanked the bolt open. The tiger bit, John's neck snapped, audibly, his head cocking sideways at an impossible angle. Linda snatched a round from her belt and smacked it into the chamber. The tiger hunkered down over its prey, growling protectively. She locked and aimed. The forehead of the enormous animal loomed in her sights. Its eyes magnetic in the firelight, iridescent green rimmed with black and white stripes, the skin above its snout rippling heavily in a snarl. Linda fingered the trigger. On John's back the words Everything is Nat… disappeared into a ragged bloody semicircle. She pulled up, breathed, reset the rifle on her shoulder, leaned into it again, cheek pressed to the smooth walnut stock and sighted on the tiger's forehead. Another breath. The mute bullet screamed to be released. A million years of evolution drummed its song of terror and vengeance through the folds of her cortex. The tiger turned and jumped, disappearing into the kair trees as smoothly and wholly as if it had never been there. Linda fired. The bullet whistled emptily into the night. A single cut twig fluttered to the ground. Another tiny red light winked its way up from the horizon into the universe.

MOSS

Moss

Exhausted from another long day at the office, Yamamoto tilted toward the subway tracks. He swayed on uncertain legs, staring past the twin strokes of polished steel that would take him home. In the wall beyond the tracks, a drainpipe wept a long teardrop-shaped stain. He saw it every day. There was never any running water, just a slow undetectable seeping. Around the edges of the stain, a halo of moss had begun to grow. Slightly mounded, velvety, iridescently green. Yamamoto looked to it each evening for reassurance.

He turned his head slowly, as if it was taking the very last of his strength to move, and peered down the long black tunnel for its promise of home. His hat was crumpled and set off to the side of his head. One shoulder drooped under the weight of an overstuffed briefcase. He straightened his back against the irrevocable pull of gravity, took a breath and sank back down, deflating with a quiet hiss. In the depths of the tunnel there was first a weak light, then a distant rumbling. The air pressure in the station rose slightly, stirring the crowd behind him. The train slipped out of the tunnel behind its electric hum and Yamamoto shuffled forward with the others. The doors opened and he was swept inside by the weight of the rush-hour crowd, caught once more in the great tidal flow that brought him to work each morning and dragged him back home in the evenings.

In the middle of the packed subway car he took hold of one of the chrome poles to anchor himself and braced for the long ride to the end of the line, leaning his head against the pole. It smelled of disinfectant. He stared blankly at the back of the person in front of him. The train hummed as it accelerated and an hour later he stepped out at his home station. Ploddingly, he made his way to the prefectural housing complex where he rented a small apartment. Along the way he took note of his special places. He did this every day, twice a day. On the way to work, and on the way home. A pilgrim making the rounds of hidden shrines. A crack in the sidewalk outside the station, the joints of an old stone wall, a rectangle of soil beneath a roadside tree, a cedar-shingle roof above a wooden gate, the empty lot at the back entry to his apartments. Each of these places luxuriant with moss. He would look and know that, somehow, it would all be all right.

me again. i've been thinkin'. i've got this idea. back up… ok, you never left komatsu so it's different for you, but listen takeshi, tokyo's nothing like that. it's all built up. i mean all of it. skyscrapers, highways. concrete everywhere you look. anyway, even so, if you look closely… and you know me, that's what i do, right? look closely. remember how you used to say that? i'm getting off the point. you used to say that too, right? well anyway, if you look carefully you'll see the world fighting to get back in. it's still small right now but it's everywhere. in all the cracks and crevices and unwatched places. and it starts with moss.

Yamamoto worked for Kawakita Kaikei Kansa Kabushiki-gaisha, Japan's largest auditing and accounting firm, better known as 4K. Their main office occupied the 23rd floor of the brand new Sun Garden building in Roppongi. There were three work areas on the floor, each one a large undivided space filled with rows of desks that were grouped into sections around a manager's desk. Yamamoto sat at one end of the room near a window. His desk was enclosed by pale-grey file cabinets, and he sat camouflaged in his pale-grey suit. In a company where new employees wore brown uniforms, junior workers wore blue suits, middle management wore black, and senior directors wore grey, it would have seemed to an outsider that he was in a position of authority, but in fact his grey clothes were allowed simply because of his age and the number of years he had worked for 4K. His spot by the window was not a position prized for its view but a place meant to keep him out of the way. He was one of the madogiwa-zoku, the window-seat tribe, people at large companies who are no longer needed but can't be fired and so are banished to a seat by the window and given busy work. The only thing about Yamamoto's little corner of 4K that was in any way special, that was in any way unique when compared to the other hundreds of desks at 4K, was what he kept on the front corner. A little mound of moss on a rough ceramic tray, which he cared for like a pet. Behind his back, his co-workers called him Kokemaro, Master Moss.

It was a Tuesday but it could have been any day. They were, for Yamamoto, all alike. He was looking over some of the company's actuarial tables on his computer, something he did every day for one reason or another. It was fundamental to his work: to review and put in order, to lend structure to the unstructured, to find errata and resolve. The long lists of text and numerical data he worked with were laid out in extensive spreadsheets, in some cases hundreds of pages long. Perhaps it was overwork, perhaps it was the fluorescent lights in the new office, but as he scrolled through the seemingly endless columns of data, the numbers flowing across the screen began to soften and blur, morphing into an image of falling water. Mist fell from the screen and floated across his keyboard, settling lightly on his fingertips. He stayed lost in those streaming images until the database scrolled to the end and stopped abruptly. He blinked, straightened up, cleared his throat, looked at the papers on his desk, touching each one in turn, and eventually remembered what it was he had been doing.

Oh, of course. Toyonaka Fabricating. Export taxes. Right.

He stood up to clear his head. Took a spritzer from a cabinet and sprayed a little water on the moss. He touched it, letting his palm rest gently on the cool surface. The wind came off the sea, the smell of the surf and oak leaves electric in his flaring nostrils. His chest lifted and fell in a sigh. Then he sat back down and started scrolling through the data again, his head gradually leaning forward as he wandered off once more, the numbers spilling down the screen as glittering mist.

these new lights they've got are easy to read by, sure, i'll give them that, but man are they tiring. you know how the mid-summer sun makes you squint and shrink away? that's what these things do to me. i'm not kidding. it's not at all like those warm incandescent desk lamps we used to have at the old place, oh they were so nice, or the candlelight at the blue lady. definitely not the blue lady. it's not like twilight, or dawn, or a full moon rising, or any of those other magic hours. it's so, i don't know, antiseptic. sure. ok. it's easier to read by but it wears me down takeshi. my eyes hurt when i get home. i feel tired all the time.

oh, one bit of bright news. bright news? weird news? something that happened this morning.... you're never gonna believe this.... OK... so i get off the elevator and i notice that there're these two new girls at the reception desk. they look like twins. real perky dressed in uniforms little ascots around their necks, you know the type. they bow to me from behind the desk and say ohayou gozaimasu real cheery-like and everything. they even call me mr. yamamoto like they know me. i mean i've never met them before. so i go over to say hello and they look up at me and smile these weird little broken smiles, eyes flat, heads kind of jerky and then it hits me. they're not people. they're androids. who makes those things? omron? no, simionics. yeah, that's right. what do they call them? not androids. what is it? oh yeah. actroids. that's it. the twins are a couple of simionics actroids.

it's kinda creepy. they look, i don't know, well like the real thing. i mean up close, anyone can tell, but from across the room? who would know?

Yamamoto felt a shadow and looked up from the email he was typing. A woman was standing in front of his desk. She carried herself with an air of severity. Trim black jacket, black knee-length skirt, a pressed white blouse. Body tense, face stern. Her hair pulled back into a tight bun. The spray she used to keep it in place gave her a faintly chemical smell.

I'm Arai, she said introducing herself curtly. I just transferred from the Berlin office.

Yamamoto stood up and addressed her as Section Chief. He had heard she would be coming. So… this is Section Chief Arai, he mused. He'd met managerial women like her before. Always dressed perfectly, never smiling, completely unforgiving of errors. In others. In themselves. Trying harder than their male counterparts in every way in order to prove themselves. She had a large packet of papers in her arms, which she dropped on his desk with a hollow thud. The side of the packet was bristling with small colored tabs. When she spoke, her words were clipped.

Yamamoto, we've come across multiple anomalies in this database from Pacific Metals. I'd like you to look it over.

Of course, replied Yamamoto, looking first at the moss, then back to his boss.

By tomorrow, she added. I have a meeting with the directors in the morning.

Yes, of course. Understood, he replied solemnly. By tomorrow.

He noticed her glance at the moss on his desk like she didn't quite understand what it was. That was a common reaction.

He patted the top of the thick packet knowing he would have to stay well into the night to get the work done by the next morning. He was used to it. Everyone at 4K put the company's needs first and, like them, he was a company man. Besides, he had never married – he lived alone. There was really nothing to go home to. He didn't have many years left until retirement. Why rock the boat now? He bowed to Section Chief Arai and stole another quick look at her as she walked away.

She was at least twenty years his junior. He was not flirting, he had no aspirations in that regard, but he couldn't help thinking that in another place (somewhere outside the company), in another light (the candles at the Blue Lady, perhaps?), in something other than that business suit (a soft dress, he imagined), she would be strikingly beautiful. As it was here in the office, under those harsh fluorescent lights, in her rigid jacket, she seemed cold and distant.

Pacific Metals. Tomorrow morning. Thank you Section Chief, he muttered quietly to himself in a voice that straddled resignation and gratitude. Yes, it was yet one more weary task pawned off on him, but it was his task. Something he actually did well. And in an odd way it made him feel like he was still a part of things.

It was two in the morning before he finished the work of proofing all the data. He rubbed the crumbs from his eyes and stretched out his shoulders, knocking on the knots in his neck with his little fists. He would have finished earlier but his mind kept slipping. As the other employees left to go home and the office became quieter, the remaining small sounds began to soften, overlapping with his drifting thoughts. The low hiss of the fans cooling the computers became soft breezes through the oak forest at Komatsu-mura. The rising and falling whir of the floor polisher being used by the evening crew in the lobby became the hiss of waves across a pebble beach.

As Yamamoto rose to leave, he noticed Section Chief Arai sitting in the unlit kitchenette. What's she doing here this late? he thought. She was sitting at the table, not moving, just staring straight ahead into the darkness. He cocked his head, puzzled, then yawned.

Home to bed, Yamamoto, he said out loud to no one.

As he walked into the elevator lobby, the twins called out to him.

Thanks for all your hard work today, Mr. Yamamoto.

He ignored them, pressed the elevator button and stepped back to wait. His foot tapped the floor. He looked back at the twins, sitting there patiently behind the reception desk, unflaggingly perky even at that ungodly hour, looking at him with those strangely believable eyes. Every so often, one or the other would blink or their head would tilt almost imperceptibly. Some programmer's idea of spontaneity. Yamamoto walked closer to them, looking back and forth between their eyes, wondering what it meant for them to be looking at him.

I mean, he thought, they can't really "see" me? Right?

He looked them over, moving around a little to see how much their heads and eyes would follow him. I wonder how much these guys know? he thought and blurted out the first thing that came to mind.

What day is it? he said walking over to the reception desk.

Wednesday, April 9th, Mr. Yamamoto, one chirped without a moment's pause. Two forty-three AM.

Yamamoto glanced at his watch to check.

OK. What's the capital of the United States.

Washington DC, the other said, matter of factly.

The square root of one thousand seven hundred and sixty four.

Forty two, Mr. Yamamoto.

How many square meters in a shaku? he asked, throwing in a bit of Japanese arcana. There was a slight pause. Their eyes seemed to go blank, bodies unmoving. One tilted her head, then answered.

A shaku is a linear measurement equivalent to ten sun or about three point zero three centimeters. It is not a measurement of area. Did you by any chance mean how many square meters in a tsubo?

OK. OK. Not bad, he chuckled. They must be tapped into a pretty big database, he thought. They've got more than just greeting protocols.

Mmm, how about this. Munja munja nerrraaww thwappp? his voice lifting at the end to make the nonsense into a question. He knew it was wrong of him to do that. He knew he was overtired. A grin lighted on the edges of his mouth.

There was a pause. The twins remained motionless for a moment. Then their eyes blinked in unison and one asked, I'm sorry could you repeat that? I didn't quite catch…

I said, ucha nagrapulitch mwwaahhh ppsst fst? His tongue pressed between his teeth as a smile spread uncontrollably across his lips.

I'm sorry, could you repeat…

No, no. No thanks. That's OK, he waved his hand at them laughing, then as if remembering, added, Oh yeah. OK. Here's something. He leaned in closer, confidentially. What can you tell me about Section Chief Arai?

The twins stopped moving. Yamamoto thought he saw them flash a quick look at each other.

Section Chief Arai is still here. Shall I call her? asked one.

The elevator chimed behind him and he heard the doors slide open.

No. No, no, that's OK. Goin' home, he said as he backed up into the elevator.

Thanks for all your hard work today, Mr. Yamamoto, the twins chirped together from across the lobby. As the elevator doors slid closed, he saw Section Chief Arai back in the work room. She was standing next to his desk, staring at the moss tray. The doors closed and the elevator dropped to the basement-level subway connection without any sense of motion.

been thinking about 4k. about the twins. we're all like them aren't we? i mean us, here at 4k. not you takeshi. out on your boat wherever you are. sunburnt skin, wind in your hair. what? me jealous? no way.

no i mean all of us little corporate robots. this complete capitulation to order and control we all submit to. so, here's a thought. what if that spiral into self-restraint we go through comes from an actual physical change? what if people actually metamorphose in places like this, our bodies absorbing the plastics of the furniture and carpets, the metal dust of file cabinets, the environmental hormones leaching from the vinyl wall coverings, the volatile solvents of the glues and the carpet cleansers, the chemicals in the energy drinks and instant foods we live on, absorbing all of that atom by atom, our cells coating in microscopic layers of synthetic materials, until one day we wake to find that we are no longer who we used to be?

Yamamoto's love for moss had begun when he was a child in Komatsu-mura. He and Takeshi would play in the forest above the cove, lazing on the mossy ground for hours, toes and fingers wriggling in the soft bedding. But his interest took a new direction when he read an article in the magazine Shizen Hogo, Nature Conservation, that was called Bioremediation

Through Primitive Organisms. The article described the projects of various scientists around the world who were testing the possibility of cleansing polluted soils. He read with growing interest about a woman in Louisiana who was using bacteria to devour oil spills in the Gulf of Mexico, a long-haired couple in Oregon who had fungi that could soak up radioactive waste, and a team of scientists in Denmark who were studying lichens and mosses as pioneer species to populate a new planet. There was a full-page photo – a close-up of the fine star pattern of moss stems holding tiny droplets of water. Reflected in each drop of water was a fish-eye view of the forest and the sky above it. The article went on about how water filtering through thick beds of moss would be purified as it seeped through. After reading that, Yamamoto had decided to make himself a little moss tray for his desk, something to keep nearby in the hope that it would somehow cleanse him.

The housing complex that Yamamoto lived in had been built thirty years before. Five-story concrete buildings that were arranged in rows like barracks. Time had not been kind. The walls were streaked with dark stains, the sandy lots between the buildings empty of plants except for some twisted sycamore trees that had been pruned back heavily each year, leaving stubby branches with gnarled fists at the ends. And yet, even there in the middle of that desolate place – one that had been bulldozed, hardened with concrete retaining walls, filled with truckloads of gravely soil, covered with asphalt roads and paths – even there, in its shadowed corners, there was moss. Buckets of it.

Yamamoto had pried some off the ground carefully with his fingertips. Back at his apartment, he had placed the mound of moss on a ceramic tray, a little dome of soft green. He had taken it to work the next day and set it on his desk. At first, people didn't notice it. Then they couldn't stop noticing it. They paused as they passed, reaching out as if compelled, touching it lightly the way they might stroke the back of the bronze sacred cows at the entries to shrines. Yamamoto watched their fingers touch the moss, sensing the transfer taking place, the reverse osmosis drawing chemicals out of their skin.

After seeing Section Chief Arai touch the moss that evening, he decided to make a second tray for her. She accepted it without a smile, not grudgingly but matter-of-factly. Put it there, she said nodding at the corner of her desk. The next day he made another for the kitchenette and one for the lounge. He scavenged more moss from around his apartment building and kept making his little trays, bringing them to 4K one or two at a time, until every desk on the 23rd floor had its own mossy filter. He became a new presence in the company where he had worked all his life, circulating the floor twice each day with a spritzer in hand like some modern-day shaman dispensing sacred waters, attending each tray in turn, making sure they all stayed moist and green. He would carefully shield the papers on each desk with a clear plastic file folder, then blow his gentle rain, a pale-grey cloud floating through the valleys of administration.

it's like a new lease on life, takeshi. this moss stuff. it's incredible how it purifies and cleans the world. a chemical sponge. and if you look at it close up, if you look really really close, it's like a microcosm of the world, a miniature diorama of a forest. i look around 4k during the day and catch people just staring at their trays, entranced, looking deeper and deeper into the fine green stems. it's like they're remembering something but it's not a memory from their childhood, it's not a place they've ever been to, it's an older forest they're looking at, more ancient even than the virgin woods that covered tokyo after the glaciers receded. it's the primordial forest that our ancestors walked out of a million years ago, wandering hesitantly out into the sunlight, their backs straining as they struggled to stand upright. it's a memory that has been woven into the very fiber of our bodies, one so old and so long-buried beneath the sediment of culture that it struggles to rise, raw and unformed like a cicada larva squiggling up through layers of dirt to awaken from its long sleep. i know they're feeling this 'cause i do. every day i look into the moss, peering way down into that prehistoric world, and hear faint echoes, strange bird-like cries, the terrible snarling of huge cats, primates chattering wildly. the last a sound that seems at times almost understandable.

Yamamoto often took his lunch break later than everyone else. As a member of the window-seat tribe, taking lunch out of sync wasn't a problem for the company. Section Chief Arai never said anything about it. One morning, he arranged the papers on his desk and took the elevator down to the outdoor food court. Like the building, the elevator was clad entirely in glass, a movable box sliding up and down a slit in the outer wall. From the higher floors, the view of Tokyo was breathtaking. The openness made many people dizzy but Yamamoto liked it. He stood right next to the outer wall, caught by a child-like thrill at seeing the world change perspectives.

When the doors closed, a young woman's voice chimed from a hidden speaker, Shita ni mairimasu, tobira shimarimasu. Then in English, Going down, the doors are closing. It was a high voice, pretty, but monotone. Yamamoto couldn't tell if it was a stilted recording or a computer generated voice. The elevator descended silently and he looked out at the city, imagining instead the ancient forest that had been there after the last ice age. Tall camphor trees with enormous trunks. Herds of spotted deer loping gracefully through drifts of ferns. Stepping lightly across streambeds thick with moss.

Yamamoto bought a sandwich and hot coffee. At that hour hardly anyone was around so he had his pick of seats. He chose a table under the camphor trees, off to the side of the courtyard. Using his pocket knife, he sliced the plastic covering off his sandwich box and began to eat, taking sips of hot coffee in between bites. The trees cast lace shadows on the courtyard and on the beds of grass bamboo that wrapped around the outside. Nice bamboo, he thought, remembering how his mother used to wrap rice-balls in their long, pointed leaves. The rice had tasted a little like the forest that way. He sniffed at his sandwich. Maybe it smelled a little of the plastic wrapping. Maybe not.

When he was finished eating Yamamoto sat back in the chair and closed his eyes, enjoying the soft light, a slight rustling of wind in the leaves, and the chirping of sparrows in the branches. He felt his weariness lift and slipped into a day dream. Takeshi and he were stretched out on the mossy ground in the forest above Komatsu-mura. They had a couple of cigarettes and were trying them for the first time. The sunlight was falling in patterns through the oak trees and there were sparrows chirping, flitting from branch to branch.

Of course. That's it, he thought. That's what reminded me. The sparrows.

It came back so clearly: the light, the softly twittering birds. The two of them posing for each other, cigarettes slung from their mouths like gangsters, coughing, laughing at themselves. A warm breeze came off the ocean carrying the sound of fishermen hauling their nets and the forlorn greeting of a passing freighter.

Yamamoto opened his eyes and looked through the trees for the sparrows. He could hear them but couldn't find them. They would chirp and he would think he had heard exactly where they were, but when he looked there was nothing. He stood up and walked around the courtyard slowly, cocking his head this way and that. As he passed one of the beds of grass bamboo, the sound became much clearer and he realized that the birds were not up in the trees after all. They were down below, hidden beneath the low bamboo. That's why he hadn't been able to see them. He walked slowly, homing in on the sound. He parted the dense leaves but found only a rock. A rock with holes in it. And still the birds went on chirping. He nudged the rock. It was unexpectedly light. It tipped it over and he found a small speaker underneath. His face flushed in embarrassed confusion and he looked around to see if anyone had noticed him.

As he put the speaker-rock back into place he noticed that at the bottom of each cluster of grass bamboo there was a small metal stake. He ruffled the leaves in his hand, bent one in two. Tore off a piece. Plastic. Very realistic, but plastic, each cluster of leaves held in place by a small iron stake. He went around the courtyard pushing the grass bamboo to the side in several places but it was the same everywhere. He coughed his disbelief, put his hands on his hips and stared. It was so real looking. And the birds! He turned slowly in one spot looking around at the courtyard. What else, he thought? He walked up to one of the large camphor trees that shaded the courtyard and tapped on the bark with his fist, leaning in to listen. Pounded once more a little harder. It sounded firm. He took out his knife and dug a little divot out of the bark. It was moist, a crescent of green showing in the inner bark.

Well, he sighed to himself. At least this is real enough.

He wondered if anyone else knew about the birds and the bamboo. He thought of himself as being a very attentive person. He saw tiny things, details, little things that were out of place. That's why he was good at his work, finding small errors in mounds of data. Most people just couldn't see things, didn't have his kind of perspicacity. They would walk by these things all their lives and not notice them. How could I have not seen this before? he wondered, flicking the knife closed and slipping it into his pocket.

That evening, Yamamoto worked late on another thick folder of data that Section Chief Arai had left with him, checking paper records against digital data. When he had finished he said goodbye to the twins and took the glass elevator to the ground floor, floating down through the nightlights of Roppongi. The elevator voice called out the floors in English flatly, Twen-ty-two, twen-ty-one, twen-ty. When the door opened, he found the food court empty and quiet. He paused for a moment, looking around. Listening. Making certain that no one else was there. The sparrows were no longer chirping. He walked around the outside of the courtyard where the beds of grass bamboo were and every few steps, he reached down and very casually, very calmly, pulled out a clump of the fake bamboo, metal stake and all, and placed it on one of the round dining tables, out in plain sight.

Tomorrow, people will see. They should know.

He went home and that night dreamt of Takeshi and the forest, of wading hip-deep in the clear pool below the waterfall with small brown fish darting past their ankles, lying on beds of moss to dry off, running down the path through the lace-shadows of tall trees, the sea in the distance a glimmering sheet of hammered light.

takeshi. what is wrong with the world? i mean what the hell are we doing? tokyo, ugh, i would so like to go back to komatsu. maybe i'll do that at golden week. take a few extra days. haven't taken sick time or a vacation in years. i think i could get some time off. if section chief arai will let me. you're wondering why am i moaning like this, right? well… there was this fake bamboo. yeah and these fake sparrows and… it's like everything's fake. fake fake fake.

i know. i'm not making any sense. maybe, it's just, you know… i'm tired. no. it's not that. it's just… you remember we used to walk through the forest and you could smell it, pick up a handful of the pine needles and just inhale them, you remember that? ohhh man that smell. and the light on the ocean and swimming under the waterfall, so cold and clear. i don't know. takeshi i just miss all that so much.

i miss you man. i miss you.

The next day, Yamamoto sat at his desk leafing through a stack of papers, stamping a red-ink seal with his name at the bottom of each page after checking the content. He thought he'd be OK. No matter how tired he got, he trusted his eyes, their uncanny ability to pick out mistakes. After many years on the job, he knew that no matter how distantly his mind wandered, if an irregularity passed in front of his eyes, he would be called back from his ramblings and awaken, staring at the error as clearly as if it had been flagged.

A faint chemical smell woke him to the fact that Section Chief Arai was looking down at him. Here it comes, he thought. Another late night. He brushed off a yawn as he stood up. She dropped a thick packet on his desk and began to ask him a series of questions related to the work she was assigning him. Small things that he thought were of little importance. At one point, he inadvertently answered her question with a question. She had asked what the probability of a certain outcome would be, and he responded by asking whether she was interested in a univariate or multivariate analysis. She didn't respond. Not right away. Instead, her head tilted to the side, just slightly to look away from him, and her eyes went blank. Her whole body seemed to freeze, her hands stopped in mid-motion, her lips slightly parted, and for just a moment she held that way. It was almost imperceptible but he caught it. It wasn't like she was thinking. Her brow didn't crease, she didn't draw characters in the air the way some people did when they thought of words, or glance at the ceiling to recall something. Her whole body just stopped. It was as if she were listening for the answer. Or, processing the answer. Then her head snapped back to look at him, her eyes came back to life, and she replied, Multivariate, of course. For a moment he couldn't take his eyes off hers, caught by the strangeness of those black circles.

Why did I never notice that before? he thought. The way they had gone blank, her irises dilating into wide black pools, holding that way while she remained frozen, then contracting again as she awoke, spiraling like the fine metal irises in a camera.

this is weird, takeshi. ok. i know. i'm tired, lot of late nights recently, haven't gotten enough sleep. i know what you're going to say. but… anyway i'll just tell you. you know i wrote you about how we're all turning into robots over here at 4k, absorbing chemicals from the air and all that, right? well, i know this sounds crazy and i know you'll just laugh at me, but i'm beginning to think that section chief arai is… you're not going to believe this… an actroid.

yeah. i'm telling you. ridiculous right?

she's not like the twins. with them you can tell they're actroids right away if you go up close. arai must be something newer. something better. she's absolutely perfect. you know i think these guys at simionics have done it.

here's what i'm thinking. what if simionics wanted to test out a really cutting edge actroid? what if, ok? so they send over two of their regular models as a distraction and at the same time they arrange to have their very newest experimental model pretend to work at the same company. tell people she's a manager transferred from an overseas office. see if anyone notices.

takeshi, this is so freakin' amazing. if this is what i'm thinking it is… if this is real… then i've met it. i talk with it. i've almost touched it. and no one else knows!!

When Section Chief Arai came to his desk in the afternoon with another packet of data, Yamamoto studied her and wondered. Her movements were abrupt, she talked in clipped sentences, the air was tinged with her chemical smell. There was the mechanical precision of her neck movements, the stilted way she held her hands. He started noticing other things, little things in her behavior. Once, one of the office girls poured her some water at the cooler and she hesitated, drawing back from the offered cup. The girl was young, new at the company, and apparently overzealous in wanting to be nice to her superior, so she pushed the cup into Section Chief Arai's hand. But Arai didn't drink any. She talked to the girl until the girl left, then poured the water down the sink.

Come to think of it, Yamamoto thought when he saw that, I've never seen her drink or eat anything.

And then there was the way she always hesitated when asked something out of the ordinary. The way she froze, like a computer freezing while it processes a long equation. He watched her at her desk with this thought, her face expressionless, hand motions precise. He thought of the twins.

Section Chief Arai an actroid? he thought and laughed, actually snorted, loudly enough to make the people at desks close by turn and look at him.

Excuse me, he said to them, hand on his mouth, then to himself, That is so good. Section Chief Arai, a robot. What am I thinking? I've got to get more sleep. Or more coffee. Or both.

He walked to the kitchenette to get a cup. But the best and worst of thoughts die hardest and he just couldn't let it go. The idea was so tempting.

Section Chief an actroid. What should I do? Slice her open and look for wires?

He touched the knife in his pocket and yanked his hand out, shocked at the violence of his own thoughts. Whenever they met after that, he would ask her a question as a game, something arcane, purposefully off-beat just to see how long it would take her to answer. Once it was a question about the selection of parametric models to estimate failure time in systems, and again she just seemed to momentarily freeze, mouth open, hands suspended in air, as if she were downloading the answer from a remote database. He would watch her eyes go blank, her head tilt in a questioning pose, hanging that way for a moment, the tendons in her neck taut like stretched cables. He would watch this and the edge of a wry smile would appear at one corner of his mouth as he waited.

takeshi. last night was another late one. i think section chief arai has it in for me. i think she knows. you know. what i found out about her. i mean, what's with all these last minute requests? maybe she wants me to get fed up and quit. no way i'm going to do that and ruin my retirement package at this point.

anyway, i worked late and was leaving the building at, what, it must have been two-thirty in the morning. so i walk into the lobby and there are two guys from simionics doing some maintenance work on the twins. they're sitting over in the waiting area tapping away on their laptops. one of the twins is slumped forward like she's… wait a sec. not she's. it's. it's slumped forward like it's been turned off. the other one has had her wig taken off and it's sitting on the counter. and next to her wig is her face. you know that thing just comes off. kind of floppy in parts and stiff in parts, just laying there on the counter staring at the ceiling. so that twin is still sitting there in her chair… hang on. not her… it. why do i do that? so it's still sitting in its chair, uniform still on all neatly pressed, hands folded in its lap, back straight, alert, everything like it usually is, but above that smart little ascot is a metal neck and a metal head with all the little levers and wires and hinges exposed. white dentures showing with no lips. eyes without eyelids. no ears or nose. not shiny. some kind of dull white metal. maybe ceramic? i couldn't breathe, it was just so, so flipping disgusting. i stopped in the middle of the lobby staring at this thing, and then its head tilts and the mechanical eyes rotate to look at me and it says… good night mr yamamoto. just like that. i nearly pissed myself. i couldn't breathe. for a moment i just stood there like an idiot and then i said good night back, i can't believe it but i said good night to this thing, and she, it, it says, thanks for all your hard work today. be careful on your way home, its lipless teeth moving as it speaks. i stepped backwards into the elevator. i couldn't take my eyes off it. and as the doors close, it tilts its metal head to one side, cutely, and lifts a little hand to wave goodbye.

Yamamoto was eating his lunch in the courtyard, five sandwiches in a plastic box, crustless soft white bread cut into perfect rectangles, identical except for the filling. Ham, egg, tuna, ham, egg. He was eating them from left to right as usual. One ham and one egg were gone and he was lifting tuna to his lips when he felt that he was being watched. He put the sandwich back in the box, took a sip of coffee, set the cup back on the table, and casually rotated his head in the direction he felt the presence. Two tables over was Section Chief Arai. She was sitting alone, with no food or drink on the table, looking straight at him. Expressionless. Their eyes met and held for a moment, then she walked over to his table.

May I sit?

Y' y' yes, of course, Yamamoto stammered, then remembered he hadn't risen and stood up as she sat down.

Please don't stand up, Yamamoto, she said. He sat back down cautiously.

I was watching you eat, she commented, glancing at his sandwich box.

Left to right like that. It's rather formal, don't you think? Almost mechanical.

Mechanical?! he blurted, regretting it as soon as he did. Me? Mechanical?

Maybe mechanical is too strong a word. Very organized?

Oh. Yes, he demurred. I guess you could say that. I've never thought of it that way.

He looked at the box and then nudged it a little toward her.

Would you like some?

Her chin pulled up and she sat back ever so slightly.

No. No thank you.

Some coffee?

No, shaking her head.

Juice? A cookie, something else? I could go get something.

Each of these was refused with a polite smile and a shake of the head.

Nothing?

Nothing.

He looked at her as if he would be able to sound the depths of her soul through her eyes.

You don't eat much do you? he asked. She smiled but said nothing. She didn't blink. Here was a new thought. She doesn't blink.

But please, don't let me stop you. Go ahead. Please.

Yamamoto hesitated and then pulled the box back in front of himself, taking the tuna. They didn't speak. She watched him eat, left to right, tuna, ham, egg, with sips of coffee in between.

She watched as if she had never seen anyone eat before. She watched him, not hungrily, but with curiosity.

You make that look so good.

Oh, no. They're just cheap sandwiches. Are you certain you wouldn't like one?

No. No thank you. He unwrapped his cookie, and she watched him eat that, too, beginning with small nibbles around the outside working his way in.

I think you are perhaps a bit mechanical, she said in a voice like a recording.

Yamamoto?

Yes, Section Chief?

About the moss.

Moss? Oh yes. The moss trays. Is there a problem?

No, no, she said quickly. Then added more softly, Not at all. I was just wondering.

Yes?

Then after some hesitation, Why?

Oh. I see. Why moss?

Yes.

He thought for just a moment about how honest to be, one of those quick calculations that takes just a second yet hurtles through years of memory, weighing honesty, propriety, fear, hope, friendship, duty, and a dozen other more primal emotions on the finely-balanced scales of the subconscious. He thought for just that moment and then slid his chair forward, leaning over the table in confidence, fixing his eyes on hers. Section Chief Arai bent at the waist to listen closer. What followed started as a sentence and ended as a prayer, a cascade of thoughts and memories that required only the occasional, Yes, I see, or, Go on, to prod him forward to the completion of his sermon. It began with a boy in a small fishing village tucked into a hidden cove. The hills that rose above the beach looked out on the endless Pacific. Oak and pine forests cleansed the air, and ocean mists teased out of the soil a covering of deep, green moss. A narrow footpath followed a stream that hurried water from the mountains to the sea. The story followed the long arc of that boy's life, leaving the village for the city, getting a job at 4K, working there for nearly 40 years, and watching the city cauterize itself with concrete, bury its rivers, pave its fields, bulldoze its forests, until there was almost nothing left that hadn't been made by man. His eyes sparkled as he said, Except for the moss. In every crack and forgotten shadow. The tide is beginning to turn.

When he was done, they sat in silence.

Yamamoto wondered, What could it mean that it listens? That it stares at me. Unblinking. Is it all just ones and zeros being referenced against a database somewhere? Is it possible that I mean something more than that to it?

i can't get over this. we meet almost every day. on lunch break. we talk. and it's not at all like when we're at work, she's not my boss and i'm not just some relic by the window. we're... like friends. we really talk. or, i really talk. she's quiet. i like that, how she listens. i've told her a lot about komatsu-mura. she never interrupts. she doesn't really react either. it's a bit creepy. her face. like talking to a mannequin. sort of. not quite.

and yet, takeshi, you know what? now i'm not really sure. i was convinced that arai's an actroid, but now i don't know. not for certain anyway. i was watching her today from across the room, the odd way she moves. the way she pauses before answering a question. but then i thought, she's not so different from a lot of the folks here. everyone's so trim and neat and bustling around with their busy work. take suzuki from the general manager's office for instance. he's a robot if the ever was one. and that new girl inoue. like a barbie doll. and that i.t. guy with the crew-cut, what's his name? tanaka? yamanaka? he's pretty much a walking zombie.

i look at arai and sometimes i just know... absolutely know for certain... she's an actroid. i've seen through her mask. i can hear her tick. and other times, well, she just doesn't seem so different from the rest of us after all.

Another day, another lunch spent together. Yamamoto was peeling an apple with his pocket knife, spiraling down from top to bottom so that the skin came off in one long strip. Section Chief Arai sat across from him, watching. A passerby might think the starkly beautiful woman was merely sitting by chance at the same table as the work-weary man, waiting for someone else to come.

Takeshi? she asked. Yamamoto looked up.

Your name? It's Takeshi?

Yamamoto paused his carving, confused. Section Chief Arai pointed at the knife. On the side of the wooden handle was carved a single character. Takeshi. Warrior.

Oh. No. No, no not me. Takeshi was my best friend. This was his knife.

Section Chief Arai's head tilted ever so slightly in what Yamamoto thought was a sign of understanding.

Everything about that kid was cool. Even his name. Takeshi. I mean, how cool is that right?

I see. Are you still friends?

There was an awkward moment as Yamamoto started to speak, then stopped, painted the air with his hands, his knife cutting back and forth unintentionally. He started peeling again.

Takeshi… he was a fisherman. His dad was a fisherman. His granddad was a fisherman. Anyway, Takeshi went out one day and… he never came back.

Oh. I'm so sorry. That's dangerous work.

Yes. But no. That wasn't it. It was a perfectly clear day. He just went out… and never came back.

Yamamoto was quiet for a while. Section Chief Arai waited calmly.

I used to think he might have made it to Hawai'i or LA. Peru. Alaska. Whatever. The years went by. We never heard anything.

Section Chief Arai watched his face as if analyzing for the first time the emotion called grief.

Yamamoto looked down at his hands and said, I've never told anyone at 4K before.

i told her about you today. now that i think about it, she must already have known. i mean, she would have access to all of 4k's email. right? wooosh, in a micro-second she'd have read everybody's daily mail. hasn't she seen all these emails i send you? to an account i own. with no answers…

what does she want with me anyway? i like being with her. i mean i really like her. i've never felt this way before about anyone. not since you left. i look around at all the other people at 4k. they haven't got a clue. i'm the only one who knows what she is. is that why? data collection. is simionics just trying to find out how i know?

That afternoon, Yamamoto made his rounds misting the moss trays. As he drifted through the company, the pale grey cloud, he imagined it all differently. The air didn't smell like wallpaper glue or vinyl carpets, but more like old leaves and forest soil. There were sweeps of ferns between the desks and vines snaking across the ceiling. Filtered light shone down through the leafy cover, falling softly on the floor and across the stacks of papers on people's desks. Everyone was dressed in simple samue, work clothes made from hand-woven cloth. A few children were chasing each other around the desks. A new born suckled at its mother's breast as she worked on her spreadsheets. Everyone seemed happy, at ease, enjoying their work. An uguisu flitted desk to desk, puffing its chest to cry its startling song. A herd of speckled deer tripped through the kitchenette looking for apples. He walked over to the glass wall that looked out at Roppongi. A light rain was falling and the distant parts of the city were shrouded in a gathering mist. The streets were empty of cars and trucks. Instead, they were covered in moss and grass bamboo through which people walked on earthen paths. Vines as thick as tree trunks climbed the sides of wrecked buildings, snaking in and out of the facades through broken windows. On top of each building grew untamed forests, like those that encircle old shrines, one ancient tree towering above the rest, its roots winding down through the empty floors.

it will come. this whole thing will collapse in on itself. people will go back to being just one of the many animals on the planet. the forests will come back. the rivers and oceans will replenish themselves. there'll be moss everywhere!

of course, i'll be long gone, but what about arai. how long can she last?

Late one afternoon, a man from the 4K maintenance staff began making rounds through the 23rd floor with a rolling waste barrel. At each desk he picked up a moss tray and threw it away. The crashing sound drew Yamamoto's attention. He jumped up and ran over.

What do you think you're doing? was what he was going to say but before he could, Section Chief Arai stepped in his way.

Yamamoto, please wait in the company lounge until further notice, she said severely.

Wh' wh' what's this all about? he replied pointing at the barrel, trying to get around her and stop the maintenance man from grabbing the next one.

Just stop, Yamamoto. Now. Go and wait in the lounge, she said in her most artificial voice.

But.... what's going on with the moss?

Yamamoto. The lounge. Now.

OK. Understood, he answered, dejected and confused. As he walked, he was thinking, What's going on here? I mean, enough is enough. If the company wants to test out an actroid, fine, but I don't want to be bossed around by... that!

He waited in the lounge as instructed. An hour passed and then two. He heard the clattering of the employees finishing their day and heading to the elevators. Another hour passed. He went to the kitchenette, got an apple and returned to the lounge. It was dark out. Through the plate glass windows, the illuminated nightscape of Roppongi spread out in front of him. He took his knife from his pocket and began to peel the apple the way Takeshi had shown him. You start at the north pole, he had said, pointing to the top of the apple, and spiral your way down to the south. Got it?

Yamamoto held the apple in his left hand and turned it slowly, letting the blade slice off a thin strip of red skin. It was careful work and he liked that. He was concentrating very hard on making the strip of skin the same width and thickness, focusing on how he turned the apple and how he held the blade, unaware that someone had come into the room. He was imagining the apple as the Earth, his blade skimming off the planet's thin crust, letting it fall in one long, continuous spiral. He had made it as far as Brazil when he smelled her.

Yamamoto, she called sternly. He jumped up, the blade slicing deeply across his thumb.

Ouch! Dammit.

Blood welled out of the cut, dripping onto the apple. Section Chief Arai was saying something but he wasn't hearing it, the pain erasing all but random words. She was holding out some worm-eaten papers and shaking them at him.

…you and your moss…

His thumb throbbed, blood trailing onto the bright white apple, dripping down the spiral curve of the Earth's crust.

…mold and silverfish…

Section Chief Arai's voice kept climbing, her black eyes creasing at the corners into fine webs.

…archives ruined. Everything chewed up…

Yamamoto tried to say something but there was a wind in his head scattering the words. He stuttered, the knife jabbing wildly as he gestured meaninglessly.

She was shouting at him, hitting the papers against her hand.

…and you, you… traitor…

He was pleading with her. Waving his hands in motions of denial, but it was an insane defense, with a bloody apple in one hand and a knife in the other. He could sense the mechanical irises in Section Chief Arai's eyes narrow, focusing on the waving knife, saw the tension on her artificial skin where it pulled, stretching thin at the corners of her mouth and around her chin.

...sabotage. How could you do this? Bring this into the company...

He could hear the framework of her spine lock as she straightened to face him. He waved his hands beseechingly, the knife jabbing as he stepped forward, pleading, trying to explain, backing her toward the glass wall, the glittering nightscape of Roppongi spreading out behind her. Her face held a perfectly designed look of confusion, her chest rising and falling as she imitated shallow breaths. Yamamoto followed her step for step, never taking his eyes off hers. She backed up against the glass, a thousand city lights flickering behind her like festival lanterns.

Yamamoto stop. Get away!

Yamamoto drew close, knife stabbing at the air.

How could you accuse me? Me. I know you Section Chief. I know what you are.

Put the knife down, Yamamoto.

How could you turn on me? Me of all people?

What are you saying?

I'm the only one who knows. I'm the only one who cares.

He had never been this close to her before, close enough to really smell her. That chemical odor. He sniffed. Hairspray?

He was close enough to see the detailing of her face plate. There were fine hairs at her temples and small wrinkles at the corners of her eyes. And chapped skin on the edge of her lower lip.

Yamamoto hesitated. Up close like that Section Chief Arai

seemed so unlike what he thought she should be. Somehow so… human. His hands were trembling as he pushed closer. The knife blade pressed against her white blouse. She parted her lips as if to scream.

Evening gave way to morning. Several million people were swept into the city on the great tidal flow, and then back out again the following night. At one time or another, they all were certain to have passed by one of those shadowed places where moss had found a toehold and was beginning to grow, but none stopped to notice. None save one. That lonely pilgrim drifted from place to place, seemingly invisible to those around him, moving in numbed silence, his eyes seeking out those corners and cracks where moss might grow. And whenever he found some, he reached out a trembling finger to stroke it as one might touch an old friend.

Two days later, dawn finds Yamamoto in Komatsu-mura. He is lying on a thick bed of moss looking up at the branches of the oak trees. Below him, just visible through the tree trunks further down the slope, is the blue expanse of the ocean. He notices that the rhythm of the waves seems to be the same as the rhythm of his breathing. That is the first thought he has had since he ran in a panic from 4K.

He is wearing only his underwear, the way he and Takeshi had done in the summer, stripping off their clothes and swimming in the bay, or walking the forest trails looking for mushrooms. His business suit and shirt lie neatly folded nearby with his shoes and socks placed carefully next to them. He is looking up into the canopy of the oaks overhead, the fine branches and tufts of leaves etching patterns on the blue sky. Occasionally, flocks of gulls fly over. He watches them through the oaks coming into view and passing from view. A single cloud spends half an hour moving across his field of vision, and he watches that too, not moving his head, staring straight up, just noting the cloud appear, cross the sky, and disappear.

The temperature is such that it feels neither warm nor cold, like there is no division between skin and air. Yamamoto closes his eyes. He can hear the wind high in the trees, a hissing like gently boiling water, but he does not feel it on his skin. It feels to him, instead, that he is the wind. That he is dissolving into the air, scattering like pollen from a spent blossom, his cells separating into a billion motes of life-stuff, floating out across the forest floor, through the crooked tree trunks to the bluff overlooking the sea, out over that precipice into the air and up in dizzy circles high, high above the beach, drifting far out over the water, and coming finally to rest far out to sea in warm currents that would carry him to a thousand unknown places. In time, he would be stippled on ice flows off the Aleutians, caught in mangrove forests on the shores of Sumatra, on the barnacle encrusted piers of the Chesapeake Bay, in the nets of fishermen working the muddy waters where the Nile spills into the Mediterranean. He would be in all these places at once. Everywhere and nowhere.

He hears the waterfall nearby, the one that he used to see cascade down the screen of his computer. He listens and tries to imagine it is the sound of a hundred people tapping away on their keyboards. He tries to bring the office into his mind but he can not. It is gone. Instead, he feels himself becoming the falls, his body dissolving into the water, flowing down the stony river and out into the bay. Warmed by the summer sun on the ocean surface, he rises as vapor to the clouds, blows inland and falls as rain on the very forest where he lies.

There is something in the way the light comes through the leaves of the trees, sparkling like a thousand electric lights, that brings him back to the lounge at 4K. He remembers now, drawing a quick breath in surprise.

Section Chief Arai was backed up against the glass wall, the lights of Roppongi glittering behind her. He was standing close to her, his knife pressed against her blouse. He was saying something like, I know what you are. I know you.

And then he wasn't sure he did.

He squinted, looking her over very closely, scanning her for those details he was so good at catching, his lips pursed, eyes darting as he tried to make sense of what he saw. He shook his head and took a step back. The chapped skin. The wrinkled corners of her eyes. The subtle hint of sweat. He saw a middle-aged career woman with a stiff posture and distant eyes. Nothing more than one of the countless uniformed workers in one of the countless offices across Tokyo.

Yamamoto stares up through the oak branches at the bowl of the sky. Another cloud drifts into view. He can hear the waves of the ebb tide against the shore. The tumbling of the waterfall. A breeze rustles the falling light. He hears himself breathing. Feels the vast rotation of the planet beneath his back.

Yamamoto strokes the soft moss. He smiles, comforted, just knowing it is there. Knowing that, in the not too distant future, there will be more. Much more.

SPRING

Spring

A covered wagon rattled westward across the dry lands of the Nebraska Territory, fourth in line among twenty headed for California. Poppy walked alongside his lead horse, one hand on the bridle. His children, Rebekah and Baby Isaac, lay in the back amid sacks of provisions. For the past two weeks there had been little else on anyone's mind other than the heat. The dust. And the lack of water. That's what they thought when they woke. It's what filled their evening prayers.

Baby Isaac cried feebly, fidgeting in the cradle of Rebekah's arm. She gave him a piece of burlap dabbed with honey to suckle on.

Now there Isaac, she whispered. That's better, isn't it?

Rebekah lay back on the sacks and looked up at the canvas tarp above her. It was slack on its bentwood frame like a pale skin draped over the ribs of some huge animal. She imagined she was riding across the plains in the belly of a whale, trapped like Jonah in a mythical beast, somehow swimming west through an ocean of dust and light. The sun showed through its skin as a blurry white circle that grew hotter and more intense the longer she watched it.

With each lurch of the wagon, the tarp would flap. A stone, a rut, a clump of sagebrush, anything in the path of the wheels, and the tarp would shudder as if gusted by a breeze. But there was no breeze. Just the relentless sun and the still air and an open plain that refused to end. Even in the shade of the wagon's cover it was stiflingly, and every day was hotter than the one before. A week had passed since Poppy started rationing water. He had opened the cork of the water barrel, poked a stick in and measured the wet mark against his fingers. Stroking his beard he announced, Four mouthfuls a day is what I figah. At's all we got to git us to the mountains.

With a flourish he had raised his ever-present bible to shield his eyes from the sun, looked up and called hoarsely, I believe you have a plan for us Lord and will not forsake us, for truly you have said, I did know thee in the wilderness and in the land of great drought.

Lowering the bible to his chest, he had added, Hosea 13:5, for the edification of anyone listening. And then after a moment of contemplating the sky, he added in a voice full of confidence, I know you see us Lord.

Rebekah's last sip had been that morning. There would be no more until they stopped at noon. Baby Isaac suckled on his burlap. His mouth made gentle sounds next to Rebekah's ear, like a cat purring. She lay there stunned, rocking with the wagon, looking up at the sun searing through the canvas. She felt it burn down through her eyes, into the depths of her brain. Her mouth opened and closed rhythmically, keeping time with the mournful squealing of the desert whale – mweeekk... mweekk... mweekk... water... water... water – high and forlorn like the squealing of a dry axle.

> high in the mountains it is snowing. impossibly large flakes falling in numbers uncountable to cloak the world. a couple of inches an hour. five feet a day. it snows without stopping, and again the next day, building up relentlessly and crushing under its own weight to make room for more. on the sides of the mountains, the weight of the snow grows in steady increments until some unseen tipping point is crossed, just a snowflake or two, and an entire mountainside releases its grip with a deep and terrible thunder. a million tons of snow gallops toward the valley floor in a headlong surge, slicing off hundred year old spruces like matchsticks. a great booming echoes down valleys for fifty miles around and then it's all over. herds of startled elk turn their heads to listen, then go back to their pilgrimages. flocks of small birds circle and settle back into whatever part of the forest is left standing. the world returns to silence. it snows some more.

Rebekah's family had left another ocean earlier that year. They had gathered by its shores to say goodbye on a day when a mist shrouded the horizon. The air cool and torn by flocks of gulls fighting over scraps from the fish-boats. The beaches where Rebekah had played, gathering clams and snails in tide pools, building cities out of sand, awaited her again on the other side. Poppy had promised that.

Clams the size of cats, Rebekah. No end to it.

That was the plan but things had worked out differently. They were only halfway to California and there they sat, languishing beneath a scalding sun, unable to move any further, a broken wheel on the ground next to the wagon. Poppy kicked it, stroked his beard, and pondered his options. In the end he decided they would drop out of the wagon train to fix it.

We'll catch you up in a few days time, he told the others cheerfully.

Let us take the young'ins, the women pleaded but Poppy would not hear of it. Their mother lay in a shallow grave along the track back in Arkansas, nothing more than an uncarved riverstone marking the lonely spot. The children were all he had left.

We'll catch you up, he repeated and waved the wagons off one by one, bible clutched to his chest, dusty hat fanning the air.

The faces of the departing spoke what they would not say. So long. Lord help you. Doubt we'll ever see y'all again.

Turns out they were right.

While Poppy worked on the wheel with his saw and hammer, Rebekah slung Baby Isaac on her back and set off to hike a wide circle around the wagon. See if she could find anything of use. Each step on the parched ground lifted a cloud of dust around her boots. She walked, she looked, scouting with a hand above her eyes. Endless tortured clumps of sagebrush were all she found. And miles of stony ground.

Halfway around her circle, the land began to rise into low hills. She climbed the first and from the top saw mountains in the great distance. Just the hint of them, as if the horizon had been torn. Faintly white-capped, they glistened like liquid paint through the hot air. She pointed and shouted but Poppy was too far away to hear.

In the hollow below her was an apparition. A crooked, tormented thing, all alone in the world. Rebekah whispered, Isaac will you look at that. A tree. What in God's name is it doing all the way out here?

She stumbled down the slope and stepped timidly into its shade. It's a miracle, Isaac, and pressed her cheek to the bark. It felt cool. It smelled green. She set Baby Isaac on the ground and lay down next to him. The sky sparkled through the leaves. The shade of a tree is different from that of a canvas tarp. Cooler, more comforting. She drifted off and dreamt of water. Not of the ocean she had left behind, or the great rivers they had crossed to get this far, but of a little brook, the sound seeming to run straight through her. It was a pleasant sound, a trickling, and when she awoke it was still electric in her mind. The sound still clear and present in the world. Trickling? she wondered. She sat up, suddenly alert. On her hands and knees she crawled and listened and crawled a little more until she came to a steep slope. The sound was right there in front of her, in the ground. Pulling out a rock, she touched the soil with her palm. It was moist. She pulled out another stone, and water pooled slowly into the hollow where it had been. She gasped, clapped her hands to her chest, then threw herself in face first, sucking muddy water that tasted of blood.

spring arrives late to the high mountains, rushing in frenzied, already dressed for summer. a powerful shamaness, she takes a thousand miles of snow and turns it into water in an unparalleled act of alchemy. onto each six-sided snowflake, each microscopic crystal of ice as sharp and faceted as forged steel blades, she breathes with just the right balance of temperature and pressure, and changes them to liquid pearls. one day winter cloaks the world ten feet deep and the next there sits a forest, a rioting meadow, a crystal lake with acres of cattails and a herd of elk licking clouds off its edges.

the snowmelt fills every crack and crevice it can, and when that's done, it overflows and runs in torrents downhill toward the sea hundreds of miles away. beneath the crystal lake, from the bottom of every brook and stream, through all the soil in the meadows and forests, water leaches downward in a subterranean rainstorm of epic proportions. unheard, unseen, unknown, through the pitch dark of the inner earth, water follows every path of least resistance to wherever it will lead.

While Baby Isaac suckled in the shade on a soaking wet rag, Poppy listened to Rebekah tell her tale. She pointed at the displaced rocks, the little puddle. Poppy ran back to the wagon and returned with a pick and shovel. The more he dug, the harder it flowed. Poppy hacked and scraped, grunting.

They did not thirst when He led them through the deserts. He made the water flow out of the rock for them. He split the rock and the water gushed forth. Do you see now, Rebekah? Do you see?

Ecclesiasties?

Isaiah. He looked at her askance. 48:21, he added, thinking it was high time they resumed her bible studies.

Once Poppy dug a few feet into the rocky slope and the

water was flowing strong enough not to simply disappear back into the ground, he dug a bathtub-sized hole and a channel from the spring so the water could fill it. In they went, hats boots and all. Two hours later, long after her skinned had pruned, Rebekah still refused to leave. Baby Isaac, pleasantly cooled, cooed and slept on the ground nearby. Poppy built a camp next to the tree. The wagon, dismantled, became the roof and the furniture. A bed a table a chair.

The next morning, his hands deep in mud by the spring, Poppy made his intentions clear.

Rebekah, with water you can live. You can drink and you can cook.

He lifted a clump of wet red clay and continued.

With water and dirt you can grow food.

He pointed a muddy finger skyward.

And, with the sun like a furnace above you each day, you can make adobe like nobody's business.

A month later they had themselves a little hut.

Next they made a garden surrounded by a tall adobe wall to temper and protect it. There they sprouted every seed they had brought with them. Collard greens and carrots, potatoes and leeks. Apple trees and peaches. Corn, wheat, amaranth. The land around them looked desolate, but it was not – the soil was rich. If only you gave them a little water, plants grew like weeds.

That year, another wagon train passed their way. Rebekah rode out to flag them down. Welcome to Hope Springs, she called out cheerfully. Passed around a jug of their spring water. A pleasant murmur rose among the people and they stopped to trade. Poppy had his water, which was for the wagon train at that point in their journey worth its weight in gold. They also had some extra salt pickles. And the horses. They had started with four, eaten one themselves the first year, smoking and salting most of the meat, grinding the bones into meal. Of the remaining three, they decided to trade away two, keeping the smallest for themselves. It would drink the least water.

Poppy spent more than a little time talking with Cordelia Smithers, a young mother on the train who had lost her husband to bushwhackers on the way out. In Arkansas of all places. They shared that and many other things. When the train moved on, Cordelia and her three little ones stayed. Rebekah and Isaac had a new mother, two brothers and a sister. Poppy built a bigger house. In the floor was a pit that held salt pickles, some jars of stewed vegetables, and a little sack of gold.

groundwater rains down through soil, falling slowly like evening mist, moving single-mindedly down along lines of gravity until it comes to solid rock. there it stops and begins to move sideways, sliding along the cold surface of the granite or basalt or limestone, forced forward by the pressure of last spring's snowmelt and yesterday's rain, the past telescoping itself into the future.

but even solid rock has its cracks and water will move through them as willingly as any other passage. down through the columnar combs of basalt fissures, across shear fractures and tectonic joints, into narrow tunnels along dissolved limestone seams, water moves elegantly through the mathematics of stress.

after a month or a year of that hidden travel, the water will reach a point where the bends and folds of its conduit break through to the surface. tinted with the essence of

> the very stone that had guided it – a touch of iron, a hint of calcium – the water bubbles back into the sunlight and runs for a foot or a mile or a hundred before diving back underground or evaporating into thin air.

In the years that followed, Poppy dug further into the slope to open the mouth of the spring. Pretty soon he was drawing five hundred gallons a day. He dug a deep channel from the spring down along the slope and lined it with stones to stop it from caving in. Off of the main channel he dug smaller rivulets, branching right and left like the roots of a tree. Some ran into walled gardens that grew select crops – greens in one, grains in another. Others went to orchards – olives, sweet fruits, citrus, and nut trees. And one fed a small pond that was used to water the livestock they now had.

As the children grew and married, Poppy built them each an adobe house. The houses were arranged around a courtyard that had shade trees and a fountain in the middle. Poppy charged wagoneers a penny to fill a jug. Three to water a horse. A nickel to fill a barrel. Sacks of gold filled the little hole in the floor of his house so he dug another. Put an iron lock box in it and slept with a gun on the bed stand.

When the first crop of olives came in, the whole family gathered to press oil. Counting all the grandchildren, and the hired-hands who now lived with them, there were thirty five people working and three babes in bassinets. They pressed a hundred gallons, of which they kept a third and traded the rest. The dregs, pits and all, went as slops to the hogs. The oil was rich and golden. They slathered it on fresh baked bread and drizzled it over their oatmeal porridge licking their slicked fingers and dipping in for more.

Bottles of the oil traveled with wagon trains all the way west to San Francisco, and back east to New York and Baltimore. Each had the same distinctive hand-drawn label of a spring of fresh water cascading out of bare rocks. Poppy sold them for six cents a bottle, sixty for a dozen. In New York's finest provisioners, under a sign reading Desert Freshness, they sold for ten times that. It was the idea of it. Bounty from a verdant paradise in the desert that had been nurtured by the grace of god.

> bedrock flows like water. only slower. its solidity is a dream held by creatures of the earth who live but briefly. mayflies. mice. people. if only they could live longer, a million years or so, and if they had the patience to sit for that time and just watch what happened in front of them, they would see waves ripple through the landscape. watch meadows rise into mountains, then subsume, fold and warp before their very eyes. oh the quivering majesty of it all.

The story grew of its own accord. Through comments made in small town gazettes, by ladies gossiping at tea parties and drunks bragging over their whiskeys, in secrets whispered in the back pews, word spread about the Preacher of the Waters. A man whose faith had brought Eden to the wilderness. Who would stand high on a boulder above the burbling spring and preach the word. His hair a white halo about his head, face and hands burned a deep brown, fissured with fine lines left by years in the desert air. He would raise his bible like a black sword against the sky and cut straight to the truth.

Behold the power of faith to change the world. Have you not

eyes to see? he would scold, his arms sweeping at the verdant acres that surrounded them.

Whether the gathered had been traveling west to stake a claim in California, or were headed back east on a return trip, whether first-timers or the traveling sort, rich or poor, the oasis at Hope Springs was a vision that would inhabit their memories forever. The tidy adobe homes surrounded by trellises heavy with grape vines. The walled courtyards, one after another, filled to overflowing with luxuriant crops. The acres of orchards, trees set out in neat rows through which they could stroll, breathing the perfume of ripening fruits. The central square with its sparkling fountain and perimeter of tall trees. People who had seen this, who had actually been there and experienced the place, had without fail been traveling for weeks under the most wretched conditions. When they arrived, their mouths were dry, bellies empty, and spirits bent to the point of breaking. They would come over a rise and see the green valley. A land of milk and honey. They would drink the cool waters, eat their first meal of fresh food in weeks and marvel at god's hand in the world. They would walk in the shade of the olives, fill their jugs with clear water from the fountain in the square. And when they returned to the hardships of the road, they would do so refreshed. With a tale to tell. And so the story spread.

> the sleepless world never rests. where lay a desolate plain, mountains rise. where once stood lofty jagged peaks, now sit low stone hills, their backs weathered down to nubs. once a tepid jungle choked with fern trees and terrible lizards the size of houses, now an endless arctic wasteland.
>
> the landscape quivers. bedrock cracks. then cracks some

more. water seeps through, then it gushes. the landscape quivers again, rhythmically, a millennial heartbeat. with each pulse, the passages of underground rivers open and close. water flows for an eon, then stops.

Late one night, as a yellow moon passed a half-closed eye across the landscape, and the family lay dreaming, there was a tremor.

Did you feel that? Cordelia hissed, nudging her sleeping husband. Poppy grabbed his gun from the bed stand and cocked an ear. A glass of water continued to tremble there, unnoticed. Poppy sat up, listened with held breath for a minute.

Just a dream, he yawned and fell back to sleep.

The next day the spring was running a little slow. A week later it stopped. Poppy and the boys took their shovels and picks and wore a hole into that hill that a wagon could drive into. A small mountain of rubble stood in the square between their houses.

This is a test, Cordelia. The Lord giveth and he taketh away, but he'll come round and give it back again. He's just testing our faith.

Cordelia thought if anyone didn't need their faith tested it should have been Poppy, but who was she to question. They talked about pulling up stakes, taking the strong box and moving to San Francisco. They had enough gold to live on comfortably for the rest of their lives. But Poppy couldn't do it. It was a matter of righteousness. He went to Fort Kearney with all his gold and came back with seven wagons of black powder in barrels piled high. The Lord would see his faith. The water would flow again. He would show the world.

The word got around. The Preacher of the Waters would

be testing his faith for all to see. A minister from Dodge City brought his flock to instill in them the kind of fervor that would carry them to the promised land. Twenty Arapaho arrived with their teepees and set up camp in the nearby hills. Cow pokes left their herds in the hands of mess cooks for a chance to see the miracle. A seller of rattlesnake oil rolled up in his cart and did a brisk business in grain alcohol. The drunks struck up a tune and danced all night. A wagon train diverted its course just to see the proceedings, burning through precious supplies to do so. On the morning of the grand event, over four hundred people were gathered in groups on the hills surrounding Hope Spring.

Poppy and the boys had spent a week rolling barrel after barrel of the powder from the trailhead up to the spring and then down inside the new cavern they had so passionately dug out. Cord fuses ran from barrel to barrel and from there down the trail to the fountain in the courtyard. Poppy touched a lit match to the end of the fuse. A puff of smoke skittered up the trail toward the spring. The sound of four hundred people gasping rose like a breeze. Ninety seconds later, the world in front of them disappeared.

They felt a bone-jarring thud hit them through their boots. Then everything moved. The spring, the stone channel that ran from it to feed the gardens, the first little house that Poppy had built and the crooked tree it sat under, the adobe houses around the square, the fountain and the shade trees. Everything jumped five feet in the air. What had risen hovered for a split second before pulverizing into a cloud of tan dust and boiling upwards a thousand feet into the air. The gasps and exhortations of four hundred people could not be heard above the roar.

An hour later, when the cloud had settled, peopled looked

down into an empty crater two hundred yards across. They waited another hour, then two, but no water ever flowed. Not a drop. One by one the groups knocked the dust from their clothes and left quietly. The Arapaho seemed unimpressed. They had expected as much. Idiots with their violent magic. The drunks, who at first had stood dumbly transfixed by the grandeur of the spectacle, began to belly laugh, rolling on the grass until they got sick. The snake oil salesman opened a bottle for himself. The minister led his flock away, explaining that true faith undoubtedly lay closer to home. Rebekah and her extended family searched the crater for days but they never found any trace of Poppy. Or the spring.

A month later, the next wagon train to pass through found them in rags, hollow-eyed amid the broken walls, unaware they were still alive. With no water, the gardens and orchards had withered to brown husks. There was nothing left to trade. The wagon master took pity on them and offered them passage to Salt Lake City. As they rose into the hills, Rebekah looked back to where Hope Springs had been and saw the crater catching the twilight like a dark spot on the moon.

> it matters not to the water where it goes. if not here, then there. somewhere it will become part of something. a tree, a field of onions, a coyote, a cricket, a cloud. a snowflake.

A Lincoln Continental hurtles down an unpaved road, raising a cloud of dust in its wake. It slows and stops in the middle of the road. The driver doesn't pull over. No need to. There isn't another car for a hundred miles in any direction. A back door opens and out spills a girl in a miniskirt, followed by the twanging pulses of A Hard Day's Night.

I'm not kidding, she screams back into the car. I gotta go. Now!

She kicks some tumbleweed out of her way and stumbles off into the dry landscape in search of a private spot to pee. Her knee-high boots gather a layer of fine dust, magnetically, changing from bright white to beige like a chameleon. She climbs up a ragged slope and disappears down the other side into an immense dusty crater.

The front passenger door opens and out steps a woman in a miniskirt, a taller edition of the girl with the full bladder. She throws her blonde hair back and squints at the sun. Lights a slim cigarette and blows clouds into the cloudless sky. The Beatles fade out and give way to the Byrds. Her foot taps, a leg swivels, hands begin to drum, neck rolls and soon she is dancing slowly in a circle around the car.

To everything, turn, turn, turn, there is a season…

The man in the driver's seat watches her through the windshield. Whenever she moves, he imagines her naked. He can't help it. An older man, a trophy wife. He looks at himself in the rear view mirror and tries to adjust the exhausted waves of his well oiled hair, his white scalp showing beneath like moonlight through willows. He takes a folder from the dash, pushes a stack of survey maps back into it and steps out. His young wife calls him over to join her dancing. He slaps the air and laughs it off. Lights a cigarette instead.

Awww come'on, Poppy. Let's have some fun.

Yeah, yeah. Sure Baby. When we get back to Dallas.

Awww. She frowns.

He takes a long look at the land around him, the folder held over his eyes to shield them from the sun. He's trying to imagine, somewhere out there in the desolate landscape, the rows of neat houses that appear in his company's brochures with their tidy lawns and beds of flowers. He can't. Who'm I kiddin'? he thinks, and oozes a long drawn out sigh. Rifling through the maps, he snatches one from the folder and spreads it out on the hood of the car. Touching the metal, he snatches his hand back.

Ouch! Christ you could fry an egg on that thing.

His wife bends over as she dances and rolls her bottom around to get his attention. You could fry one on these Poppy, she teases, touching a fingertip to her rocking bottom and making the sizzle sound.

He sees a glimpse of white panty and imagines a puff of blonde hairs peeking from the hollow where her legs meet. He takes a long draw on his cigarette and sweeps his arm across the landscape.

I see a thousand homes out there, Baby.

He says this optimistically, but doesn't really believe it himself.

His wife stops dancing long enough to look around and see if she had missed something.

Poppy, who the fuck would want to live in this God forsaken place? He snaps around to look at her angrily.

Language, baby, language, he says wagging a finger and nodding his head in the direction their daughter had gone.

Yeah whatever, she sneers back and starts dancing again, singing along with the music, A time to dance, a time to mourn, a time to cast away stones, a time to gather stones together.

The man puts his hands to his mouth, megaphone style, and shouts, Becky! Come on sweetie, we got to go. A few minutes pass and a blonde head appears above the distant ridge. The girl stands on the crest, mini-skirt and beige-white boots, waving like a Siren to lost sailors.

You guys gotta see this.

Come on Beckster. We have to get back, her father says dismissively.

No really. You gotta see this. There's all these ruins down here, walls and shit.

The man turns to his wife. See what I mean about your mouth. Where'd she learn to speak like that?

His wife shrugs, chucks her cigarette. The song changes to one by Orbison. She starts doing the Mashed Potato, pointing to herself and singing, Pretty woman, walking down the street. Pretty woman, the kind I like to meet…

Hey! Don't you guys wanna see? It's like an ancient Indian village or something, shouts the girl.

The man begins to fold up his map, but stops short and looks up at the next thing she says, suddenly interested, his eyebrows lifitng as his mouth forms a small o.

Yeah. And there's like a huge pond.

in the high mountains the nights are getting cold. the valleys glitter with aspen and birch already turning gold. elk gather by a lake to begin their pilgrimage downcountry. geese lift into the air by the thousands, circle and head south. some mornings there is a skin of ice on the lake that crackles in the slightest breeze. any day now it will snow.

A
PEACEABLE
KINGDOM

A Peaceable Kingdom

The streets of Chestnut Hill are quiet now as the good people wind down their days toward dinner. The only sound is the distant hum of a solitary lawn mower beating back the sun-drawn urges of someone's Kentucky Blue. You look around, enjoying the peaceful air as you drift slowly down the sidewalk. The houses, painted softly in well-mannered tones, sit poised on velvet lawns, snuggle comfortably into beds of clipped yews. Tall elm trees arch over the sidewalks casting dappled pools of shade that flow back and forth with the breeze like shallow tides. The newly repaved streets release the heat of the day and the smell of hot tar – that warm aroma of suburban civility – and you pause for a moment, letting it pass through you. Nothing, you think, speaks more clearly of human dominance over the world than asphalt. Chestnut Hill is a ministered place, a place of comfort and safety. Like the rolling meadows in the Cotswolds with their meandering old stone walls and cottonball dots of grazing sheep, or the terraced rice paddies that cascade by the hundreds down hillsides in Bali, Chestnut Hill is a well-tended place. A peaceable kingdom.

You think back to how it was in ancient times, when stories of the great ice fields were still told at the evening fire. You remember a band of hunters making their way home through the forest. They came over the same rise you have just now crossed to find the huts of their village in the valley below. Smoke from small fires drifted in the evening breeze. The fields ripe with grain and greens. Immediately they knew. Here is food. Here is shelter. Here is safety from the wild. It was not a thought but a feeling, an ancient understanding hardwired into the human fiber from eons of walking the land. It was true back then and true even now for the good people who settle in Chestnut Hill. Maybe stronger so because they do not realize why.

A noise rises behind you and you turn to find a group of boys hurtling down the street on their bikes, chasing each other in full-out battle. The throaty sound of weapons firing grows louder as they approach. One boy pops a wheelie and loops off the street up onto the sidewalk, back tire skidding then catching, leaving a small black stain. He rushes toward you pedaling as hard as he can, his attention focused on a boy next to him. His bike is blue with long red tassels that flicker flame-like off the ends of the handlebars. He points a finger at the other boy, cocks his thumb, and fires a spray of bullets, spittle shooting from his pink lips. You are so dead, man, he screams. Obliterato, and rides straight through you unaware. The whoops of the war party billow and fade as the bikes turn the corner. The gang disappears, leaving in their wake the scent of fabric softener and hair gel.

You turn and continue down the sidewalk, the afternoon sun already low, the world tinted by the magic hour of amber hues. The lawn mower you heard whirs away in the backyard of a nearby house, reassuring the neighborhood of its vigilance, a metal hound snarling at the wild. It calls to you and you float back there to see. You know this place. You've been here before. It belongs to the Man of Few Words. As you pass through the side yard, the engine of the mower cuts and the world stills. A sparrow flies overhead and lands in an old sugar maple. It angles its head in a series of stilted jerks, scanning in your direction with one eye then two then one again, almost as if it can see you. Then it ruffles its feathers and flies off in a blur of wings. You continue floating into the backyard where you find the Man of Few Words pushing his mower across the lawn to the tool shed. The machine is still hot from its hour of forced labor, smelling of motor oil and crushed leaves. The warm aroma of suburban authority. The man walks with his head down, looking back and forth in a pendulum swing, checking for chickweed and clover. A lawn only looks this good if it's kept weed-free, he thinks, and you can see in his smooth face the immense sense of pride and relief he feels knowing that all his hard work is paying off. His gait is reserved, almost mechanical, his clothes pressed, his hair clipped short halfway up the side of his head. It is a walk and a style that fits well in the bright halls of Morgan Standard Appliances where he works, and only the trace of grass stains on the cuff of his pants and two dark crescents of sweat on his shirt suggest he is anywhere else.

From time to time he pauses and glances up to check the borders of his property, scanning the neatly clipped hedges for stray twigs. He notices a leaf poking up awkwardly, like a cowlick, walks over, slips his handshears out of the leather holster at his hip and, in one deft motion, nicks it away. He looks around for others, snipping here and there at places that don't need the attention, appeasing his hand which seems to need to cut something. As he searches he raises the shears like a barber, clicking in the air, daring the world to grow. Satisfied that there are no more strays, he goes back to the mower and pushes it around the corner to the toolshed. You float along behind him but as he makes a wide circle around the hedge, you continue in a straight line, passing through the hedge as easily as water through cloth.

Within the hedge the latticework of fine branches surprisingly open considering how thick and lush it looks from the outside. You linger there for a moment. In the crotch of one of the branches is a bird's nest made of fine twigs and pine needles, with a bright piece of sparkly red ribbon woven through as if for decoration. Three sparrow chicks are poking their heads up from the edge of the nest waiting for the return of their parents. It's spring and the chicks are only a few days old. You watch their gaping triangular beaks and gawky neck movements for a moment, then pass out the other side of the hedge and back into the sunlight just as the Man of Few Words opens the door to the shed.

Nailed to the gable above him is a pressed metal sign, the same size and shape as a license plate, that says Jack's Shack. Underneath it, in smaller letters, is the name of the lawn care company that made the sign. He got it by sending in labels from five of their products. He had nailed it up there one bright Saturday morning several years before, grinning like a kid naming his fort. He takes a rag from a hook on the door and wipes down the mower, cleaning off the grass-clippings and oil, running the cloth along the red metal curves until it shines. The shed has the chemical smell of gasoline, fertilizer, insecticides, and herbicides – all useful to the Man of Few Words in his subjugation as he carefully selects what will and will not live within the borders of his land. The bottles and bags sit in well-organized rows on shelves at the back of the shed. On the wall next to them are his hand tools. He hangs his shears on a hook surrounded by a tracing of the shears. The real shears fit inside their outline snuggly. Other tools hang on the wall in the same way, each nestled into a tracing of its own shape. Shovels, rakes, sickles and hoes. He pushes the mower into the shed, closes the door and heads back to the house. You follow, floating along behind, watching his slow, careful walk as he patrols for weeds.

When he reaches the house he opens a control box attached to the wall, fingers a little switch and looks to the lawn. A second passes before the system reacts, and then there is a loud hiss as sprinkler heads rise from the ground. They ascend like slender deities from their subterranean shrines, whirling and casting rain to deluge the world. The ease with which he brings forth this miracle is lost on him. Everyone he knows can do it. He closes the box with a firm click of its latch and continues to the terrace overlooking the backyard. He sweeps a few leaves away and takes a seat in his favorite chair. Perched on the flagstones like a man on a beach, he gazes over his quarter acre of perfect lawn and watches sunlight glint off the wet blades, as calming as gentle ocean waters. He stretches, and locks his fingers over the close-cropped hairs at the back his head, enjoying the deep green lawn textured by a pattern of mown bands. The dancing water gods spin in their slow revolutions, spraying arcs of crystal rainbows. Tzitt tzitt tzitt tzitt. From behind him, the scent of fabric softener pumps out of a dryer vent. Not lemony not soapy not lavender but all of those at once. The warm aroma of suburban cleanliness. He breathes in deeply, closes his eyes and lets his mind soften into the smell and the evening song of the water gods.

After a half hour, the Man of Few Words gets up and turns the sprinklers back to time-control. The little metal deities slow, sigh, and ease back into the ground. He takes another look around the backyard, cool and fresh in the last light of day, and goes inside. Just as he turns his back, a sparrow loops across the yard and disappears into the hedge without so much as slowing down.

As he goes through the screen door you follow, passing vaporously through the clapboard wall. The space inside the wall is filled with fiberglass insulation, pink and soft as cotton candy. Something small and dark is nestled in there, curled up tightly around itself, sleeping. You linger for just a moment close by it, listening to the quiet breathing, sensing the rise and fall of its little warm body. It stirs, lifting its head to smell the air as if it senses your presence, then puts its head down again. Then once more, it lifts its head and sniffs, this time more vigorously, its fine paws patting at the insulation around it. Awake now, it jumps up and scurries upward through a fiberglass tunnel of its own making. This is new since your last visit.

Are you pleased?

You pass through the sheetrock painted rosedust and light French gray into the living room, catching up to the Man of Few Words as he settles into his recliner, clicks on the TV and eases back into the naugahyde. The sound of dinner being prepared comes from the kitchen and he sniffs at the air, calling out to no one, Something sure smells good! Pot roast?

He smiles and pats the arms of his chair. He loves being home. He loves coming home, driving back from work in the evenings, or after running errands. When they'd first moved here, he found himself going out on some excuse, just to be able to drive back, to see it all again as if for the first time, dropping off the highway and working his way up the hill through all the quiet, well-kept streets: Millbrook Way, Meadow Street, Orchard Place, Pine Street. It never occurred to him that each street had been named for something that had long since fallen to the chainsaw or the bulldozer, and that the green and white street signs on their handsomely carved wooden posts were no more than lonely grave markers.

Between Meadow and Orchard was where the apple trees had been, a haze of sweet white blooms and honeybees this time of year. There had been a small woods and a pond nearby. On the night of the first warm rain in Spring, hundreds of yellow-spotted salamanders would crawl out from under fallen logs and deep beds of leaves, and stagger across the meadow to mate at the water's edge. Lower down, by Millbrook, was where the houses of the miller and his sons had been, their gardens and stables. The brook that traced the hollow there took its name from their work, but now it trickles silently through a heavy concrete pipe deep underground. The paddock for the miller's horses and cattle had stretched up the hill from the brook. Above the paddock, where the view was best, six generations of their family were buried. They still rest there beneath the plastic jungle-gym of number 43 Pine Street, pranced on unknowingly by the many light feet of the neighborhood children. No disrespect intended. People are simply oblivious of the world they live in. They forget and move on.

Why not you?

West of Pine was an Iroquois settlement long before the mill was built. Eight feet below the neat lawns, black carbon circles record the songs of their campfires. Post holes from their longhouse rest in neat, parallel rows, filled now with a lighter soil carried in from other places. The Man of Few Words drives down these streets every day without a clue.

He rests in the recliner, the scent of fresh-cut lawn still lingering on his sleeves, and imagines driving up through the streets, turning at last onto Ridge Circle, the cul-de-sac where he lives, easing off the pedal to take the last bit a little slower. His New England Colonial sits at the end of the street where the old sugar maple spreads over the front yard, one of the few trees remaining from the original farm. The shrubs around the house are nicely clipped, the driveway just resurfaced to a deep liquid black, the house painted teal and cream, and embracing it all – his perfect lawn. It is a dream he replays during tedious meetings at work, lying sleepless in hotel rooms on business trips, even sitting right there, in his own living room. Once more, he takes himself through the journey but just as he gets to the point where he is about to pull into Ridge Circle and find his house waiting calmly at the end of the street, his train of thought is broken by a sound. A skittering. Or was it a scratching? He's not sure. It's a sound so faint he's not certain he heard it at all, but still he sits up to listen better, his head cocked to the side. His son comes galloping up the stairs from the basement with a thick textbook in his arms, turns the corner and pounds up the carpeted stairs to the second floor.

Must've been the kid or something, he thinks, and eases back down to watch the game show that has just come on.

You watch him for a while longer, clean-shaven, boyish, laughing at the TV as if it were his old friend, and then float straight up from the foot of the recliner, pausing at the ceiling to look down on the Man of Few Words stretched out in his chair, hands behind his neck, feet out on the ottoman, a minor American sultan relaxing in his palace waiting to be fed, the light of the TV throwing shifting patterns across his smooth, satisfied face.

You pass up through the ceiling into the cavity between the first and second floors, entering the empty space between the joists where the cables for the telephone and electricity pass in stapled bundles. The air moves as something passes by you. Something fast and light on its feet. Small, but not so small. Below you, the Man of Few Words glances up at the ceiling, ear cocked, pausing for a moment, then eases back into the chair to lose himself in the TV again. You continue upwards, passing through a tiled floor into the bathroom that is shared by the children. All the lights are on and a clinical brightness fills the room, like the operating theater at a hospital. At the sink is the Ice Princess, absorbed with her evening ablutions. The little lights that encircle the round vanity mirror she is using are flicked on to their 'daylight' setting and the young Princess is staring deeply at her own reflection with a frightening intensity that reveals both her artistry and adoration – part surgeon, part Narcissus bending to the pool. When her younger brother had first heard the name, vanity mirror, he had snorted, That's a good name for it, don't you think?, a critical insight that had earned him a quick punch to the fat part of his arm.

In the Ice Princess' hand is a pair of tweezers with which she is perfecting the line of her eyebrows, her fingers slim and nimble, the nails an explosion of glitter. The mirror hangs off the end of an extendable scissor-arm over the sink. She has it flipped to the magnifying side so her pretty face, which is just inches away from the glass, looms large before her, every hair, every pore, enlarged and brought into hyper-sharp focus. With each pluck she winces, the corners of her eyes briefly squeezing at the pain. Then her face recovers its steely determination and she plucks again.

What won't we do in the name of self-improvement? was another comment her brother had offered, this time from the safety of the hall beyond the half-opened bathroom door, drawled cockily before dashing to his room unscathed.

On the wall of the bathroom are shelves of various heights and depths, holding all the items necessary for her work, everything lined up in a specific order, placed according to their association with parts of the body – a taxonomic chart of personal hygiene. There is a shelf for hair that holds shampoos, conditioners, highlighters and the like. There is one shelf each for facial skin, eyes, and mouth. Armpits get a half-shelf. Breasts, consisting mostly of various enhancing pads, have the other half. Groin, hands, and feet each get a shelf, and nails occupies a long narrow shelf filled with a rainbow of small glass bottles each holding a measure of syrupy polish. From time to time, she turns from the mirror to these shelves, her fingers scanning along in front of her eye, searching for the right item like an apothecary in her storehouse. Her brother keeps a toothbrush in the holder by the sink. And a tube of toothpaste in the medicine cabinet.

As the Ice Princess whittles away at herself, the process almost entirely automatic at this point, her mind wanders. She thinks about her day at school. About what people said. About what people said about her. She makes mental lists that order and reorder her social networks. She imagines herself in clothes she can't afford. As her mind plays back the day's conversation, she remembers something distasteful, a nasty barb she received from one of her classmates, and her face goes blank. Her head drops slowly as her eyes roll up to the mirror with a chill look of contempt. It is a look she has perfected over time and she wields it professionally.

She is completely aware of what she is doing at the mirror. She knows why these long hours spent preening are required of her. This body of hers, this vessel she was granted at birth to carry her through her life, is not bad, but neither is it outstanding. A partially suitable vehicle. The parts that don't suit her, she willfully corrects. She *will* be beautiful, she *will* be perfect, and she is ready to endure almost anything under her own hand to achieve that. She is both sculptor and sculpture, fully committed to carving out of herself a better self.

You float off to the side, to the wall of the bathroom where the light switches are, pausing to take a last glance at the Ice

Princess who stands with her slim back to you. She wears only a white tank-top and Hello Kitty panties (a last vestige of once-innocent days), with her long, golden hair sliding down her back. You see her face reflected in the mirror, mascara eyes and frosted lips made huge by the magnifying curve of the glass, stretched into a fiendish mask. With that last glance, you pass through the sheetrock into the narrow cavity in the wall where the wires for the switches run. It is filled with cobwebs and dust. In one corner a small spider sits in a new web, awaiting even smaller things that cruise the perpetual night of that inner highway. It spins quickly on its delicate legs, facing you as if sensing your passing.

Continuing through the wall, you come out into the room of Anpanman, otherwise known as Little Brother, Johnny, John-boy, Lil' Jack, Butterball, and Pudge Face. His plethora of names reflects the fact that he is not yet fully formed. Not yet pigeonholed. He has been an anime freak since he was old enough to watch TV and, like 50 million other kids (albeit, mostly Japanese kids), Anpanman is his favorite. Even now, as an 8th grader, he still watches reruns and has somehow come to resemble the character: round-headed, red-cheeked, chubby, good-natured and curious (irritatingly so), always seeming to show up out of nowhere, and burdened with a fierce hero complex.

The room is dark. Mechagodzilla and SonGoku can be just made out, peering into the room from the wall like visitors from another world peeking through poster-shaped wormholes. Next to the bed there is a reading lamp in the shape of a dragon. The long, scaly neck snakes up from a heavy base, then curves over so that the horned head points down toward the pillow where Anpanman lies. Two spots of light shine from its LED eyes onto the book he is reading, lying face down on the bed, book propped up on his pillow, feet kicking in the air excitedly. It's a university level textbook of human anatomy and physiology, and he's flipping slowly through the pages of illustrations that depict the human body in various states of dissection. A muscle man walking around with no skin on, another showing all the blood vessels suspended in air like red and blue tree roots snaking out from the heart, a third with skeletons striking sports poses: throwing a javelin, crouching to release a bowling ball. When he'd first seen these drawings at school, he spent the rest of the day envisioning everyone he met in various states of disassembly. In the cafeteria he watched his skinless neighbors chew their lunch, naked sinews flexing in their jaws, food bubbling down through ribbons of intestines. In the hallway, a group of girls tripping along in front of him lost first their clothes, then their skin, then their muscles, then organs, until he walked behind a coven of chattering skeletons, humeri and ulnae wrapped around their textbooks like ivory clasps.

He flips another page of the textbook and it opens to an article under the bold heading Gut Flora. He breathes an audible awe~some into the air. Gut flora: microorganisms that live in the digestive tracts of animals.... ten times as many microbiota and microflora in the intestines as there are cells in the human body.... mostly bacteria which make up 60% of the dry mass of feces. He glows with interest and rereads the whole section. He imagines the gut flora of his own body. He knows they are made up of bacteria and other microscopic organisms, but the word flora keeps tumbling through his mind and he can't help but see them as plants. In his mind, his stomach appears as a New England meadow in spring, a riot of wild flowers growing amid the oaks and maples. The duodenum is a Swiss highland of deep green firs, the jejunum a wide sweep of prairie grasses, the ileum filled with acres of the Amazonian jungle. Strange colorful birds fly tree to tree, passing over muscular cats that silently prowl the ground like shadows. Gut Flora. Awesome. It would be just like him to quote this section during dinner.

You ease away from Anpanman and his book, and float down through the thick, shaggy carpet on the floor of his room, passing into the floor cavity, which is dark and empty, if you don't count the billion mold cells that have populated the area ever since the clumsy boy knocked over his fish tank some years ago. The murky water seeped down through the floorboards as Dipterus and Thrissops, his pet goldfish, smacked around on the broken glass, gasping for breath. Since then, mold has grown on the joists and the underside of the flooring in dark patches like sooty lichen. Continuing down through the floor, you emerge into the kitchen. The black and white checkerboard floor there is scrubbed, the dishes stored, the counters free of all mess, holding only a few electric appliances arranged as neatly as family heirlooms on a mantelpiece. You pass down through the linoleum floor, into another floor cavity. That same dark shape that passed you earlier scurries by again. You wait until it disappears around the corner. Sinking further, you arrive in the finished basement where Succor Mom is hard at work doing the ironing while dinner cooks.

She has a heavy professional-grade iron, its steam line

hanging from the ceiling to keep it clear of the ironing board. The newer model that the Man of Few Words had bought for her, one that is lighter and easier to use, sits on the shelf nearby, untouched. This is, after all, her job, and she wants very much to do it well. Even when she was a little girl she cared passionately for a whole family of dolls, naming them, dressing them, caring for them when they were sick or injured. As she grew older her love was transferred from dolls to friends at high school, and later college, washing and sewing, tending to their personal needs like a chambermaid. Now married with a family of her own, this need she has to care for people has shifted to the three of them. The need to lend comfort. The need to give support. Whatever they require, she is there for them, putting food on the table, washing, ironing and mending their clothes, cleaning the house, holding them when they are frightened, hurt or lonely, making them feel proud of themselves for doing whatever it is they are doing. She is a mute well giving up its water without so much as a whisper, quenching the thirst of whomsoever comes before her. A fold here a press there, a wipe a tuck a hug a smile, she shapes her home into a place of comfort and security. Do the others understand this? Her silent husband, her haughty daughter, her dreamy son? No, not really, she thinks. But no matter. She is a deep well and not easily run dry.

She is putting the finishing touches on a few of the white shirts that Jack the Elder, the Man of Few Words, wears to work, pressing the collars into sharp triangular blades, setting creases down the back as crisp as rolled steel. She stacks everything gently in piles according to the room she will bring them to, and sets the piles in a large plastic laundry basket. At the top of the stairs, she flicks out the basement light and closes the door gently, walks through the kitchen where she stops briefly to check the pot roast and wipe a dot of gravy from the counter, then out through the living room and up the carpeted stairs to the second floor. As she rounds the corner to head up the stairs, the Man of Few Words looks up from his program to catch the gentle tucking of her skirt, the restrained sway of her hips. Stepping up onto the first step, she turns her head just long enough to catch him watching her legs and blushes before heading upstairs. After all these years, she still blushes at the thought.

Succor Mom puts the clothes away in their respective drawers, not tossing them in but tucking each in neatly and patting them down before closing. She straightens the covers on the beds in each room, fluffs the pillows, and heads downstairs to the kitchen to finish preparing dinner. On each plate, she serves up a slice of pot roast with peas and mashed potatoes, and calls her family. They gather around the square table in the kitchen, drawn by the meal to spend a few minutes near each other. You hover by the salt and pepper shakers, listening. The Man of Few Words pulls his plate a little forward to center it on the placemat, fingering the knife and spoon to straighten and align them. Grace is said and they eat quietly. Succor Mom's falsetto cheer breaks through the light clattering of cutlery on plates, What did we do today?

The Man of Few Words says, Lawn's done, jabbing a knife into the air to press his point.

The Ice Princess offers the single word 'nothing' in the most desultory voice she can manage, not bothering to look up from the food she is stirring around her plate. When his mother's gaze shifts to him, Anpanman also offers the requisite 'nothing' but then remembers that, in fact, he does have something to tell. His face lights up and he begins to rock excitedly on his chair, breaking into a high-pitched recitation, the words piling up on his lips in their rush to be spoken.

Hey, did you guys know we have all these microscopic creatures living in us, he says and shivers. This is way cool, you gotta check this out, there are all these little-little things, his fingers pinching in front of his eyes to show how absolutely tiny he means, all these microorganisms living in our intestines, at which word the Ice Princess's face blanches and she drops her fork and knife onto her plate with a loud clang, that help us digest stuff and like without them we'd probably die, like we're not alone you know in our bodies? like there're these thousands of other species that we have inside us and we like depend on them to live, his parents can only nod quizzically at the idea of having other species inside of them. Anpanman takes a brief pause for air and continues.

It's weird. I mean, things living inside us? It's like we're possessed. His eyes roll back to show their whites, limp hands floating out in front of his chest kyonshi-style and in his best Vincent Price he moans, Weee aaaare poosssessed.

The Ice Princess turns her palms up, her mouth dropping open in exasperation, eyes rolling back in a mask of disgust miming the silent cry, Why have I been burdened with this turd brother?

The parents look across the table at their children, both with their eyes rolled back to the whites, and manage uncertain smiles. The Man of Few Words mumbles, That's… um, that's great Lil' Jack.

Succor Mom chirps, Who wants dessert? Jell-O! Everyone loves Jell-O.

Dinner over, Succor Mom gets elbow deep in sink suds, cleaning everything once before their final sterilization in the dishwasher. She hums as she washes. The Man of Few Words heads back to his recliner to re-enter his well-deserved state of repose. On the way he adjusts the magazines on the coffee table, restacking them by size and aligning their spines. He scoots down into the chair, kicks back and flicks the TV on with the remote, hoping to catch a sit-com that he likes. His fingers lock behind his neck, armpit hairs puffing out from his t-shirt, and he sighs. The Ice Princess is back in the bathroom, face to the mirror. Anpanman lies on his bed, lights off, watching an old episode of Dragon Ball Z. The nuclear family, nicely compartmentalized.

The Man of Few Words is chuckling along at the antics of the heavy-set guy who is always messing up in his attempts to get dates, coached from the shadows by the acerbic hostess of the show, who regularly punches holes in his ego. He is just about to call to the kitchen to get Succor Mom to bring out a bowl of chips when he thinks he hears the sound again, like a skittering or a gnawing. It's a faint sound and he still isn't really sure he heard it. It might have been the TV, so he mutes the volume and listens carefully. The ear that he has tilted toward the ceiling lifts a little as he strains to listen. He holds his breath for a few seconds, eyes wide, face frozen with attention, then gives up, shrugs and flicks the sound back on. Not a minute later, from the upstairs bathroom where the Ice Princess is grooming, comes a long, high-pitched and utterly frantic shriek. The Man of Few Words throws down the remote and leaps to his feet. By the time he reaches the stairs Succor Mom is already in front of him and they storm up the stairs together, pushing open the door to the brightly lit bathroom and pressing as one into the opening. Anpanman comes from behind and wedges in between their legs for a glimpse, the nuclear family compressed to a critical mass. You follow, hovering above them, sensing the fissioning that has already begun. There stands the Ice Princess, hands limp, comb dropped in the sink, her face ashen and streaked with mascara. She's trembling and breathless. It takes some time to decipher what happened, but after piecing together the few gasped sounds her daughter could make and carefully examining the comb and preening through her luxurious hair, Succor Mom concludes, yes, in fact, she does have lice.

The word hurtles through their well-scrubbed minds. Lice. It drags into their thoughts a host of other words unbidden. Syphilis. Scabies. Leprosy. Plague. Their imaginations just won't sit still. The ever-helpful Anpanman says, Now all we need is rats. He says this to himself but, knowingly, loud enough to be heard. Loud enough to warrant a fatherly wallop in the arm that will leave a small bruise. Rats? thinks the Man of Few Words, but says nothing. He runs his hand back through his close-cropped hair and looks to the ceiling. Succor Mom pushes the boys out of the bathroom and shuts the door. The Ice Princess collapses into her mother's arms, ready to be quarantined on a desolate island. They sit on the edge of the tub, the girl sinking her face into her mother's neck, letting herself be wrapped by strong, protective arms. She snuggles into their safety, shivering.

Mo~m, she moans. What am I going to do? her mind trapped by the image of her classmates walking by her, faces averted in disgust. The ice inside her melts and becomes surprisingly warm tears.

Ohh baby, don't cry, says Succor Mom as she rocks her daughter making tiny shushing sounds in the girl's ear. It's OK Sweetie. Really, trust me. Lice are no big deal. Most kids get them. It's OK baby. A little special shampoo and they'll be gone. You'll see. She strokes her daughter's hair, but in her mind are the neatly-pressed women at the PTA meeting, standing across the room from her, looking scornful. What kind of mother would let her kids get lice? In this neighborhood?

She thinks this but mumbles instead, You'll see. It'll be all right, and pulls her daughter's head to her chest.

Pushed out of the bathroom, Anpanman goes to his room and begins googling lice. He finds some close-up images that remind him of the Om creatures from Nausicaa, so he prints out a few of them and tapes them to the wall near SonGoku. In the days to come, this blasphemy will earn him a quick bruise on his other arm. The Man of Few Words pads slowly down the carpeted steps to the living room. He sits back down in his recliner but he doesn't switch on the TV. He just sits there, very still, listening to the little sounds a house makes. The sounds you never hear. The soft low whump when the air conditioner comes on. The creaks in the floorboards when someone walks by upstairs. The creaks in the walls when the wind blows. The creaks that happen for no apparent reason. He sits there listening for well over two hours but that scratching sound, the faint skittering he thought he had heard before, never reappears.

For a week, the Ice Princess stays home from school, quarantined like a smallpox victim, having her homework delivered to her door by worried friends. On the third day, just after dinner, the doorbell rings and the Man of Few Words answers it. Outside are three well-dressed girls smelling of perfumes with names like Endless Passion and Asian Orchid who crane their necks to see if they can catch a glimpse of their schoolmate. The Man of Few Words stops them at the door. Kathy's still too sick to see anyone, he says snatching the papers from the startled girls and closing the door in their faces more abruptly than necessary. As he walks back inside, he hears a scratching coming from the kitchen, and then a gnawing. A definite gnawing sound as if something was trying to chew through wood. This time he'd really heard it and it stops him in mid-stride with the stack of homework held out in front of him like an offering. He hears it again, clearly. He walks quietly into the kitchen, turns off the light and lies down on the floor. He lies and waits, hardly breathing. He can smell the lemon wax on the linoleum and is still lying there when Succor Mom comes into the room, flicks on the light and gasps. She takes a breath and asks calmly, Um… what are you doing? He stands and looks at her shyly but doesn't say anything. He steers her to the living room by the elbow, and they sit down to watch TV until bedtime. The next morning, the Man of Few Words yawns as he plods downstairs. He can smell coffee already brewing. As he reaches the kitchen door, Succor Mom cries out, What the beejeezus?!

What's up, hun? he calls. Walking into the kitchen he sees her standing by the faux-granite counter staring a fruit basket in her hands, motionless, as if deep in thought.

What's up? he asks again, cheerfully.

She puts the basket down and picks out two apples, one in

each hand. They each have a long, toothy gash in them, a deep white notch through the red skins.

Every one. Every last damnblad one, she says shaking the apples at him as if she was about to hurl them. The Man of Few Words starts to say something, but finds he hasn't the words.

In the days following the discovery of the Ice Princess' lice and the nighttime visitor to the kitchen, Succor Mom begins to feel strange. At first, she thinks that she's upset at the possibility that she might have lice, too. She peers into her bathroom mirror and rakes a nit-comb through her hair, examining the teeth carefully. But there are no lice. It isn't that. She thinks, if it was a rat that had bitten her apples, then maybe she has contracted plague from it. The Man of Few Words has a word to say about that. She can't get the image of strange, invisible creatures living on the skin of her beautiful daughter out of her mind. Of Anpanman's vision of microbes in spongy webs growing inside her like mold under the sink. Her clothes begin to feel too tight. Her heart races at times for no reason. She notices the smell of her own body, touches herself and smells her fingertips, alarmed and excited. She dreams of wolves.

This nervous unraveling builds until one night when she is preparing fried chicken for dinner. The whole bird is set out on the cutting board ready to be butchered into parts. It's a task she finds disturbing if not repulsive. She gets a fresh-killed bird from the local farmer, rather than buying precut pieces, because she feels it is fresher and cheaper. But she doesn't enjoy the cutting. At least, she didn't used to. This time, impulsively, she thrusts her hand into the cavity of the bird to clean it out. The rubber gloves she normally wears lay forgotten on the counter. You're there behind her. She digs her finger into the giblets and pulls them out with an audible sucking sound. They smell of blood. She looks at the mess of organs in her hand and squishes them, enjoying the cool, sticky wetness. She sways, feeling something like vertigo. A sudden fever. A realignment of her nerves into a more ancient pattern. She swoons wiping the back of a hand across her forehead and leaving a bloody streak.

Do you know about this? Is it something to do with this place, something long-buried like the miller's family, or the people of the forest, that has risen once again. Is it you?

She slaps the counter and laughs, throwing off uncertainty, plunges her hand into the bloody cavity again and again, yanking out all the remaining organs in a series of muscular jerks. You watch her as you float above the counter near the neatly arranged appliances. Her hand wet with blood, she grabs the cleaver and lifts it high above her head. With one quick downward stroke, she hacks the bird in two, whack!, straight down the backbone, the heavy butcher block resounding with the force. Her hair begins to slip from its moorings, falling in loose strands around her neck. Her movements reflect in the polished surface of the stainless toaster, in the food mill, the espresso machine, the juicer, in all the neatly arranged appliances, a dozen frantic women hacking at their prey. She switches to the small bone knife, grabs half a bird and starts to slice and tear it into sections. Not the neat cutting she normally does, slicing the cartilage cleanly at the joints to separate leg from thigh from body. No, this is a slaughter, wolves at the carcass shredding with their long yellow teeth. Bloody bits of chicken splatter on her white blouse, on the countertop and the Italian tile backsplash. She rips and shreds until she reaches some point of satisfaction and then stands back, breathless, utterly amazed at the carnage that lies before her as if she had just walked in on it. She brushes the hairs from her face with a bloodstained sleeve, trying to calm down, wondering what had happened. And, what to do about it. There'll be no fried chicken tonight. After a minute's thought, she grinds the meat into a chicken-noodle casserole to hide her work. Her family will spit out all the little bits of bone they find and look at her askance.

Are you pleased? Was this your work, or are you only watching?

As Succor Mom is wiping the last bits of bloody cartilage from the counter, you float through the Italian tile and the wall behind it, into the laundry room closet. There are brooms and mops, a bucket, and shelf after shelf of cleansing products. It smells lemony and soapy and lavender all at once. On each bottle and box, pretty women smile below their outrageous promises. You look at them one by one, intently, as if checking their sincerity. At the sound of footsteps you pass into the laundry room as Succor Mom strides around the corner from the kitchen. She pulls off her blood-splattered blouse and skirt, grabs the bucket from the closet and throws the clothes in. You watch her, standing in front of the utility sink in her underwear, her shoulders rising and falling as she kneads the stained clothes in cold water. She pours some bleach in and stands back, catching her own reflection in the glass of the side door. Hair half loose, underwear like a white bikini, a slender trail of blood running down one cheek. She likes what she sees, and shivers.

You leave this half-undressed woman and continue through the next wall to find, in the inner cavity, a completely nude one, a Playboy centerfold fixed to the sheetrock with dry and curling duct tape. The carpenters who built the house had kept her up in different places until they grew tired of her and let the rock-hangers board her up. Their little joke. The owners would never know. Buxom Miss July remains there, smiling, spread-legged on a perpetual summer beach, a fertility goddess sealed in her shrine for eternity, listening to the endless perambulations of the washing machine. You pass through her silver navel-stud and into the garage just as the light comes on and the automatic opener engages. The heavy-paneled door begins to slide up, letting sunlight flood in, illuminating shelves on the walls filled with neat rows of polishes, oils, and brushes, everything a man might need to keep his car in perfect shape. As the door rises you see the Man of Few Words pulling into the driveway, returning from HomeHelper with the rat traps he'd bought.

He had found them in the Sanitary Items aisle – sturdy panels of wood, about four by six inches, on which were mounted thick steel coilsprings. He picked them up off the shelf, feeling their weight and the strength of the steel through the thin plastic wrapper. He imagined the wire snapping across his own fingers and shuddered reflexively. He pictured the rat, neck snapped, eyes-bulging, skittering its back feet across the kitchen floor in the last moments of its life and hesitated. In the recesses of his brain, in whatever tangled web of neurons these thoughts are woven into being and weighed for their value, the life of a single rat hung momentarily in balance with the tranquility of a well-kept home. The home proved the heavier. He picked out three traps and went to the checkout counter. As he walked down the aisle, a purple finch trapped inside the building flew overhead, flitting from beam to beam along the ceiling. A moment later, another finch chased behind it, following the same route, and the pair fluttered their way in little spurts out of sight. He did not notice them. He walked to the checkout and slid the traps on the steel counter, careful to place them face down, like the first porn magazines he had purchased so many years before. Back then, the edges of his cheeks and ears had tinged red under the watchful eyes of the pretty young cashier. This time, he pretends to be busy with something in his wallet.

The Man of Few Words is unloading the bag with the traps from the backseat when the Ice Princess comes howling up the driveway, eyes red from crying, long trails of mascara dripping down her cheeks. She races through the front door, slams it shut with a sound clearly meant to announce both her arrival and her distress, and disappears upstairs. The Man of Few Words watches this performance, perplexed, but says nothing. Succor Mom will take care of it. As he walks into the house with his bag of sprung death, you float up through the garage ceiling and into the Ice Princess's room. She runs in and throws herself on the bed, weeping theatrically into her pillow.

During her confinement, after the discovery of her head lice, she had undergone a regimen of medicinal shampoos that slowly worked their wonders. Succor Mom spent endless hours preening her long hair with a fine-toothed nit comb, removing tiny white eggs with surgical care, working over her head section by section like a mine-sweeper in a field of flax. When the all-clear was pronounced, the Princess had returned to school to a flood of expressions of concern from teachers and classmates alike. They, of course, had thought that she had been suffering with the flu. She reveled in the outpouring of sympathy and enjoyed being back at school immensely. Heading to the cafeteria, she found a cadre of the older girls waiting for her in the hall. The Gang of Five. The prettiest girls in school, the clique that the Ice Princess aspired to join. Aspired is too gentle a word. Acceptance into their inner circle is what kept her at the mirror morning and night. It is what she pondered in dreamy moments when she should be listening to her teacher, when she was idly texting friends or reading in bed. This desire lay at the very core of her being, and she needed only their approval to be complete. And now, there they were. They had come for her. The girls formed a tight semi-circle to block her path, shoulder to shoulder, eyes set. The Ice Princess stepped inside their circle, textbooks clutched protectively to her chest. They did not look to be in an approving mood. She tried to breathe and found the hall empty of its oxygen.

Hearing the Ice Princess burst into the house, sobbing, Succor Mom hurries up the stairs and into her daughter's room. She sees the girl crying on the bed and tries to hug her but gets pushed away, forcefully.

I jus'… just want to be… left alone! she howls, whacking the bed with her legs and burying her head into the pillow.

What happened dearest? asks Succor Mom stroking her long, nit-free hair.

I just want to die!!

Come on hun. Tell me what happened. Through many hesitant false starts, weeping and gasped expulsions, the broken

Princess lays out the tale. How the Gang of Five had trapped her against the cold cinderblock wall, poked at her hair with their pencils and rulers. There were no words to be remembered, only a blur of faces: heavily mascaraed eyes filled with disgust, flashes of white teeth through frosted lips, haughty and snickering, pressing in on her, flicking at her hair with their instruments of torture. And then, as suddenly as they had started, they stopped and left, walking arm in arm down the hall away from her. She had rushed to the girls room and vomited.

And you, hovering there, watching her tell this story. Is this what you expected to happen? Is this why you've come?

Ohhh my poor girl, says Succor Mom wrapping her arms around her miserable daughter. I am so sorry.

How could they have known? the Ice Princess snarls, pushing her mother away, suddenly alive and ready to fight. How did they find out? Mother and daughter as one rotate their heads in the direction of Anpanman's room.

You float sideways through the wall, passing a swarm of lady bugs in the void that will erupt like confetti come autumn, and drift into Anpanman's room just as mother and daughter burst through his door. He is caught with his pants down, literally, half on half off, teetering on his bed. Many shouts, angrily raised hands, and passionately expressed entreatments of innocence later, the ladies sit down on the edge of the bed, deflated. The Ice Princess moans, If buddy-boy here didn't wikileak the news, who did? She swivels her head up to look at her mother.

Um, Mo~m? which is answered with a strong and insistent, No, not me, hun. I didn't tell… any… any…. Her eyes turning thoughtfully to the ceiling.

Mo~~m?

No, Sweetheart. I didn't tell anyone. I promise. I wouldn't.... I wouldn't do that .... Her voice trailing off, wondering.

Mom! What are you saying?

Well dear... I was just thinking... her hands rolling in explanation, that when I was in the drugstore buying your lic... your, you know, your special shampoo, Debbie Candor's mom was in the same aisle, too, and we chatted for second. You know, just hello goodbye.

The Ice Princess's face freezes.

Well she may have seen me buying the shampoo is all.

Her mother and brother fade away as the Ice Princess relives her persecution. In the middle of the pack of girls, front and center in the Gang of Five, was Debbie Candor giving her the Look of Filth. She voices this memory into Anpanman's room in a dull monotone, breathing it out into the air as if there's no one there to hear. They all sit in silence. The double-cross revealed and no one to blame.

So it was Debbie Candor? says Succor Mom. What I don't get is...

Ice Princess spits out a pained, What?

Well, you know, it's just that Debbie... She looks at her daughter and matter-of-factly says, Debbie's had lice, too.

The Ice Princess looks at her in open-mouthed disbelief.

Twice!

After a moment of silence, in accidental coordination, from three different mouths, come the slow cold words, That little bitch.

The Ice Princess goes to bed early. You look down on her from above as she lies curled on top of the covers, a Renoir maiden at rest. Her beautiful hair spreads out around her on the white sheets, chest rising and falling easily with her breaths. When you drop closer, you see her eyelids fluttering with sleep-thoughts, her hands and feet twitching ever so slightly. You leave her to her unsettled dreams and float down through the floors to the basement. On the way, you pass a place beneath the living room floor where the carpenters had used a rougher grade of lumber. The beams there still have bark on them in places, and pressed into the bark, is some dirt. From the dirt hangs a tiny fern, now dry and shriveled. You pass that wasted forest, slipping down into the basement to find Succor Mom at the ironing board again. She's working on a stack of pretty lace napkins that she uses when guests come for dinner, enjoying the process of pressing and folding them. It's a calming job, each square of fabric made flat, folded, and flattened again. Repetitive. Precise. You watch her at her work. You pass close to her, around to the front to see her face. As you do, she feels a hot itch flash over her skin and rolls her shoulders to shake off the feeling. She continues ironing as you circle her and she feels the itch again, shivers and hisses out a held breath. She watches her own hands put the iron down. Her index finger extends and presses its nail into the napkin hard enough to score a long, deep line. She watches this as if it's someone else's finger. Then her hands pick up the napkin and with one quick outward convulsion, tear it in two. At the sound of fabric ripping she jumps back from the ironing board as if burnt and stands there, confused. Strangely excited. Chuckling in low slow gulps like a crazy woman.

Look at you hovering there. Who are you anyway? Do you know anything about this?

With Succor Mom in the basement and the kids upstairs, the Man of Few Words googles 'rat bait'. Cheese, peanut butter and chocolate all seem to get the most hits. He has in mind a cartoon image of a rat with long, long whiskers holding a chunk of cheese in its paws and munching happily. We'll start with cheese, he announces confidently. That night, after everyone has gone to bed, he baits the traps with cheddar and sets them out, one each in the basement, kitchen and living room. The thick, coiled wires rest there patiently on their wooden beds, each bent to its purpose, each having but one thought. Release. He turns off all the lights, washes his hands, and goes to bed. He lies for hours staring at the ceiling, listening for the whack! but it never comes. The air thins and stretches, and fills with tiny sounds that could be a faint gnawing or skittering, or just the wind, or his wife stirring in bed next to him. He falls asleep listening. The next morning he gets up early, anxious to see what he might have caught. Anpanman pokes his sleepy head out of his bedroom door and tags along yawning as they make the rounds. You follow, floating nearby. First, the living room. Nothing. The wires coiled tightly as ever.

Nothin'? asks Anpanman.

Oh he's been here all right, say the Man of Few Words. He points. All the cheese he had scattered to draw the rat to its execution is gone. Only the bit on the trigger is left untouched.

Everything but this one piece. Gone. Clean as a whistle.

Smart dude, said Anpanman nodding his head in admiration.

We'll see about that, says the Man of Few Words coldly.

In the kitchen they find the same thing. The cheese around the trap gone, the chunk on the trigger untouched, wire still bent at the ready. No rat to be seen. In the basement, the same story and a smattering of little black droppings left for them to clean up.

Oh my God, this has got to be the smartest rat in the world, chirps Anpanman. This guy's like Einstein.

Einstein, huh? We'll see about that sonny boy, says the Man of Few Words, vexed but just a little impressed himself.

Over the next few days, the play repeats unchanged. Setting traps at night, checking in the morning, finding nothing but collateral damage. The Man of Few Words tries changing the bait from cheese to peanut butter (no good either), and then to chocolate (Anpanman seemed more attracted to it than the rat). After finding a plastic container of birdseed he kept in the basement gnawed opened and spilled, he switches to that.

You like birdseed, you'll get birdseed.

Each day at breakfast the family asks, Any luck with Einstein? to which he offers a crestfallen, single-syllable answer. No. And with each failed day, as his frustration deepens, much against his will and better judgment, a feeling of respect grows within him for this intelligent rodent that refuses to be caught. He copies Anpanman and takes to calling him Einstein.

On the fourth day, he comes back from the hardware store with an electric-zapper trap but catches nothing. On the sixth day he tries glue traps which are so sticky he gets himself caught just trying to set them out. The next morning he finds, as usual, all the bait spread around the traps missing, and the traps themselves completely untouched, except for in one glue trap where he sees the faint impression of a rat's paw. A little star pattern of fine pale lines on the clear glue. He imagines Einstein nibbling his way up to the trap. The glue looks like a little pool of water in the moonlit kitchen. Einstein places a paw on it, delicately, then snaps back at the realization, looks up toward the upstairs bedrooms where the family sleeps, and narrows his eyes.

Einstein you son of a gun, mutters the Man of Few Words as he throws the glue traps in the garbage, and yet, he is smiling as he says it. At first horrified by the idea, just the idea, of a rat in the house, he now feels nothing but respect for Einstein. He imagines the rat peering through a small hole in the sheetrock, watching him as he sits at the computer late at night googling 'catch rat best method,' whiskers twitching as a sly grin spreads across his narrow, toothy mouth. Eventually, the Man of Few Words throws out all the traps and comes back from HomeHelper with a live trap. He sets up the little wire cage in the kitchen with a piece of cloth inside so the bottom of the cage and the trigger mechanism are hidden. Less cage-like, he thinks. He makes a trail of birdseed leading inside the cage. On the first morning, all the seed outside the trap is gone. Einstein 1, Man of Few Words 0. He spreads more seed. The next day, all the seed outside the trap and just a little bit right inside the trap is gone. Einstein 2, Man of Few Words 0. But when the Man of Few Words sees the seed gone from inside he can sense this is going to work. Eventually. He just needs a little more patience. In the meantime, he gets from the basement the old aquarium that Anpanman used to have. It has a wire mesh top. Perfect for a cage. When Anpanman asks him at dinner why he was cleaning up the aquarium, he tells the family, For Einstein. You know. As a pet.

Excuse me? says Succor Mom, disbelievingly, slapping down her fork and knife. As a what?

Him or her? questions the Ice Princess, stirring her peas.

Awesome! blurts Anpanman, mouth full.

You're not really going to keep that rat in the house are you? continues Succor Mom, tapping her knife on the table.

What makes you think it's not a her? demands the Ice Princess, in a B-movie attempt at being aghast.

This is so awesome! squeaks Anpanman. C'c'an I keep him in my room?

Her! Keep her! says the Ice Princess coldly and definitively, pointing her knife at no one.

Can we talk about this later? asks Succor Mom, arms crossed.

The Man of Few Words says nothing more.

Days go by. School lets out for summer. When not at work, The Man of Few Words loses himself in the rat hunt, sleeping less and less, yearning to hear the click of the trap door snapping shut. Succor Mom's fevers continue. A mirror punched. A drawer full of socks hurtled across an unsuspecting room. Her clothes wrinkle, her bun slips, her eyes become the distant pools of a person rigged with grenades, at once empty and on fire, trembling at the thought of what the next moment holds. For the Ice Princess, climate change is afoot. She finds herself a loose berg calved off the pack and pulled by hidden currents into uncharted waters. Having been double-crossed by Debbie Candor, her passion to be one of the pretty girls in the Gang of Five dissipates.

Like, who do they think they are anyway?

She falls in with a new group of friends, kids who are into horseback-riding and hiking, for whom 'makeup' means 'the composition or constitution of something', whose nails are torn and filled with dirt from working in their community garden, whose skin is colored only by the sun and wind. She spends a long weekend with them at a sleepover and comes back with her hair in dreadlocks, reams of sparkly beads woven into each long braid, the heavy smell of burnt hemp suffusing her clothes. Seeing her, the Man of Few Words is speechless. Succor Mom looks, pauses for only the briefest of moments, and wraps her arms around her new daughter. Anpanman offers her a huge, Awe....some..., and a high-five, which she plays down real cool-like but, still, its nice to know someone's got your back. She winks at her brother and gives him a friendly noogie. The Ice Princess has channeled her inner tree hugger and morphed into Gaiagirl. Of course, she spends more time than her new friends tending her dreads in front of the mirror, but in many other ways she really has changed. Deeply so. She responds to questions at meals. She plays with her brother in the backyard. And, she smiles. Which is nice. All in all, it's southern waters she's floated into, and the Ice Princess has all but melted.

One afternoon, Succor Mom goes to the mall, one of those cavernous places, seven floors of sugar-coated consumption built around a large central atrium, filled year-round with the strains of a vaguely Christmassy music. She decides to start at the top and work her way down, and takes the elevator up to the seventh floor. When she gets out at the top, she hears trumpets and chimes. A marching band from a local high school is beginning a fundraiser down below near the water feature. She can hear them tuning up and walks over to the railing to look down on the spectacle. As she nears the edge, the air lofting up from below with the smell of French fries and warm chocolate, she is possessed by an overwhelmingly strong urge to jump. To leap out into that space, arms spread wide, and cast herself upon the wind. It is not a desperate feeling. It is a completely self-confident belief that she can fly, a feeling welling up inside her uncontrollably, crackling up her spine, out along her shoulders and down the skin of her arms to the tips of her fingers. She can feel with every fiber of her body that this is possible. She will launch herself over the railing headfirst. The air will hold her up, no question, arms spread like wings, blouse fluttering as she turns in slow circles down toward the amazed people below. Her calves tense in preparation. She takes a long slow breath and rises onto the tips of her toes, her hands pressed down on the railing to lift her chest, her head leaning out and over the precipice. The band strikes up Semper Fidelis. Little children waiting at the Frosty Cream behind her hear the music and rush to the railing, knocking into her legs. She surges forward, her chest lurching over the edge. Startled, she yanks back and fights very hard to move herself away from the railing, unable to catch her breath. She finds the emergency stairs and hurries home with nothing bought. You see her pull into the driveway and tumble from the car, hair out of place, shirt untucked. She walks with nervous speed to the front door and disappears into the house. You float after her, passing through the foyer and into the empty living room, but she has already rushed upstairs to the bathroom.

The Man of Few Words is outside on the flagstone terrace, so you float out the back wall to where he stands, staring at Anpanman sprawled face down on the lawn. It's hot, one of those lazy summer days that seems to just stretch on forever, the sky filled with motionless plumes of cotton candy. The Man of Few Words walks over to Anpanman, but the boy doesn't look up. You float next to him, watching. Even when his father's shadow crosses where his hands are, holding a small magnifying glass, Anpanman doesn't turn from what he's doing but only says in a slow voice, Dad, you are in my light.

What's up kiddo?

No answer.

I asked you something, John.

Belly botany.

What?

Belly… oh! awesome. Hey, come check this out. Without looking up he calls, Come on Dad. C'mere, check this out. Here, you can use this one, and he takes another, bigger magnifier from his side and sets it on the lawn next to him. The Man of Few Words looks around once, thinks about it for just a second, then crouches down, then kneels down, then cautiously lies down next to his son. He picks up the magnifier and peers at the grass where Anpanman is looking. You hover above and watch, trying to look through the magnifiers too. The boy has a flip type with two lenses that increases the power when both are used together, and he is holding it right up to his eye, his face jammed almost to the ground.

Oh man check this guy out.

The Man of Few Words, leans in a little and peers through his magnifier to where his son's hands are.

What am I looking for?

Can't you see it? The earwig. Dermaptera. Check out those pinchers, ohhhh man. Way cool. As he watches the bug crawl through grass blades like trees, the boy starts making crashing noises with his throat, a soundtrack to the monster movie he's imagining. Hey, there's a pillbug.

Where?

There, right next to him.

Oh yeah.

The pill bug is stretched out, crawling along just near the earwig.

Hey I wonder if Dermaptera will see him? What's his name, Arma-something. Arma, what is it? Arma-dilly-dally-something.

Here comes the earwig, kiddo.

Oh yeah. Then, in his World Wrestling Championship announcer voice, Anpanman blurts, Battle of the Bugs. Final Countdown.

Father and son press their heads together, looking. You lean in as well, hoping to catch a glimpse. The lawn is rich with the gunpowder smell of fertilizer and herbicide. The pinchered earwig, looking like some alien war machine, draws nearer to the pillbug, proceeding at a slow pace until they finally cross paths. A light touch of the earwig's leg and the pillbug reflexively rolls into an armored ball. The earwig walks across it and disappears in the grass forest. Father and son let out audible sighs in unison, having hoped for something more violent. This goes on for the better part of an hour. They watch two ants lock in a tug-of-war over a grasshopper leg. A white grub poke its fat snout out from deep down among the grass roots, sense the light and retreat.

A chinchbug tumble into view, a sign of a devastation yet to come that somehow passes through the Man of Few Word's protective radar without triggering a chemical attack.

They lie there pressed in against each other, new best buddies, each hyping their latest discovery – ohhh, you gotta see this! no way. check this out – feeling the warmth of the sun and each other's bodies through their summer clothes, continuing the hunt just to prolong their filial touches. Belly botany bonding. The world in those few square inches of grass beneath their gaze is teeming with life. Scanning through their magnifiers, they are transported above an endless forest filled with ancient arboreal creatures. Anpanman feels that any moment a flock of pterodactyls might lift into the air and circle about his hands, tiny winged creatures landing on the tips of his fingers. How awesome is that? The Man of Few Words finds himself floating over a forest like the one that existed in that very place a thousand years before it succumbed to settlers, farms, villages and, finally, to the carefully planned development of Chestnut Hill – an endless sea of tree crowns extending as far as the eye can see, within which live entire kingdoms of animals just waiting to be discovered. Mowing the lawn will never be the same.

As they lie there, lost in their dreams of ancient worlds, Succor Mom calls out to them that she is going out to mail some packages. They raise hands to wave goodbye without looking. Succor Mom stops in front of the mirror in the foyer to check herself, smoothes her hair back and tucks a few strays into the bun, then closes the top two buttons of her blouse that had somehow come undone. She looks with a measure of doubt at the woman in the mirror, not quite liking the gleam she sees in her eyes and then drives to the central post office. She waits patiently in line for ten minutes, listening to the footsteps of the other customers echoing from the high, domed ceiling. As she waits, little scraps of memory bob up, unwanted. The marching band at the mall, seen from high above, scented air rushing up from the atrium. The sudden, loud rip of a napkin. The echoing footsteps grow louder and she finds her breath shortening with excitement. Whack! goes the cleaver through the back of the chicken. The footsteps sound like a landslide and she is stricken by the urge to howl. To drop her packages, rip off her blouse, rake her hands through her hair, fling her head back and really, really scream. An urge so strong, the image of herself berserking so clear in her head, that she knows she has to just do it or flee. She steps out of line, hugging her packages tightly to her chest, and drives home, knuckles white on the wheel. You are waiting for her when she pulls into the driveway. She passes through you on the way inside.

Who are you? Were you one of the miller's children? A tow-head kid who played under apple boughs dizzy with humming blossoms, dreaming of honey on oatmeal? Did you love this place too much to leave?

Were you an Iroquois boy, a shadow with a bone knife and bow who never returned home without game? Were the forest and meadow your books, each bent blade, gentle hoot, pile of scat, and paw print a story in themselves? Do you want them back that much?

Were you a Marsh Owl, winged death with yellow eyes that missed nothing? A pink-tongued buck?

Were you the pines along the bluff, redolent with sap in

August's heat? A fiddlehead in the hollow by the brook unfolding upward into light?

Were you the clearwater spring? The black earth?

Why do you linger so in this Peaceable Kingdom?

It is the fifth day of trying the live trap when the Man of Few Words hears it. He is lying in bed, watching the ceiling, waiting for sleep to draw him in with its gentle opiates, when he thinks he hears a faint clunk from the kitchen.

What was that? asked Succor Mom.

Lordy pancakes, says the Man of Few Words and rushes downstairs in his pajamas, Succor Mom right behind him. In the trap is a large rat, much bigger than he had expected, with a fat rump and a long tail, thick as a finger at the base. It's scrambling madly side to side, scratching at the bottom of the cage to tear the cloth away and try to dig itself out. The Man of Few Words takes the aquarium off the kitchen counter and puts on the leather work gloves he had prepared for this purpose. The trick now, he thinks, is getting Einstein from the cage to the aquarium. He puts one hand on the trap and the other on the aquarium. From the cage to the aquarium. He looks back and forth between them. Cage to aquarium. He rubs his hands together. He hadn't really thought this through. Anpanman and Gaiagirl, having heard the commotion, are now gathered with Succor Mom at the side of the kitchen watching things unfold. The Man of Few Words decides to just dump Einstein into the aquarium and slam the wire cover shut.

Easy, he mutters to himself.

What's that? asks Succor Mom.

He slides the wire cover halfway opened and tilts the trap so it points down into the aquarium, releases the trip-lock on the door and slides it open. Einstein grips the wire cage tightly, refusing to come out. The Man of Few Words shakes the trap, but Einstein holds fast inside. At a loss for what to do next, The Man of Few Words gives the back of the trap a hard whack and knocks Einstein loose, sending him tumbling down into the aquarium.

Rats are the scurrying kind of animal. That is what the Man of Few Words had thought. Their legs too little, their rumps too fat, to actually jump. Big mistake. Einstein drops from the trap to the aquarium floor and as the Man of Few Words begins to slide the wire cover closed, the rat rebounds and leaps up against the cover, throwing all its weight into it. Bam! The cover pops up. With stunning speed and strength the rat drops and jumps again, and again. Bam! Bam! each time moving closer to the opening where the wire cover has yet to close. All this in the space of a second. Adrenaline rushes through a panicking Man of Few Words. The rat is fast and powerful. Each time it hits the wire cover, the cover pops up and shakes, vibrating through his gloved hands. Einstein leaps up once more and jams its snout into the corner where the cover has yet to close completely, scrambling and biting and scratching at the sides in a desperate attempt to get out. Its eyes are intense, staring straight at the Man of Few Words without even a hint of fear. He whacks the rat on the nose with his gloved hand and yanks the cover closed. Holding down the cover with one hand, he pulls a heavy stew pot out from a nearby cabinet, sets it on top of the wire mesh cover as a weight and only then, sure that

Einstein cannot get out, flops back on the checkerboard floor, huffing, seriously out of breath. Looking at his glove he sees that the leather is bitten straight through on one finger. In the corner of the kitchen Succor Mom stands with a child in each arm, crouched down in protection mode. They all stare at the aquarium in which Einstein continues to rage, leaping up to the cover, hanging from it by his claws, biting furiously at the wire to try to cut through, dropping down and scratching madly at the glass floor in an attempt to dig its way out, its mouth smeared with its own blood. Keeping him as a pet begins to seem like a very bad idea.

Later that night, the Man of Few Words loads the aquarium into the family station wagon and drives to the hills to get rid of Einstein. A one-way country vacation, in Anpanman's words. He's driving carefully, Einstein riding in the back seat, the heavy stew pot still on top of the wire cover to hold it closed. Despite this, the Man of Few Words remembers the way Einstein had furied against the trap and worries what would happen if he got out. He imagines something jumping in front of the car, braking too fast, the aquarium tipping and spilling Einstein onto the floor. He imagines hearing the rat scurry over the seats and climb up the back of his shirt collar. He flinches as he imagines long sharp teeth making quick angry slices into the back of his soft neck. He shakes his head to clear his thoughts but all the way out to the country he drives very, very slowly.

An hour later he arrives at an abandoned quarry that was one of his haunts back in high school. He would go there with his friends at night to go skinny-dipping, watching with shy wonder the supple bodies of the girls who joined them. It was a magic place at night, especially when the moon was full and the world alive with its silver light. A deep, open pit, the quarry had white-marble walls drilled and blasted into terraced cliffs that looked like frozen waterfalls. Forty feet down, at the bottom of the pit, was a bottomless pool of water. His friends and he would sneak into the quarry at night and climb down the narrow path to the bottom, strip and dive into the cold water, their bodies and the walls glowing white in the moonlight.

It was a place to howl and laugh. Loud. Carefree.

It was place of a wet first kiss, and of many furtive touches.

It was a place where, on a moonless night so dark he couldn't see his hands he looked up from the bottom of the pit to the star-pocked sky and saw countless fireflies swarm overhead in endless rolling waves like liquid constellations.

As he drives up the quarry road now with Einstein, the voices of his friends come back to him, the smell of beer and weed, the sound of bodies splashing into still water, endless starry skies that record the infinite possibilities of their lives. He passes the rusted Keep Out sign and parks the car in the old saw yard still littered with jagged blocks of unfinished marble. He takes the aquarium from the back seat and sets it on the ground. Einstein looks frightened, cowering in the corner.

This sucks, says the Man of Few Words, seeing the once-fearless Einstein laying low, shivering. He kicks the aquarium over. The glass cracks and the wire top flings off. Without a moment's hesitation, Einstein springs out and disappears into the nearby grasses, a tailed shadow gone forever. The Man of Few Words stands there, looking hard into the meadow, listening for the sound of Einstein scurrying, but there is none. The rat is vanished. After a few minutes, he shrugs and walks over to the quarry, looking down into the pit, his toes on the very edge of the shattered cliff. He stares down into the depths of the hole for a long time, not moving, leaning against the weight of many years, breathing quietly, as if waiting for something or someone to appear. Behind him, a single firefly blinks its way across the lot, over the car and out into the meadow. The moon rises from the horizon, impossibly large and red as if heated from within.

The Man of Few Words returns to the house, driving up the empty streets. Millbrook, Meadow, Orchard, Pine. A herd of deer bound out of the bushes and cross the road in front of him. He stops to let them pass, watching them move gracefully through his headlights and into the trees on the other side of the road. Arising from darkness and returning to darkness, illuminated but for a minute. When he gets home, he heads straight upstairs. You float up from the living room where you've been waiting, sliding up into the bedroom as he slips into bed next to Succor Mom, trying not to wake her. He lies there listening to the small sounds of the house. The low whump of the air conditioner, the little creaks. There is no gnawing, no scratching. He misses them and remembers the quarry. The deep pool of black water. The moonlight. The wild grasses. Succor Mom slips her hand lightly over his shoulders. You're awake? he asks but she doesn't answer. Her hand drops slowly down along his chest, skimming lightly down to the fine hairs that gather below his belly button. It's not Saturday, he thinks. The candle-shaped nightlight flickers, illuminating the soft touches and slow passionate kisses that follow. The sheets slide down off them with their gentle wrestling. Without warning Succor Mom lurches up to straddle her husband as if hoisted by quick ropes, pulling him into her and yanking her chemise over her head to free her heavy breasts. She flings her head back, dropping her long hair down her back as her spine convulses in cobra rhythms. You float slowly down, her desperate earthy moans echoing from above like a distant thunder as you settle into the plush carpet. Deep within the thick mesh of fibers you find thousands upon thousands of dust mites. You watch them for a while, oblivious to the grunting and pained gasps that echo from above, absorbed by the sight of these microscopic creatures, eight-legged pincher-mouthed things that roam like prehistoric herds through their woolen forest. The room goes quiet. You rise up from the floor to the window and look out at the moon rising above the trees. What's this?

Chestnut Hill erased, replaced by a towering structure of glass and metal that rises to cut the clouds, lived in by countless millions, colored by gardens that spill down its terraced sides. Babylon redux.

The scene morphs into a scorched wasteland of festering open pits so hot with irradiated effluent the only life that remains is what can feed on silicates and liquid iron. Poisonous clouds lift from the pits, shrouding the scene.

The clouds break to reveal an orchard by a brook that tumbles clear and bright over small stones. Children playing naked beneath apple limbs heavy with fruit are watched over from the nearby wood by their parents as they harvest acorns and mushrooms.

Are those dreams? Or have you just seen what is to be? Does it unfold like that, in that order? Or are those futures existing in parallel, librettos waiting to be chosen?

You look over to Succor Mom who lies exhausted on her husband's chest, his fingers tracing the hollow of her spine like water through a creek bed.

The Man of Few Words wakes, having nodded off without realizing it. He lies still for a moment, eyes barely open, slowly coming to the realization that he's no longer asleep, no longer dreaming, but has once more been cast out into the solid world. Words lift into his mind, quarry… rat… sex… as he sorts out what is real and unreal and rediscovers the present. It's still dark. Moonlight comes strong through the window. Something is wrong. He rolls over. The other half of the bed is empty. The bathroom door is open but Succor Mom isn't there. He listens for sounds downstairs. Nothing. He slides out of bed and pads his way quietly on the carpeted floors, looking in the children's rooms as he goes. She's in neither of them. Where on earth has she gone? He descends the stairs, his hand running lightly on the banister to steady himself in the dark. He remembers her candlelit face crushing as she rode him in ecstasy. Or was that pain? You float down through the floors to follow, passing the chandelier with its unseen cobwebs and descend into the living room.

All the lights are off. The Man of Few Words reaches the bottom of the stairs. He listens for sounds. The air conditioner gives its distant whump, the floor creaks somewhere, and each little noise gives him pause. He thinks that maybe she's sitting somewhere in the dark, with a drink or something. He looks into the living room. She isn't there. He doesn't want to turn on the lights or call out. If she is just sitting quietly that would startle her. He gets as far as the kitchen door but before he can check inside, he sees her. Through the windows that look over the backyard, he sees that she is out on the lawn. Bathed in the bright sliver-white moonlight she is luminescent. Her silk chemise, pale skin, and blonde hair, all glowing against the dark expanse of lawn. She is walking slowly in a circle, a graceful long-legged motion like a Lipizzaner strutting around a paddock, her arms spread wide, palms up, neck pulled back, wading joyfully through the moonshower. Every now and then she bows and jumps, then prances quickly in one direction then another, a suburban woodelf. When she leaps, he sees she's naked beneath her chemise.

She doesn't seem drunk, unless on the night air. She doesn't seem loopy or lost. He sees it in her face. Even just by the moonlight, he can see it. He watches her move through her ecstasies, frozen to the spot where he stands near the kitchen door, peering through the glass into a diorama of the pixie world that has somehow materialized in his carefully-tended backyard. His heart is racing the way it did when he watched the girls at the quarry so long ago and he feels like any moment he might whoop. Or cry. Or both.

Then something moves. An axis shudders and tilts, a shift that is momentous yet somehow effortless, and he walks silently out the back door, careful not to make any noise, letting it close lightly behind him. He strips down to his boxers and walks across the terrace to the stone steps that lead down to the lawn.

He crosses the grass toward her. If she notices him, she gives no sign of it, continuing to prance in circles, a wonderling in the moonlight. When he reaches where she is, he stands quietly, turning on his heels in one spot as she prances around him, breathless at her beauty, the fibers of his body crackling with nervous delight. The axis wobbles again and he leaps. A little ballerino leap, an elf-jump, a frog hop. And then another. A spontaneous act as strange and wonderful as diving off the edge of a cliff into dark waters. There's no turning back; he's over the edge and gone. He prances after her, caught now in his own rapture. Not mimicking her, just caught in the same circular path. She makes no sign that she knows he's there.

Somewhere around the corner of the house, a tiny timed pulse of electricity sends three small gears turning against each other and a valve slides open. Into the besotted ears of the prancers comes a sudden hiss like baskets of snakes and a million droplets of water burst out from the lawn to fill the night air with glitter and moon rainbows and the singsong tzitt tzitt tzitt of the water gods. Soaked and surprised, the two nightelves look at each other for the first time and burst into giggles, continuing to prance through the evening shower, drenched in the unexpected.

About this time, Anpanman wakes, thirsty, and stumbles his way to the bathroom to get a drink. From the little window he sees what is happening in the backyard and bolts to Gaiagirl's room. There are some unpleasant words exchanged and not a few slaps and counter slaps before the sleeping sister can be fully woken and the tale told.

What?

No shit. I swear. I saw it from….

What? Are you for real?

God's truth. Cross my heart and hope to….

Oh My God…. and out the bedroom door they go on wings.

They transport themselves downstairs, appearing in the living room next to where you have been hovering and press their faces to the window in utter disbelief. They look at each other, wide-mouthed, then back through the glass. Gaiagirl feels the inexplicable movement, the axis mundi pitching wildly, and whispers to no one in particular, I'm gonna get some of this shit too, and dashes for the back door, leaping outside in her tank top and Hello Kitties. Anpanman stands there, alone with his reflection for just a moment of sleepy indecision, then yanks off his jammies right down to his Anpanman shorts and sails out after his sister with a whoop and a howl. The banshee child incarnate. You float after them, passing through the wall on your way with its now-empty fiberglass tunnels.

Sometimes acknowledging each other with a smile and a wink, sometimes just circling madly in their private raptures, the wilding family leaps and dodges, arms flung wide, dancing in the warm wet night, bathed in moonlight and irrigation mist, circling and circling until they wear the lawn thin. You watch them for a while in their happy deliriums and then float off to the side of the yard, passing slowly through the hedge. Inside, you see the sparrow chicks asleep, curled tightly in their nest. They look full-grown. Perhaps even tomorrow they'll fly. Perhaps tomorrow. You float out of the hedge and back into the moonlight, then through the wall of Jack's Shack. Inside, all the machines and handtools, nicely wiped and polished, shine in the light that streams in through a small window. They seem somehow changed. Then you notice it. Handshears in the hammer spot, a shovel and rake reversed. From there you float straight up to the ceiling of the shed where paper wasps have built their elegant, pendulous nest, then out and above the shack, above the hedges, past the tops of the trees, high above everything to where you can look down at the revelers in their yard. Now flung in exhaustion on the ground, they lie with their heads and arms and legs tangled with one another, staring bewildered at the moon high above them, lightly touched by a glittering mist that settles to cover them and cleanse them of themselves.

THE ESSENCE
of BEING

The Essence of Being

It was well past noon when Fiona finally began to stir, struggling up from the depths of an intense, narcotic dream.

She was swimming through thick beds of kelp, kicking her way up through cold water toward a bright patch of light at the surface that shimmered like brushed metal. Tantalizingly close and yet impossible to reach. She knew if she could just touch the light, just break through to the other side, she would be saved. She kicked, she clawed at the kelp, but a powerful current was pulling her back down, an almost sentient force that willed her to stay, to sink back into the darkness. She panicked. Her lungs burned for lack of air but the more she struggled the more long strands of kelp wrapped around her arms and legs, clinging, holding her under water. Just as her last bit of air was about to run out, when she felt like her lungs would explode, she woke abruptly and found herself tangled in sheets of red satin, blinking madly at a sun-filled room. Sitting bolt upright she gasped and gulped air. With quick bird-like turns of her neck, she glanced around the room, eyes alternately squeezing and opening in the brilliant afternoon light, looking at the world as if seeing it for the very first time. A Bang & Olufsen clock she thought was some kind of wire basket, clothing strewn across the room like a closet had exploded, a life-sized charcoal drawing of a businessman jumping like a rock star with his face lit from within. She drew a hand over her eyes to block the light and tried to remember exactly where she was and how she got there. Her mouth was dry and pasty, her head thick. She smacked her tongue uselessly across puffy lips, then lay down and tried to sink back into the dream, squirreling her head under the downy pillow, but it was gone. Whatever somnolent landscape had existed for her up to that point, it was no longer there, and she rose once more reluctantly into the bright light, squinting and scraping cobwebs of hair from her face.

Fiona groped for a glass she saw on the bedside table, drank a sip, and recoiled at the taste of warm, flat champagne. Shit, what the fuh, she slurred, her forehead crushing into a mask of disgust. She slammed the glass down, almost shattering the slender stem. It hummed, the noise a live wire in her brain, and she shushed it, laying a diamond-studded fingernail across her lips. She swung one leg out of the tangled sheets then the next and sat on the edge of the bed, wavering. With its ceiling-high glass walls, the room felt like an aquarium. She waited as she adjusted to the light, gradually becoming aware of the sweeping view, an avenue framed on both sides by tall office buildings, an angular canyon of grey and brown stone with hard light casting down one side, reflecting and re-reflecting in countless sheets of tinted glass. Confused, she looked again at the clock, the clothes, the still-humming glass. Pieces began to fall into place and she mumbled groggily as she ticked off the names of places she had been the night before. Gallagher's. Tooting lines off the table.

Oh god, OK, she murmured, remembering. Studio Seven. Watching herself in the smoky mirrored walls, dancing topless.

Oh yeah. Ohhh yeah. Fuckin' pah~tay, she sang poking a finger into the air and popping her chest, then collapsing at a fresh stab of pain in the back of her head. Her hand tapped clumsily down through the air as she walked herself through the rest of the night: club to cab, party to limo, another club to meet Dannie.

Dannie! Oh fuck yeah. Now she remembered. She rose unsteadily from the bed, put a hand to her head and bellowed nasally, Dannie! Yo, Dannie, what the fuck?, but there was no answer.

She stood, grabbing on to a dresser to prop herself up. On top was an open box of Puccini Bomboni chocolates, half-eaten, the wrappers scattered around like something feral had been rummaging through the trays. She looked closer, her hand gliding over the box, wavering and hovering as if divining the contents. Her fingers slowed, dropped, snatched a dark ball with gold flakes and popped it in her mouth. Biting down, the soft mousse center oozed outward and melted over her tongue, sliding creamily down her throat. She felt it dissolve into her blood and course through her arteries, sticking immediately to the sides of her hips, her belly, the soft parts of her upper arms, depositing onto her body like fine clay at the bottom of a pond. She took another.

I'll work out fifteen extra today. Swim a couple more laps, she said to herself, sticky-mouthed, shrugging. No worries.

She walked slowly from the bedroom to the living room, dragging her feet, glancing at random objects, trying to put it all together. A 15th-century Buddha peered out serenely from its alcove at the end of the room. A Klimt looked down on her from the wall, knowingly. She looked back at the gilded figure. It seemed to be smirking and suddenly she realized that she was wearing nothing – not a stitch. She stopped and glanced back at the bedroom but couldn't be bothered, slapping at the air dismissively. Fuck it, she grumbled, scratching her pubes and continuing to prowl through the apartment. She enjoyed the feeling of her toes pushing into the deep carpet and had a brief, vivid flashback of crawling across the same carpet the night before, cat-like, her long glittering nails digging into the plush fibers as she meowed, back swayed, ass high in the air for the amusement of the people watching. She wiggled her toes in deeper, remembering, a grin growing at the corners of her now-blurrily rouged mouth. As she brushed past a Chinese armoire with large metal handles, a sharp jolt of static electricity sparked to her finger. Shit! she said snapping around to look before realizing what had happened.

What the fuck? This place is so friggin' dry! she grumbled, her face pinching into a well-practiced look of distain.

Next to the armoire, a buffet table held the remains of a smorgasbord. Sliced meats, olives, fruits, pastries, and a wheel of ripe Brie well past prime, melting across the cutting board and down onto the furniture. Half-eaten fans of crackers sank into the rising butter-tide. She slid her finger through the ooze and scooped up a dollop, licked it and smacked her tongue. She took another. She could feel the cheese drip down into her like a fine white putty, a kind of semi-liquid wax building up inside her, on the soft parts of her neck, her swollen breasts, the sides of her already ample hips. She slid her hands over her body to check.

Oh god, she muttered, pulling at roll of baby fat at her waist, hearing Lisa scold, You are what you eat! An image of the wiry yoga teacher doing Down Dog flashed across her brain.

That skinny bitch. What does she know? Fuck her.

She sauntered over to the plate-glass wall. Thirty stories down, the street looked like a scale-model. Taxis and trucks plied the roads, the sidewalks were busy with hundreds of people, but they all appeared as miniatures, little toys being moved around by invisible wires. In the distance, where the avenue ended abruptly at the river, she could see a narrow glimpse of blue-grey water flowing from left to right between the tall buildings, dotted by little boat-shaped shards of white. She watched them aimlessly, swaying, focusing on the water and feeling herself drift slowly in the same direction.

On the sofa was a newspaper, scattered like it had been flung there. The picture on the cover was of her: a beautiful woman in black walking down a city street looking remarkably like Jackie O, with a broad-sweeping hat, large dark sunglasses and an elegantly simple haute-couture dress. The flash of the camera had illuminated the skin of her face and arms so they looked like porcelain or white alabaster, too pale to be human – a statue frozen in mid-stride on a busy street, expressionless, oblivious of the photographer. The headline snarled, Fiona's

Latest Fiasco. Fiona looked at the paper and remembered.

Oh fuck. That's today. What time is it? Shit, shit, shit. I am not ready for this.

Some bottles of Pellegrino were set out on the sideboard near the sofa. She opened one and drank a long draw from the bottle. She was so parched she could feel the water sliding down her throat and into her stomach, actually feel it outline the intestinal passages as it descended through her mapping the very structure of her inner self. The strong afternoon light angling in the windows warmed her legs. It felt nice. She looked down at her feet where the light fell on them and ran a hand through her hair to pull it back from her face. As she did, some of the dry skin from her forehead flaked and fell, tumbling as a fine powder down through the beams of light to the carpet. She watched it fall like light snow.

Jesus, look at that, she spat. This place is so fuckin' dry. Yo, Dannie, she called to no one. Put in a fuckin' humidifier, what?

She raked her fingers through her hair again, ruffling her nails back and forth on her scalp, and watched a cascade of dry skin fall slowly through the light.

I am friggin' dissolving, she giggled.

She was mesmerized by the feeling that her body was falling apart cell by cell before her very eyes, that she was watching her very being dissipate and melt into the plush carpet. She scratched her head again, watching the cascade of skin-dust fall slowly through the air and disappear into the thick fibers around her feet, then scratched some more, erasing herself from the world. There it is, she thought. It wasn't just her career breaking apart. Her body, her actual physical self, was crumbling and falling away and she couldn't stop watching.

As she stood there staring at her toes, absorbed in her self-dispersal, the air around her seemed to thicken and draw close. The city outside the windows with its ponderous buildings and frenetic street life was forgotten. The penthouse suite, its fine carpets and antiques, the food, the spilled glasses of wine, the newspaper announcing her latest shame, all gone. There was nothing but her bony feet on the carpet and the motes of skin falling through sunlight. As she watched the flakes of skin drift, feeling utterly alone within herself, she became aware of a gentle sound: her own breath unexpectedly apparent, the air sliding in and out over her lips with a slight rustle like wind through leaves. She felt her heartbeat in her chest, then in her wrists, then heard it in her ears. Clearly. The rhythmic squeeze of slick cardiac muscle pushing thick, warm fluid through arteries. Absolutely apparent to her. She felt her skin as a taut, lit surface, defining her outer shape, stretched over a frame of bones and cartilage like a tent. She felt the food she had gorged on the night before passing through her and into her and becoming her, even as she watched the dust of her body fall away into the angled light, and she had a clear recognition of herself arising into the world and extinguishing from the world at the very same moment. It was an extraordinarily beautiful feeling, like finally.... finally, she had accidentally touched on something important. Something essential.

She breathed. Slowly. Afraid to move and scatter the feeling.

The carpet was soft underfoot. The sunlight pleasantly warm on her shins.

And still it was there, that awareness of coming into being and going out of being.

She heard the slight hiss of an air conditioner in the next room and a clock ticking in the hall.

And still the moment was unchanged.

She looked out the window and the city was there again. In the distance, a long rust-red freighter slid on the blue-grey water, moving sideways between the buildings, appearing on one side and disappearing on the other.

And still she felt herself drawing her existence from the world and returning it to the world all at once.

A reflection in the window caught her eye. Her focus readjusted. The sight held her for a moment. A woman, naked, frizzy hair scattered wildly like a modern-day Medusa, shoulder tattoo, dark circles under her eyes. The fact that she was standing stark naked in front of a plate glass window for all the city to see hit home. The word paparazzi shot through her mind and she took two quick steps back out of the light, crossing one arm over her breasts and hunching slightly forward, hand on her crotch.

Fuck!

She glanced around the room, then back outside at the windows of nearby buildings, but saw nothing. Stepping back a few feet more, she let out a small sigh of relief and her shoulders sagged. She ran her hands through her hair to pull it off her face and took a deep breath. She looked back down at her feet and held very still to try to recapture the sensation but found only her own bony ankles. She touched herself – her wrists, her heart, her forehead – but there was nothing there but cool skin. The moment was gone. Her face collapsed into a petulant frown. She threw her hands up in exasperation, and stomped off to the bathroom to take a shower, raking the newspaper off the couch and planting it into the sea of Brie on the way.

Later that day, at a press conference called by her agent to address the latest run of bad news, as she sat at a desk jammed with microphones in front of a roomful of aggressive reporters, she thought for a moment that she felt it once more. That wondrous feeling. The essence of being. She paused, mouth slightly opened, listening for it, probing her body with her mind to capture the sensation, but as soon as she tried to pin it down it was gone. Disappointed, her lips creased into a well-practiced pout and a hundred flashes lit the room.

GARDENS
OF THE
SOUL

Gardens of the Soul

FERUS

In the first days of spring when the world is cool and endlessly wet, and aches to be alive once more, the air in the lowland forests grows thick with smell of winterkill as it begins its slow dissolution into soil. Some is plant, some animal. Everything succumbs in time. Mushrooms sprout by the thousands, pale amorphous gravestones marking the fall of winter's dead. For those few weeks the forest lingers in a false sleep as the spoils of the dark months fall prey to the alchemy of the season. They disintegrate then ignite, and release their inner essence to rise through trunk and stem up to countless swelling buds. In the space of a week the forest is reborn as leaves open and spread, forming a living ceiling fifty miles square. Fresh winds dry the air, and the once melancholy forest turns into a verdant place filled with half-light and the scent of new life. The heaviness that had pervaded it disappears, carried away by one more turn of nature's wheel. Morbidity passes into profusion. Clouds of small insects blur the air. Tiny animals scurry unseen through fallen leaves in numbers uncountable. Wild ivy snakes its way over the ground like a spreading tide, choking all before it with anxious fingers. Summer to winter and back again, the forest is always reeling from an overabundance of itself.

HORTUS

The garden awakes to spring at the urging of many hands. Someone plays the lute and cries the morning song as crews of young boys strip the winter cloak from the garden's shoulders, draping the rough burlap on racks to be aired and dried for the next year. All the rich black soil that lies cold in long beds where herbs will be planted, all that rests beneath the leafless rose and hydrangea, beneath the lilac and the willow, that which waits quietly in circles around tree peonies and crab apples, is turned and lifted and brought to life. Curved-back women lean into their hoes, working to the sound of the lute. The wet earth sucks back as they hack into it, and they cluck softly with each pull, cleaving the soil to draw it out of its months-long sleep. Men work along the hedges with shears, the sound of their blades chipping at the air like a roomful of clocks.

A stocky man with bark for skin pedals a whetstone. It casts a steady stream of sparks as he presses sickle and scissor to the wheel. Newly sharpened, he returns one to its owner who tries it on a nearby hedge. Snick! An unwanted twig falls, guillotined and gone. The hedge-man smiles at the smith and turns back to his work.

Those parts of the garden that had loosened and softened

through the winter months. Those which had died and withered on the harshest of nights, when fingers of moonlit ice traced every edge of every thing. Whatever had begun to grow unbidden – the burdock and bramble, the oxtongue and thistle. All those are now excised with blades of iron and removed from sight.

Order will return to the garden.

It has been so proclaimed.

FERUS

In the middle of a forest awakening to spring, a four-horse coach is sunken to its axles in a stretch of deep mud. Three days of relentless rain has softened the roads, and the horses strain at their harnesses, trying to extricate themselves and the sinking coach. Shoulders slick with sweat, they throw their weight against the straps, panicked by each crack of the driver's whip, snapping leather and buckles to the point of breaking. The driver stands on his perch, yanking the reins with a gloved hand and bellowing at the horses, the boards squealing under his weight each time he strikes the whip. His high boots are already greased with mud from an earlier sink. He does not want to have to get down and deal with things from the ground again. Reaching back long he cracks the whip over their heads, the lash-tip whitening the air with a cloud of spit. Leather and buckles sing. Foam sprays from curled lips as the horses shake their great necks and stamp holes into the mud, struggling against an impossible weight. Once more the driver strikes, nicking the tips of their ears. Then again. Working the coach forward measure by measure with each strike until at last with a final surge the carriage straightens and lifts, and with a great shuddering, clatters out of the hollow onto higher ground.

Long dark arcs of mud sail up from the tall wheels as the coach picks up speed and hurries down the forest road. It seems to ripple as it moves through shadows splattered down by overarching trees. The driver sits back on his perch and looks around anxiously at the endless tangle of green that closes in on the road. He had not wanted to drive to the moors. He especially had not wanted to pass through this ancient forest with its deep shadows and hidden movements. He calls to the lone passenger in a voice made coarse by too many years of wind and dust.

One more like that Miss an' we'll be in it for the night, Lord 'elp us.

His voice drops off suddenly at the end, eyes turning backward furtively. He had been warned. She was not – this alone had been made very clear to him – not to be unduly upset.

The passenger is a few days past her fourteenth birthday. Too old to be called a girl, too young to be the woman she is. Her hair is pulled back tightly into a braided bun, her clothes black, covering her from wrist to shin. Her skin, what little can be seen, is uncommonly pale, made more so by the color of her clothes and the green forest light. Shadows hang about the hollows of her eyes like the soft blush of lampblack that collects on the sconce of a tallow candle. Her thin hands flit, nervous birds that smooth her dress then her hair then her dress again. She stretches forward and arches her back. The welts she carries itch badly but she wills herself not to scratch at them. It is for her an old game she knows well how to play.

HORTUS

Ashford Hall had been built of a light-brown sandstone, an entire quarry split, hauled, carved, burnished, and stacked into a graceful thought as if the raw stone had simply reconsidered itself and sat down in another way. A more intellectual posture. The Hall is of solid build, and has already weathered more than a century, but its many large mullioned windows give it a feeling of lightness that belies its true weight. The local children turned it into a rhyme – Ashford Hall, more windows than wall.

The view from those windows at the back of the main hall is one of many gardens, each framed by high stone walls and yew hedges that form outdoor rooms. The most important and largest of those gardens is in the center, placed directly on axis with the main hall, so that the center of the garden is in line with the center of the hall. Balanced with the same intention as weights on a scale. The carefully penned map of the estate that hangs in the third-floor library shows this clearly. In bird's eye view the map depicts the symmetrical house – large main hall bracketed by smaller east and west wings – with its long tree-lined entry drive approaching from the front, and in the back a straight path leading away from the center of the house to the central garden. Surrounding that garden are smaller gardens, and surrounding them, orchards of apple, pear and nut-trees, and then further out, fields of potatoes and leaf-greens. Enclosing those cultivated fields the map shows acres of wheat and barley in soft brushstrokes, and beyond them large swaths of meadow for grazing sheep and cattle. Finally in boiling patches of grey-green at the edges of the painting, like dark clouds gathering at the horizon, is the ancient forest. The whole design expanding outward from the center in a purposeful gradation of civility.

The central garden is called the Sun Garden. It is composed of variously-shaped parterres, neatly-clipped foot-high hedges that create intricate patterns. The garden has been laid out by Thomas Ashford following the strictest biaxial symmetry. The shapes and patterns of the parterres on the west are reflected in mirror on the east, and likewise the south is identically reflected in the north. The patterns used in the parterres are based on the simplest forms of geometry such as squares and triangles, circles and arcs.

Thomas inherited the title to the estate while still in his teens, upon the accidental death of his father. On a summer day a few years after that, he experienced a moment of head-spinning rapture. Sitting on the lawn near the Hall, he was squinting at the sun in a cloudless sky. He looked too long and suddenly the sun seemed to flare in a great corona of electric fire. He winced and looked away and, when he looked back, the sky buckled and burst, showering all-but-transparent geometric icons that drifted down and settled gently around him. A triangle on the lawn. Polygons hung up in the trees. A circle in the center of the old garden, glowing. That was his epiphany, his singular revelation in what had been up to that point a singularly uninspired life, and he began working it into his world in an attempt to keep the rapture alive.

Now, if one knows where to look, they will find tetrahedrons hiding in the buckles of his elegant shoes. Ellipses and chords insinuated into the silver and porcelain of the tableware. Polygons peopling the wallpaper. This obsession with geometry is more than just a matter of design. For Lord Ashford, geometry is the language of God. In the garden each parterre, each boxed hedge, each geometrically clipped topiary, is a word from the vocabulary of His language.

The whole garden, His earthly sermon.

FERUS

On the coach seat opposite the young traveler is a large cloth bag with the letters E. B. D. embroidered on one side. If there had been other passengers they might guess her name to be Elizabeth or Emily, but they would be wrong. It is Faith. The bag is not hers. Other than the dress she wears, she has nothing left in the world she can call her own. The bag and what few items it contains were given to her by the village priest.

For pity's sake, he had said. For pity my child.

He had made the sign of the cross and mumbled something about fate, about her uncle, about God's will, his eyes lifting heavenward at this last thought.

A blessing in disguise, he had muttered before shuffling off to kick through the ashes.

All that was hers, and that was never much, now lies smoldering in the remains of the ruined cottage she had once called home. An ancient pile of wattle and daub, cruck-framed with a frizzy thatch hat, the cottage had huddled up against the edge of the forest like a lost child, tilting sadly away from the winds of the moors. There was a barn, buckled at the knees, and a pig sty, which had lost its borders through neglect and now more or less rambled everywhere. In the fire it had all burned up in a few hours – house, barn, everything – alchemized into carbon dust and sucked into the night sky.

The previous owners, who had lived happily and prosperously

in the home for many generations, had given the property a genteel name. They called it The Heavens. Under the unsteady hand of Faith's father, however, that name had become a painfully implausible deceit, one that never occurred to Faith until that very morning when she left, never to return. As the coach rose above the vale, she turned back to see a black scar singed across the heath. The name flew threw her mind and the absurdity of it struck her. She winced and looked away.

She may have no possessions but she carries with her more than she wants. Memories that form her physical self as surely as the food she eats and air she breathes. There is the wind that rolls off the moor and slips uninvited through the thatch into the attic corner where she slept. The voice it had. Its winter teeth. It fills her lungs still and is her breath.

There is the sideways glance she gave her reeling father. A look that hadn't pleased. His jaundiced eyes narrowed, suddenly intent. Then the angry whoosh of a walking stick. The world shredded as the gnarled handle dug into her cheek. A little tooth sailed clean out of her head, and with it went her voice. Try as she might, after that she could not speak.

There is the silver lacquer which the moon poured over the forest and moor grasses, that dripped down along the stream in the valley, over the barn and the pigs in their broken paddock, purging the world of color. It flows inside her now, whitening her bones.

There is a moonless night, a bonfire giving objects what little form they have. Dancers, singers, a horse tied to a tree, long grasses twitching in the meadow. Her mother half hidden in the bushes, shirtless, mouth pressed into a farmhand's crotch. This, too, remains within her, a prickly heat that wakes with the touch of the afternoon sun through the fabric of her dress. With the touch of her own vespertine fingers.

Riding in the carriage, her tongue seeks out the familiar gap, its pink tip pushing out like a snake head from a stone wall, and her shoulders hunch in fear.

The coach clatters across an old bridge. Below the low arches, swollen waters bunch up in muscular brown streams, the relentless weight of the water shivering up through the stone. Faith hears in it the forest calling out to her – a farewell rattle, a hissed good riddance. On the far side of the bridge is a low hill and the sound of the river softens as the coach climbs out of the lowlands. Within the hour they crest the hill and roll out from the shadows of the trees into daylight. The coachman stops to let his passenger take in the view. From where they sit, high on a bluff, Faith sees the road descend in front of them across open farmland and meander through patchworks of small fields and meadows dotted with lazy flocks of sheep. The fields are bordered by low stone walls and hedgerows forming an irregular pattern that is broken only occasionally by stands of ancient trees, the last remnants of the old forest she just traversed. Remnants that have not yet succumbed to the farmers' axes.

A few miles west, in the middle of that quilted farmland, stands Ashford Hall – grand and proudly symmetrical. The long alleé that leads up to the front entrance, bordered on both sides by tall oak trees. The terraced gardens and neatly arranged orchards. An orderly place of mythical proportions. It stands out within the wild landscape as dramatically as does a lighthouse on a desolate shore. A beacon toward safety.

Faith tries to speak the name but only the winter wind comes hissing from her lips.

She brushes a loose hair from her cheek and, as she does, catches a lingering scent of oil. She sniffs quickly at the tips of her fingers. A memory flickers, and her charcoal-smudge eyebrows crush under the weight of a frown. She irons her dress with her palms. A long breath whistles through pressed lips. Her tongue tip probes the old gap. Shoulders hunch.

HORTUS

In the center of the parterre garden at Ashford Hall is a circle, the purest and simplest of all geometric forms. In the center of that circle stands a pedestal of white marble and, on top of the pedestal, a sundial. The whole arrangement is designed so that the sundial sits in the exact center of the garden, and is aligned precisely with the mid-point of the main hall. Precision and alignment, that is key. Every day that the sun shines, the elegantly-detailed metal framework of the sundial does its work. Silently, faithfully, judiciously, it turns the perpetual, mute cycles of the sun into meaningful slices of time.

Two men lean over the pedestal, being careful not to cast their shadows on the dial. One holds the base of the armature in his thickly calloused hands. The other holds, in a slim, pale hand, a small pocket watch.

Again, Wilyam. Counter-clockwise. Counter, he stresses, pointing as if the man helping him will not understand by words alone. Just a little more.

Yes m'Lord, comes the gravelly reply. The burly gardener shifts his weight onto one leg and pulls, moving the dial just a quarter of an inch. The pale man looks down at the hands of his pocket watch and back at the sundial, then back at his watch again. Satisfied, he steps to the edge of the circle looking at the sundial the way an artist might survey his sculpture, although it is not the aesthetics but the accuracy that compels him. He looks back up the long path to the house. There, on the third floor, inside the tall windows that fall like sheets of ice down the façade, is the library. He pictures the table that stands in the center of the room, and the brass chronometer that sits in the center of that table. Sundial in the center of the garden. Chronometer in the center of the library. The two, now perfectly aligned in time and space.

You know Wilyam, he intones, My great-great-grandfather, Edward, was the first Ashford at Ashford Hall.

He mentions this as an aside, as if the old gardener after all these years isn't fully aware, or properly aware, of the long and illustrious history of the house and family.

Edward used to set his pendulum clock by the sundial. With my chro-no-meter, he intones, ruffling the word across his tongue, I no longer set my clock to the sundial. I set the sundial to the clock.

He harrumphs a little air to drive home the point.

Yes, m'Lord, comes a politely detached reply. Wilyam has never stepped foot in Ashford Hall, has never seen the chro-no-something-or-other, and thinks he would be just as happy to get back to his work tending the garden.

Lord Ashford looks back up at the house. The windows hold huge squares of cloud-pocked sky. He taps his pocket watch, gives another short self-satisfied grunt, and glances at the gardener, wondering why he is still there.

That will do Wilyam, he says waving him away with a loosely turned hand.

The gardener nods, releases the dial and steps back.

Will there be anything else, m'Lord? he says poised in a short bow.

No, no. Well done, Wilyam. Well done. Then, remembering, calls out. Oh yes! Tell that idiot with the lute to stop playing. We are here to work not play.

With that he tucks his watch back in his vest pocket and turns slowly to take in the rest of the garden. From beyond the hedge comes the sound of many shears snipping. A pleasant sound he thinks. A tidy sound.

From the corner of his eye he catches a maid hurrying down the path from the Hall toward him. He swivels on his heels noting the herbs and flowers that fill the patterns of the parterres, each planting held neatly within its hedged frame, the whole arrangement making a complex brocade. He extends his cane, pointing where he looks as if to detect the scene better, and turns once more to take it all in, checking off a mental list.

Hedges well clipped, yes, soil turned, lawn edged neatly, good, sundial set, right.

The maid's shoes crunch the gravel as she hurries up to him and hands him a note from the butler. He looks down at it briefly, grunts his understanding, and begins to make his way briskly back up to the hall, cane swinging and pumping as he goes.

She's come, he huffs to himself. Well, what of it! Come what come may. Time and the hour runs.

FERUS

Faith waits in the third floor gallery, mouth unconsciously agape. She is trying to absorb the shape of her new home, her travel bag dropped on the floor by her feet. A pink tongue pokes through the tooth hole. The corridor-like gallery extends a hundred and fifty feet from where she stands, its coffered ceiling twenty feet above her. Cloudlike. The sheer volume of the space anchors her. Her now-burnt cottage, the barn, the pig sty, all of it, could easily fit within this room. On one side, huge glass windows overlook the gardens. On the other side, the high paneled wall is covered from floor to ceiling with portraits, entire lineages of the Ashford family and notable friends stacked one above the other, the expired occupants of the Hall eternally inspecting the living ones. Occasional pieces of dark-stained furniture that were gathered on trips to the continent wait patiently along the walls, each dented in one place or another with a memory of its use or misuse. Persian carpets spread on the floor depict scenes of gardens in a geometric simplicity that rationalize nature beyond what even Wilyam's iron shears can do. The afternoon light angles through the imperfect panes of the leadlights, rippling on the floor. The gallery shimmers and warps as if filled with water.

Faith stands in that paragon of civility feeling nothing but the weight of her past. It clings to her as palpably as the pig muck on the hem of her dress, and the scent of smoke that refuses to leave her hair. It lingers in the long white scars flung up her pale back like cracks in ice. In her moor-wind voice.

Invited or not, she thinks, coming to Ashford was a terrible mistake. She could not have felt more self-conscious if she had been wearing one of her father's costumes, the wolf coat or the jester hat with striped bunting and dangling bells that jingle at every movement calling to all the world, Come look! Here stands the fool, the freak. She tongues the gap and hunches, trying to disappear.

She becomes aware of a quiet ticking, far away and barely audible. A delicate metallic pulse that seems to arise from nowhere in particular, as if it is coming from the building itself. Not a heartbeat, but, yes, she thinks, like a heartbeat. She listens intently, at first unsure if what she hears is real and then, with each passing moment, increasingly unable to ignore it.

Among the portraits there is no one she recognizes. Her parents of course are nowhere to be seen. They had never told her anything about her family. The only relative she had known of was Lord Ashford and that was only through the books he sent each year, along with her parents' annual stipend, an amount carefully calculated to allow them the freedom to stay idle and ruined. The Heavens had not been in her parents' name. They had owned no means of transport and nowhere to go even if they had. They had spent their days sitting by the smoky peat fire or staggering across the moors, and soothing their self-pity with port-wine and laudanum.

Faith's response to her parent's excesses was her own silent prudery. She sewed herself a simple black dress that concealed her from floor to hairline. The sleeves ran down to her thumbs, more of a cassock than a dress. My nun! Where's my nun, her Mother would bellow in contempt when she wanted her daughter. No parent enjoys a wilding child who lives beyond their control, but just as truly no parent loves a child who is embarrassingly more chaste than they are. In her mother's final year, as the stay-ties of reality loosened and she circled only partly within the orbit of her former self, she would rail against her daughter, scolding her to her face.

Thinks she's better than us, does she? Won't speak, won't dance, all buttoned up are we? Priggish bitch.

She would push her own ample breasts up with both hands, swelling them through the low-cut bodice just to watch her daughter's face crush. Faith was too naive though. The thought that her own propriety would somehow act as a gravity to center her mother's increasingly elliptical path, that her taciturnity would counterbalance her father's incontinence, working in opposition to it like black bile to red blood, was wholly wrong. Not that the theorem was bad, her uncle might say, but the scale of the problem, the convoluted layering and history of their disease was beyond the curative powers of a hopeful child. A high-necked dress and perennial silence were not sufficiently medicinal to alleviate the ingrained demons of a lifetime.

The ticking that Faith heard so distantly now takes on a new shape within her ears, growing louder and changing into the sound of someone walking, the regular clicking of boot-nails on floorboards. The sound comes from a dark stairwell at the far end of the gallery. Faith watches a figure rise up out of the shadows and stride into the well-lit gallery. The angular line of his face, his high cheekbones and heavy brows, the way he leans into his stride, it is surely the ghost of her father, she thinks, walking through the watery light, wraithlike. He draws nearer and, as he does, gradually solidifies into a living man. A different man. Finer in dress than her father ever was, not as tall or robust in body, but uncannily like him. His feet a metronome, he clicks his way briskly to a point an arm's length away from Faith and abruptly stops. Cane in hand, he pops open his silver watch, glances at it briefly and slips it back into its pocket. He gives Faith a hard look-over, head to toe and back.

A wolf howls mournfully off the moor, loping down her spine.

Frightened pigs shuffle and grunt in circles through the muck she feels low in her gut.

Sunlight from the leadlights hits the skin of her face like a house on fire.

Her tongue slips itself into its toothless home and down drop her shoulders like hung men.

HORTUS

Faith? You will be Faith, I assume? he asks, but he knows. How could she not be. The face. The demeanor. When she does not react he adds, I am your uncle. You will call me Lord Ashford.

He waits, but she says nothing.

You must be tired from your journey.

He does not phrase this as a question, but as an explanation to himself for her silence. He sees a girl slimmer than she ought to be, nervous, chiseled face (his face), dark-eyed, wrapped in a high-necked black dress and a funereal air.

Funereal, he thinks. Of course, I must say something.

Your parents, Faith, then he stammers, unable to find the words. Tragic!, he blurts but it is not what he thinks. Good riddance. Got what's coming to them. La dee dah. Any of those would have been closer.

Faith presses her lips together and draws a finger across them. Her head cocks slightly in a question, Did you not know?, eyes pleading.

Lord Ashford clucks, Mute? Nonsense. Then softer, to himself, Mute? But how?

He looks her up and down, circling her as if she was a gelding he was considering acquiring.

I imagined she'd be a more vigorous specimen, he thinks. Seems well behaved enough, but who knows what she'll do.

He sniffs the air indiscreetly. She has a vaguely feral odor and he remembers her father as a boy coming home from a hunt, bloody game on his shoulder. That wilding musk.

What is it? he thinks. She's been traveling for days. Needs a bath. But there's something else. Smoke?

He remembers the reason she had to come, and with that he is suddenly back on a hot summer night, fifteen years past. There had been fires that night, too. He looks at the girl askance, worried.

Is it too late for this one? he wonders.

Lord Ashford is a man of thoughts, proudly phlegmatic. The way he sees things, structuring his thoughts in the science of his day, emotion is a contagious entity, a spore trying to penetrate the tinder of his body. It is a foreign thing that would imbalance his natural disposition toward calm, his phlegm, with the disturbing cholera of too much yellow bile. The violent outbursts of his brother were all the proof anyone needed of the ill effects of emotion. When some report of his brother's latest scandal arrived, he would scoff, An untenably changeful man, clearly too much liver.

He looks at his strangely silent niece and decides a diversion is in order. A device to put her humors back in balance.

Come, Faith, let me show you the rooms.

He extends his hand, not to be taken but to guide, and turns slowly down the gallery, pointing with his elegant cane at the portraits that watch over them, calling off the names of each. He leans into his left leg, effecting a strut, and speaks louder than necessary to draw Faith out of herself.

If she is going to live at Ashford, he thinks, she will need to be shifted. I'm not going to have your father back. Not in any form. Not even you.

He points with his cane at a portrait of a man on a tall, grey horse. Timmoth Ashford. Great huntsman. It was he who built the moat along the front of the Hall. And here, Lady Emily Darlington, third cousin to the Queen, wife of William Ashford. One of the finest gardeners of her time, he adds with a wink. The Rosarium was her addition. Wonderful singer they say, and Faith nods in admiration. Having never met any of her relations, she is enthralled at such sudden company, greeting them willingly through their linseed oil windows.

Walter Ashford standing on a rocky outcrop (a fine painter himself), Diana and her beagles (pretty girl… not much else there), James and Alexander (sons of the second Lord Ashford, both died fighting at Clatterford, good boys) and so on until they come to a large door in the center of the gallery.

In we go Faith, Lord Ashford says. You will enjoy this.

He swings the doors open with obvious delight and the sound that had captivated Faith before comes again, more clearly. That subtle ticking. Lord Ashford strides in, talking to himself, before he realizes that Faith is still waiting behind him at the door.

Come on, girl, he calls loudly, then once more in a softer voice, Come in, Faith.

He extends his hand and she walks slowly into the room.

In all of Ashford Hall, this library is the place I love most and you are welcome here any time. Please. Feel free, he added earnestly to drive home the point.

The floor is an intricate parquet based on repeating polygons that grow in complexity from the center outward. The high walls are covered with shelf after shelf of books, floor to ceiling. In the corners of the room, spiral staircases lead up to iron catwalks that trace the walls so that every book can be within arm's reach. Lord Ashford looks at Faith, her mouth opened, eyes scanning in blocks as if counting.

Thousands, my dear. Thousands.

Lord Ashford stands in the middle of the room by a small table. On top of the table is a carved wooden stand holding a metal instrument with many interlocking rings and gears. On one side is a dial with three hands which Faith understands is some sort of clock, but unlike the heavy pendulum clock in the rectory near The Heavens, with its sonorous slow tock tock, the sound of this clock has a nervous excitement about it. Lord Ashford clears his throat.

This my dear is a chronometer. Again he stretches the word, Chro-no-meter. One of only a dozen or so in all of England, he adds to make clear the import of the machine that stands before them, and with that he launches into the short lecture he always gives to visitors on how the device gave measure and cadence to an otherwise unformed world and how, sitting in the center of the library it was both physically and metaphorically the center of Ashford Hall. Faith listens but hears only three words.

Precision. Control. Order.

And here, says Lord Ashford turning his attention to a side table, are the globe and armillary sphere. Faith sees two metal spheres surrounded by polished metal rings, but neither means anything to her. Lord Ashford begins to turn the globe slowly for her to see, explaining that it represents the entire Earth, pointing at the different countries, drawing her in closer.

Here is England. We stand right… about… here he says pointing lightly. This is France and this extended shape is Spain, and here, the boot, this is Italy, yes? he glances at her to see if she is following. And this large mass is the dark continent, Africa. He continues to recite as he rotates the globe but Faith is no longer hearing, caught instead by the images of serpents, their heads rising from frothing seas. Her uneasy look stops Lord Ashford's speech.

Oh yes. The serpents. And next to them it reads, Hic Sunt Dracones, Faith. Here be dragons.

The word dragons forms a question in her eyebrows.

Yes. Dragons. Metaphorically speaking, of course, he says and adds with a tilt of his head, I think.

He turns to the next object, not a solid globe but a series of open metal rings, each nested inside another.

This, Faith, is an armillary sphere. It models the celestial worlds.

Rotating the armature, he describes the names and intentions of each piece: the celestial poles and the axis that connects them, the celestial equator, the ecliptic marked with the various signs of the zodiac, four rings parallel to the equator to represent the Tropics of Cancer and Capricorn and the Polar Circles, two rings perpendicular to the equator for the Equinoctial and Solstitial Colures, and calibrated Meridian and Horizon Rings, all of which depict the rotations of the sun, the moon and the planets. He pronounces the name of each slowly for her benefit and watches as her lips silently mimic the shape of those words.

Taking hold of a brass handle on the base, Lord Ashford turns the gears driving the device and the heavens begin to rotate. In his best professorial voice he intones, The world as we know it, Faith, is etched in lines of geometry. All things, from the smallest mote to the heavenly planets, follow rational courses. If we understand this and align our own lives to that inherent truth, we too can live in harmony with God's plan.

Faith nods slowly, unable to understand the terminology but completely seduced by the tenor of the room – the elegance of the devices, the precision of the sounds they make, the clarity of the light, the smell of the books. Lord Ashford, who has no children of his own, finds himself reveling in the attentive audience. Lady Ashford and her fashionable young friends would never venture near the library. It was the parlor for them, or the gardens. Gossip and music. He smiles at the sight of Faith's eyes glowing beneath her father's charcoal-smudge eyebrows and thinks, She can be fixed.

FERUS

Faith stands naked in a shallow tub of water. A translucent marble slip of a girl, a pale map of veins and bones. Her dark hair, released from its binding, hangs in loose cascades to her waist. She trembles, shoulders rounded forward, arms crossed uselessly across herself in shame. Miss Hickes, her governess, stands by the tub looking at Faith, appalled, her hands cupped over her mouth to hide her feelings.

Oh child. Oh you poor, poor child, she moans. Her hands lift and rattle the air.

When Lord Ashford handed Faith over to Miss Hickes, he did so with a whispered instruction, Bathe the girl, burn the clothes. But she had not expected this. Not this. In all her time as a governess, she had never seen such a thing. From the small round curves of the girl's buttocks up to where her neck disappears into her fine black hair, Faith's back is covered by a splayed pattern of whipmarks. Raised welts across the white skin like claw marks on birch bark. Slim ones from a willow cane, wider stripes from a leather belt, the occasional impression of a chain. Faith's father had been nothing if not inventive. The older marks are scarred over into raised white welts. Others are new enough to still be caked with dry blood. Miss Hickes turns to the young maids in the room and scolds, You'll tell no one. Not a soul! You hear? Not a word or you'll get a taste of the same from me, Lord help you. Understood?

A delicate lady's maid manages a, Yes'mum, before dropping her eyes. The charwoman, stocky of build with a man's hands, does not avert her eyes but looks at Faith with respect. Not pity. Respect. She has a few of her own to show if anyone cares but nothing like this.

And after all that, the girl doesn't let it show, she thinks, imagining the strength that takes.

Miss Hickes regains her composure and helps Faith lie down

in the bath. Tenderly, with exquisite care, she washes her with a lambswool mit, slowly erasing the layers of Faith's history. The bath water tints red, then black as a fine soot leeches from her hair. The governess calls for more hot water.

And have Mrs. Albright send up her box of herbs, she calls after the maid.

Afterward, in her bedchamber, scrubbed clean and smelling of lavender and rose oil, Faith notices a wooden box set out on her bedside table. On top is a letter, rolled and sealed with red wax. Opening the box she finds inside yet another box, the second more refined, carved and coated in red lacquer. The surface holds words from many languages in bas relief. Wissen, Connaissances, Conhecimento, γνώσεων, قفرعملا, 知識, עדיה. She runs her finger over the raised letters, as if by knowing their texture she could delve their meaning. Lifting the lid, she finds a blue velvet cushion with a small depression in the center holding a silver orb the size of a quail's egg. A delicate chain flows from it off to one side. The orb is finely wrought with a pattern that recalls leaf veins.

Faith takes the orb from its cushion and lies down on her bed. As she rolls the pendant in her hands, pressing lightly on the sides, it begins to tremble, as if alive. It whirs quietly and makes a faint click as the outer surface separates along unseen lines. Slowly, the outer casing unfolds like the petals of a flower, revealing a complex mechanism within the orb. Miniature gears, springs and levers propel elegant rings in slow orbits. It hums in her hand, the sound drifting lower, the movement slowing, and gradually coming to a stop. Faith closes it with a delicate click, then presses and opens it again. Enthralled. The refinement of the metalwork, the precision of the mechanism, the way the outer shell fits together so perfectly when closed that not even the slightest gap can be seen. It mesmerizes her. She holds the orb close to her ear to better hear the tiny sounds it makes – the delicate clicks when opened and closed, the gentle whirring of the gears in motion, the cyclical hum made by the revolving rings.

As she sits on the bed, listening, there is no wolf howl from the moor. No cold wind in her throat. No prickly heat on her skin. Those old memories entirely sublimated by this weightless perfection. She spreads the chain and hangs the orb around her neck. Picking up the letter, she breaks the seal. Penned in a man's careful script, it reads:

Dearest Niece.

God has created the world in accordance with an intelligible plan that can be apprehended only through the light of reason. Inside the smallest thing, there are yet smaller things, each of which obeys the Laws of Arithmetic and Geometry. From the sprouting of an Infinitesimal Seed to the Periodic Motions of the Heavens, there is but one Reasonable Plan. In this way the Lord has made his world. Know in your Heart, Faith, that His order lies abundant and transparent in all things. Seek and you shall find it.

HORTUS

Lord Ashford feels light. A little bit of the hound in his steps. He springs two stairs at a time as he ascends to the terrace. His cane paints the air. He attempts a whistle. Seeing his niece, he calls out and waves her over. She still insists on wrapping herself in black clothes, but the cut is finer that what she arrived in. He saw to that. Her back is straight, none of that hunching, her presence more poised.

Come child, look at these, he says, and sweeps an arm toward where his servants are working on glass cases set out on a table. Next to the cases are wicker trays in which they have collected samples of ferns and moss, pieces of bark and stone, and other things from the outer grounds. Methodically, they are setting them piece by piece into the cases, building little landscapes within.

What do you think, Faith? Splendid aren't they?

Knowing she cannot answer, he glances to see her expression and is pleased. He watches her press her nose to one, looking as if through a window onto another world.

Is it possible, he wonders? To distill out of her everything that was her father – the coarse, the violent, the lascivious – and make her new? What a challenge. And yet, he thinks, possible. And just the thought makes him light.

He straightens his jacket, fingers the hexahedral buttons on his waistcoat, checks his pocket watch, and closes it with a distinct click before depositing it back into his pocket. Faith, he calls, and with his cane echoing his words in meaningful swooshes and jabs, he begins his lectures, leading her down into the garden.

They pass the sundial and make a long loop through the Water Garden with its playful fountains and hidden jets that can be surreptitiously triggered to spray unwitting guests. From there they stroll through the Chinoiserie with its barrel-shaped bridge, red-lacquer towers, and strange rockeries. For parties held there, girls ball their hair into double ox-horn buns and wear soft flowing robes, babbling to each other in a Chinese of their own invention. Passing through a moon gate they leave the Chinoiserie and enter the Physic Garden filled with medicinal herbs, local plants like yarrow, thyme, sorrel, sassafras and tansy, and others like snakeroot and ginseng that come from the colonies, all of which are used by the house surgeon in his practice. Lord Ashford stops to explain.

There are four basic components, Faith, of which everything is composed. Earth, air, water and fire. These are correlated to the four humors. Black bile, blood, phlegm, and yellow bile, respectively. These each have their associated organ. The spleen, heart, brain and liver.

Wilyam's grandmother, working on her knees in the garden, overhears this but it is lost on her. She knows the herbs simply by their 'signature', their God-given shape and color.

Cuckoos-meate's fine this year m'Lord, she says showing a basket of leafy greens she's picked. Be right sour by summer.

Lord Ashford glances at the basket, then turns to Faith as if to interpret, whispering across the back of his hand, Cuckoos-meate. That's sorrel. It cools the liver. Strengthens the heart.

As they make their way into the Rosarium, Lord Ashford is just getting started on Linnaeus and the concepts of genii and species. He has a first edition copy of Linnaeus' Systema Naturae in the library – one of his most prized possessions. The clarity, the organization.

Classes, orders, genera, species. Faith, everything is explained right there. Everything has a lineage. Everything has a place.

It is the underlying structure of the world that catches his fascination. Not the beauty. The fact that the garden smells so nice on this warm summer afternoon, with the light falling just so across the hedges, illuminating and giving form to every bush and tree, and the sound of the fountain in the next court making silver bubbles in his ears, and the grass path a velvet cushion beneath his soft cloth shoes. None of this ever crosses his mind.

He does, however, notice Faith. And smiles.

FERUS

Faith sits on the edge of her seat in the library, ears peeled for the bell, glancing from her book toward the door expectantly. Life at Ashford revolves around two meals: dinner at eleven and supper at six. A chime is sounded before each. Faith revels in the meals. Not for the splendor and the pomp. Not for the food or the lavish cutlery and bone china. For their predictability.

For a girl who lived most of her life in a house where people rose when they wished, ate when they were hungry, drank all day and fucked all night, where all semblance of regimen had fallen victim to the satisfaction of corporal whims, the regularity at Ashford was a wonder. An anchor and a guide. The chimes before meals like church bells calling in the faithful. As was customary, some people changed their clothes for dinner. Everyone did for supper. Faith wore black for both. It was not mourning cloaks. It was who she was.

She set up residency in the window seat of the library, reading voraciously. When anyone needed to find her, that was where they looked. On the side table she kept Reverend Staynoe's Instructions for the Good Education of Children along with a copy of the Bible, to lend a certain propriety to her indulgence. In fact, she spent most of her time swimming through Defoe and Swift, the titles sometimes stories themselves. Defoe offered, "The Life and Strange Surprizing Adventures of Robinson Crusoe, of York, Mariner: Who lived Eight and Twenty Years, all alone in an uninhabited Island on the Coast of America, near the Mouth of the Great River of Oroonoque; Having been cast on Shore by Shipwreck, wherein all the Men perished but himself. With An Account how he was at last as strangely deliver'd by Pyrates."

When not reading, she walked the gardens, absorbing the symmetry of the parterres, the stillness of the clipped topiary, the poise of the immaculately maintained hedges. The order of the house and garden – the routine schedule, the balance of the design, the tidiness – was her salvation.

The core of her new world was the library – the repository of knowledge and civilization. Surrounding that literary heart was the sectioned body of the household, an architectural nautilus curling out from its center, each chamber holding its muse – food, art, music, religion. There was the parlor for meals, the drawing room for music and conversation, gallery for art, a chapel to pray in, the kitchen, buttery and pantry for food, the mangle room for cleaning, and bed chambers for rest. And sex. Oh yes, she knew all about sex. At The Heavens everything lived on the surface. The loving embrace. The bloody claw.

To keep memories of her wilding past from rising, Faith kept close to the house, a little black moon orbiting the library, passing in her cycles through the gardens and the drawing room, the gallery and the parlor, settling into a cyclical pattern of life.

The discipline of the place flowed into her and expelled what had been there before. Days went by without her thinking of her father's whip. Then weeks. Memories of her mother's final descent – hair wild and torn off in patches, cracked lips spitting mad sermons in languages undecipherable – softened, dimmed, and eventually evaporated altogether. As Lord Ashford had predicted, swayed by the virtue and steadiness of the place itself, Faith was born anew.

HORTUS

The day is glorious. High wisps of cloud, the air crisp, tinted with the smell of wood fires, the kind of autumn morning that stirs the blood. Lord Ashford thinks this as he walks down the long expanse of meadow that leads from the gardens, out past the orchards to the pastures, and from there beyond to the forest and the moors. At the far end of the meadow the land drops into a swampy hollow. Dozens of men with horse-drawn carts are hard at work there, digging out the wetlands to create a lake. On the hill just beyond them, masons clamber on scaffolding as they set up the stone columns that will support a Greek temple. In another month or two, if the weather holds, the work will be complete and the view from the upper floors of the main hall will look out over the gardens across a great lawn to the new lake and temple in the distance. A picturesque terminus to the Hall's already grand view. Another small colonization of nature by the well-meaning Lord Ashford.

Today, he is taking Faith out to see the work in progress but she has fallen behind as they walk. He turns to find she has gone, and sees her lingering at the grand iron gate that separates the gardens from the meadow, hanging onto the ironwork the way a swimmer might linger in the shallows, clinging to a dock before setting off to swim across unknown waters. The meadow grasses are spotted pink and yellow with foxglove and buttercups, alive with fatly humming bees. Quail bolt from the tall grasses in startling eruptions of tan and white. In the shadows of the woods that border the meadow, slender deer can be seen loping through the trees. They stop to stare, round eyes filled with nervous tension, then spring away and are gone. Even if Lord Ashford notices these things, he surely does not sense the queasy feeling that they produce within Faith. The heady rush of the untamed. He raises his cane like a flag and calls her name. Faith keeps glancing back to see the roof of the hall above the garden hedges, calling to mind the room in the center, the books and the comfort of the chronometer. She looks at the meadow skeptically, stretches out an unwilling leg, and lets go of the gate.

The excavation of the lake bed is proceeding methodically from one side of the hollow to the other, turning a lush green marsh, still choked with frogbit and hornwort, into an open pit of brown mud. Yellow wagtails, startled by the work, shoot like sparks through the reeds. The men are knee-deep in the muck, sweating heavily as they lean into their shovels, the smell of their bodies mixing with an odor that rises from the earth. An ancient musk derived from centuries of rot, now being exorcised. A thousand autumns' worth of fallen leaves. The perennial crops of withered water weeds. The carcasses of untold numbers of animals, wild and domestic, that had entered the marsh and never left. The bones of a hundred slaughtered Roman centurions who had died terrified in the shivering cold on this very field, dreaming of Mediterranean breezes. The dissolved remains of all those luckless souls who, since time immemorial, had been banished to that wetland. The old, the sick, the unwanted newborns sent hurtling still wet with their mother's blood into the all-consuming muck. It is this, all of this, that Lord Ashford would subdue and reform. Pygmalion with a drafting pen for his chisel, and all the world his ivory.

He senses from the corner of his eye Faith's interest and begins to swing his cane vigorously, stabbing at things, calling out to the men.

Deeper there. Wilyam, take note! Deeper man deeper. Let's not go light on this. And flatten out around the edges so we have a place to walk. And gravel, man, throw down some gravel or we'll all sink to our knees.

Feeling Faith's eyes on his back, he thinks, This is the way it's done, girl. You reach out and take what lies fallow and you make something of it. It is nothing until it has been given shape. If you can see this then you can also see that this is what you were born for.

He leads Faith up the hill to look at the temple works. The circular colonnade is almost complete and the men are building a wooden scaffolding that will support the construction of the dome.

I think I shall call it the Temple of Natural Philosophy. Put in statues to the worthies. Copernicus, Kepler, Galileo, Newton, Linnaeus, all the other men of Reason.

On the way back across the meadows, his talk shifts from gardens to the cosmos, the orbits of celestial bodies in the heliocentric interpretation. He plays the part of the sun. The tip of his cane tracks Faith as she runs circles around him, his little black planet, carving spiral paths through the buttercups.

FERUS

Faith sits on the bench in the library kicking her feet as she reads a prayer book that Lord Ashford left out for her. She is looking at a full-page illuminated drawing of The Man of Sorrows. The margins of the drawing are covered with simplified images of nature. Strawberries heavy with red fruit, flowers, vines, a bird, a snail, a butterfly, even a small worm. Held within that garden-like frame is Christ, the Man of Sorrows, naked except for a cloth wrapped around his loins. He appears to be sitting back against some invisible object. From a wound below his right breast, blood cascades down his chest and across his legs. From his head many thin lines radiate outward in a glory, looking more like needles than rays of sacred light. His face is a blue-grey mask of pain. Faith strokes it with the tip of her finger. Lightly. His sorrow now her sorrow.

She jumps, startled, as the door to the library swings open, and Miss Hickes steps into the room.

Oh, says the governess huffing with her deep manly voice. There you are, Faith. I didn't mean to give you a fright.

Faith shakes her head to say, No, I'm fine.

We missed you at dinner, Faith. The governess looks at the pile of books on the bench.

Reading is fine dear but you must not skip your meals.

Faith nods as if to say, Yes Miss Hickes.

The governess looks at her sternly for a moment, as if

gauging something, then delivers the message she came to give.

Faith dear, Lord Ashford wants you to join him in the Physic Garden. Straight away, Faith.

She looks at the girl still sewn up in a black dress, well past the time of mourning, and shakes her head disappointedly.

What would you be reading today, Faith? she asks. Faith holds the prayer book out for the matron to see. Miss Hickes recognizes the book and nods.

Ah, Hortulus Animae. I see. Well that's fine then isn't it? Little Garden of the Soul. Beautiful title don't you think?

Faith nods in agreement but in fact she is no longer listening. Those words have gone into her ear and pushed out everything else.

Little Garden of the Soul.

A year has passed since she came to live at Ashford Hall. Countless times Lord Ashford has talked to her about natural philosophy, the cosmos, the balancing of the humors, but it was all vague notions up until that moment. Now it is as if all that she has heard is tumbling into place. Suddenly she has a mental image of why she is the way she is. It happened just like that. She heard the title of the book and could see it all.

She sees her heart as a red, gourd-like object like the ones depicted in the color plates of her uncle's volumes on anatomy, but now she also imagines something else that isn't in the illustrations. In the middle of her heart is a glowing light in the shape of a silver orb, slowly folding and unfolding its petals – each motion a heartbeat. This she believes to be her soul. Orbiting around that, like planets around the sun, are little glass spheres, like miniatures of Lord Ashford's glass cases. Each sphere is filled with a miraculous garden. Tiny plants with tinier leaves, small but perfect fountains sprinkling bright pearls of water, elaborate rockery, and long winding paths. One sphere holds the parterres of the Sun Garden. In the middle of it she imagines the sundial glinting in the afternoon light. This sphere, she decides, is Reason. Another sphere holds the Rosarium. That would be her Corporal Senses. A third holds the Chinoiserie. Surely, she thinks, this is Wonder. In a fourth is the Water garden and that is Vigor.

Then comes another thought. The glass spheres can open. They are divided into two halves, top and bottom, that are hinged with fine clasps and able to open of their own accord. When they do, they allow the essence of the garden within them to escape. The primordial aether of that garden spills out and races through her veins, swaying her into a particular mood. When the sphere closes, that aether evaporates through her skin and the effect of that garden's atmosphere ends. The opening and closing of the little gardens orbiting her heart controls the rising and falling of her humors.

When Lord Ashford talks about the movements of the stars or the theories of species, it is the sphere of the Sun Garden within her that opens. She can see that now. When sunlight in the library warms her body through her dress and she feels her nipples hardening, she realizes that it is the Rosarium releasing its perfumed breath. The water garden, the Chinoiserie, the Physic garden, the opening and closing of each turns her to a different mood. As she imagines it, these little glazed worlds are the gardens of her soul.

HORTUS

She is not like him, Lord Ashford mutters to himself as he circles the sundial, thinking of his brother. They say the fruit falls close to the tree but, nay. I say this fruit is of a different tree, somehow tumbled down below it. That's all. It must be God's will. She is, a kind soul. A gentle soul, who has been forced to live under the most egregious conditions during her youth. I wouldn't think there is a dark fiber in her.

He is watching his engineers drag out a Gunter-chain to survey the Sun Garden. It rattles across the gravel walk and catches on one of the parterres.

Stop, you imbecile, he shouts. Watch what you're doing.

The young man drops his end of the chain and hurries over to extract it from the neatly clipped hedge. Lord Ashford shakes his cane at him and swivels away. He is planning to produce a book about all of the gardens at Ashford Hall, a large format edition with many detailed drawings in plan view, section and perspective. The original impetus was to give one as a gift to Earl Temple on his birthday but he has since rethought that.

Might seem presumptuous, his wife had suggested.

He walks to the other side of the sundial and peers through a theodolite to scan the details of a distant gate, then steps back and takes in the big picture. He lifts his cane to draw circles and polygons in the air as if sketching over what he sees. Dimensions drawn in fine red lines appear in his mind paralleling the shapes, reminding him of the mathematics behind his plan. The Golden Mean that decided the height of the surrounding hedge. The iterations of pi that lay hidden in the parterres.

FERUS

Faith is walking the path down to the Sun Garden bordered on both sides by rows of topiary cubes and spheres. She is trying very hard to make sure she is moving down the very center of the path. The purpose of the exercise is to align herself with the garden, to get the symmetry of her own body to match that of the space she is moving through. She spreads her arms out to both sides and walks, one foot in front of the other as if on a tightrope, her body fitting into the alignment and balance of the built world. If she puts herself exactly in the center of the garden, she thinks, she will absorb its equanimity.

Passing through the various garden courts, Faith takes a new turn and comes upon a garden she has never seen before. It is surrounded by a tall hedge and closed off with a locked wrought-iron gate. The garden inside is completely overgrown. A vine slithers out, snaking up the bars of the gate. Wilyam, on his way to the Rosarium, sees her and calls out.

G'morning, Miss.

Faith smiles at him and points through gate at the unkempt garden, eyebrows knitting a question.

This garden, Miss? Yes, Miss.

He looks once up toward the house as if to see if anyone was looking, then says to her sideways and softly, 'At would be yor father's garden, Miss.

Faith's head cocks. A finger points to her own chest.

Ay, your Father's. 'Ere now Miss. Didn't you know? Her expression told him she didn't.

Oh yes, Miss. Yor father's alright.

His face lifts and he pushes out his lips as he recalls some long-forgotten time, then continues.

He were a fine young man yor father, full of 'venture.

A fine man?, thinks Faith, astounded, and wipes the air to show her disbelief.

Oh yes, Miss. As I say it. I know'd him well. Know'd all of Lord Richard's boys. Thomas, 'at would be the present Lord of course, was the first. The second son, John, God rest 'is soul, was taken by the croup when 'e was but two year.

Faith shakes her head in disbelief.

Oh my, yes, Miss. You never hear'd of 'lil John neither did you? Wilyam says sadly. Well, when 'e died, Lady Ashford, Lady 'lizabeth that is, was hard-pressed for more'n a year. No music in the house at'all, Miss. Nothing. Not 'till your father, James, was born. Then there was noise again. 'N plenty of it, he grins.

Faith sits down on a stone bench by the iron gate, and points to the other side for Wilyam to sit.

No Miss, t'ank you kindly. He leans into his weed hoe instead. She rolls her hand to say, Go on. Wilyam purses his lips.

Well yes, le's see now, Miss, yor father James. He wor a 'andful alrigh', always in motion one way or another, like the wind Miss he was, you'd feel 'im pass-like more'n see 'im if you know what I mean. Riding 'bout the meadows with his lads. Out to the 'ills. Down by the stream. Never could settle down like.

Faith points at the garden.

Oh yes Miss. The garden. I wanders a bit when I gets started. He drags his cap off with his dirt-blackened fingers, wipes his brow with it and slips it back on.

Well, let's see. Come 'is 16th year, well, 15th or 16th Miss if I re'clect, Sir Richard fancied James needed some'in to set 'is mind on, some'in to get 'im to settle in as it were. Told me 'isself, the Lordship did, right 'bout here where we are now, Miss. It was still all sheep meadow then. 'Is Lordship marked off this plot of land and told me to plant out the border 'edge, which I did. Said what 'appened inside would be left to James' own doin'.

Faith peers in through the barred door. Her raised palms ask, And? What happened?

Well Miss, full of life and 'venture, your father was, like I said, always looking for the latest this and that, so he took himself down to Bristol to meet the ships, the big ones Miss, coming in from Indy and the Carybian, and came back with the strangest what not, plants you never 'eard tell, Miss, nutseed big as cats, Miss, snaky vines and, Lord knows what.

Faith points west toward the seaport many miles away.

Yes Miss. He'd go up there and buy them plants at the dockside. Brought the seeds back in boxes, and live ones in those glass cases. He'd bring the plants and we'd plant'em out jus' the way 'e told us to.

Faith stands and looks cautiously through the garden gate, pressing her face close to the bars to see in. The lush foliage is almost solid, huge leaves overlapping, dense as the shores of Defoe's jungle. There are star-shaped leaves of the deepest purple mixed in with silver greens and long trailing branches covered in a white down that seemed to be hair or fur. Old fruits from the past year still hang in places, dark and shriveled like cannibal booty. There are vines as thick as her arm, a bush with four-inch thorns and in the shadows, some kind of cat or ferret with enormous round eyes is staring back at her.

Well, we planted what we were told and laid in the manure, and brought water through that summer, Miss. Some of 'em died in the first winter anyway. He looks up at Faith. Me'thinks that Indy is a bit 'otter than these parts, Miss?

Faith nods in agreement.

A long sight 'otter if you ask me, Miss. So some died t'at first winter like I said, but others took off like 'ares, Miss. Couldn't cut'em back for trying. Was a right magical place if I do say so meself, Miss.

Faith looks at him questioningly.

Well, yes, Miss. Magical. Strange and all. Weird plants and animals. Weird spirit to the place, Miss. James would come out of a late night with 'is lads, and we'd put out cressets so they'd 'ave some light, and they'd be up all hours, Miss, singin' and dancin' and what not.

Faith points to Ashford Hall, mimicking Lord Ashford with his pocket watch.

Sir Thomas, Miss? The old gardener shakes his head and sighs emphatically. No, Miss, no Sir Thomas never 'ad a light foot Miss, if I may be so bold.

Faith lifts the lock on the gate and looks at Wilyam.

Can I let you in, Miss? Oh no, Miss. Tis forbidden. Ever since James left. We had the smith make this gate and it's been locked up. 'Is Lordship's done t'rown away the key if you ask me Miss. More 'n like that old lock's rusted shut anyway. Wouldn't open if you it wanted to.

Then he pauses for a moment. Looks down the path as if he just remembered something.

Will there be anything else, Miss?

She smiles a thank you and waives him off. For the next hour she lingers there, gripping the bars of the iron gate, fingers entwined by the vines that seem to have grown even in the time she stood staring at the garden. A breeze drops over the hedges and rustles through the broad-leaved plants. She sees those enormous eyes again. They lock onto hers without fear as if they know her.

HORTUS

Lord Ashford stands by the window of his bedchamber high above the gardens in the east wing. He can see Faith, a black dot among the greenery like a bumblebee in the chrysanthemums. She seems to be motionless, peering into the gate of a garden. For an hour she doesn't move. For the same hour Lord Ashford doesn't leave the window. He knows what she is looking at.

What Wilyam had not told Faith was how the brothers had fought over that garden. Thomas had chided his brother, pressed him to clean it up, harangued him at the supper table in front of guests, always the pedantic lecturer.

A garden, brother, is a place of order. Man touches the natural world and, through the ordering of that world, he brings its feral and barbarous sentiments into a state of calm and harmony.

Here, here! the table of courtiers and hangerons cheered, knocking spoons on cups, always in support of hierarchy and order, always rallying behind the next-in-line. It didn't phase James a bit. He took a long draft of wine and rejoined.

The garden, brother (this last slurred, a hollow-cored word, filled with old venom), is not a machine. Its order, as you call it, is beyond the imagination of your geometry. A garden… pausing for effect and rolling his thick hand in imitation of his brother's thin one… is a place of beauty into which man enters to rediscover his sense of wonder. Man, and wo-man, he added with a nod to the lady on his left, one hand slipping onto her heavy thigh for a deep squeeze while the other stabbed a bite of cold meat from his plate. And because he knew it would irk his brother, said, A garden is a place of magic.

Thomas choked, coughing out a hunk of boiled potato.

Magic? Poppycock. Stuff and nonsense.

The table grumbled its disapproval. James just let his dark eyebrows wander around his forehead and drained another glass of wine.

Over the years, James and his entourage, his lads as Wilyam called them, spent more and more time in his garden. They had a rustic lodge built, and ordered food and drink to be carried down from the kitchen, often spending days apart from the others on the estate. James wandered in his garden like Adam among the first things, reeling from wine and wonder. On one warm spring day, the kind that calls awake! to the very fibers of a young man's heart, while climbing a strangely twisted tree he had imported from some distant land, he noticed that the bark smelled like spice. Cardamom? he wondered. He peeled off a piece. It was leathery and moist. He sniffed it and tore off a bit with his teeth. As he chewed, it released a dark red juice, bitter and numbing to the tongue. He swallowed the juice, tore off a new piece, and chewed some more. His stomach grew warm. His heart raced heart. His tongue grew numb, then his throat, his chest, and finally his whole body at which point the feeling turned from numbness to fire. He was lit. He was incandescent.

The entire night was spent in rapture, gawking at sheets of color that descended from the stars to paint the world, pummeled by long threads of unraveling thoughts that shredded his softened mind. The next day, when he told his lads about what had happened, they all had to try some, too, nibbling their way from one end of the garden to the other, their teeth flecked with bits of bark and leaves, eyes swimming with iridescent waters. Weeks passed unnoticed.

From his window, Lord Ashford looks down at Faith peering through the locked gate but in his mind it is fifteen years earlier, a hot August night, standing at that very window. Outside, the moonless garden was almost imperceptible, no more than silvered patterns on black cloth. Within that blackness, his brother's garden was glowing, columns of sparks crackling up from the cressets into the night. Shadows leapt through the trees, growing grotesquely large then disappearing. He opened the window and caught the strains of bagpipe and fiddle.

Such good fun is it? he pouted. Well I never!

And, in fact, he had never – so many things disallowed to the eldest son. He was the first-in-line, the heir apparent, the housebound, the pale one. He never did as he wished, only as required. He would be shadowing his father on a fine summer's day, listening patiently to a lengthy description of Ashford land holdings, hear some distant thudding and look up to see James pounding across the meadow on his black horse, long hair flying. He would yearn to run with him, but his father would reprimand, Are you getting all this, Thomas? reeling him back in.

Yes father. 150 acres in barley and rye in Tupton.

He would be crossing an orchard in spring through the sweet

apple blossom haze and come across James circling the silk dress of a young guest, fox scenting the hen. They would nod to him respectfully as he approached, their m'Lords washed away by waves of giggles when he passed, and he would feel his ears ignite.

He would be walking from the library or the chapel wrapped warmly on a chill autumn day, and meet James and his lads back from the hunt, dressed in leathers, braces of hares and pheasants slung over their shoulders, smelling of sweat, blood and gunpowder. He would clutch whatever he had in his hand to his chest, his reader or his bible, but it was a weak substitute for a still-hot flintlock.

These memories mixed with the bagpipes as he looked down on the burning garden.

Such good fun, eh?

He went downstairs, got his spaniels and a stick, and walked down to see. Laughter and cries echoed out from the hedges of James' garden, insane cackling followed by a throaty animal moaning. Someone was banging out a jig on the pipe and tabor. Thomas got as far as the clipped opening in the hedge and stopped, his small dogs pressed in at his feet, growling. Half-hidden by trees, the lodge glowed with lamplight. Shadows of dancers flashed across the oil-cloth windows, keeping rhythm with the drumbeats. He made his way into the garden, pushing through the tangled trees, tripping over roots. Cressets bled pools of light in the distance, silhouetting strange plants and pieces of clothing thrown carelessly over their branches. He pulled down a branch to see. In clutches of twos and threes, naked boys and girls copulated noisily. Through the parted branches,

Thomas saw his brother with a young girl. She was down on all fours and he was mounting her from the back, their moonlit bodies an unearthly white, shiny with sweat and highlighted by the cressets. James' long hair was wild about his shoulders, his bushy eyebrows splayed above mad eyes. Grunting with each thrust like a braying satyr, he pounded his hips into the girl, her face a twisted mask of pleasure. She grimaced in ecstasy, mouth widening, neck stretching in a low breathless moan.

Thomas gasped. He knew the girl. Sara Whitbread, the daughter of a neighboring landowner. She visited often, ate at their table, and there she was, rutting with his brother on the ground like beasts. He shuddered and pulled back into the branches, watching stunned as they climaxed and collapsed on each other, panting and sweating, showers of sparks from the cressets falling next to them like the cascades of Abaddon. Thomas' heart beat in his throat, horror and jealously racing each other across the fertile landscape of his young mind.

He tore out of the garden, dogs yipping at his heels, stumbled back to the house, raging at the thought of what he had seen.

Beasts! On each other like that, right there on the ground.

He made his way through the dark corridors to his room. To admit to himself that he wanted exactly what his brother had would be to fall from grace. Saving himself meant destroying them. He passed a sleepless night and in the morning spoke with his father. The old man fumed. The girl's father was well-known, the scion of a shipbuilding family.

Appearances must be kept! he barked.

That afternoon, James and the girl – both painfully hungover and only blearily aware of what was happening to them – were stuffed into their clothes, dragged before a priest in the family chapel, forced to mumble some vows, and packed off in a coach with a trunk of clothes and a gunny-sack of coins, never to return. They made it as far as a local inn and retired to bed to consummate what had already been consumed. They ordered gin sent up and weren't seen for three days. The way things turned out, it was a prophetic wedding. A harbinger of still bolder days to come.

FERUS

It is a late summer day of small white clouds. Faith sits on the window seat of the library beneath diamond-shaped washes of green and white, crystalline fragments of the garden held up for view by the leadlights. She had come into the library in search of something new to read, spiraled up to the top level and walked around the catwalk, her hand brushing along the leather-bound volumes, fingers thock thock thocking on the spines. She stopped abruptly and pulled from the shelf the book her hand happened to be touching. It was a thick leather-bound volume embossed with the name Las Casas. She took it back down to the window seat, placed it on her lap and flipped it open. Nothing could have prepared her for what she would find.

Her uncle is a man of science and a man of God. His library holds within it all the noble thoughts of the world. And there, in that very sanctuary, right there where the chronometer sings its most equitable song, she finds horrors as old as memory.

My God, she silently mouths at seeing the woodblock. You poor soul!

Executed in strong simple lines, the drawing depicts a naked man tied in a seated position to a framework of sticks, a few feet off the ground. Below him is a roaring fire, the flames already rising and burning his flesh. Crouched down on the ground next to him, a soldier is feeding more wood into the fire while another fans the flames with a bellows. Standing behind the burning man is a third soldier looking down with an expression of detached fascination, as if he is watching dinner cook. The burning man has his face turned heavenward in utter desolation. In the background, helmeted soldiers are chopping the hands off of naked women.

Faith feels something orbit inside her.

She stares at the etching for a few minutes, disgusted and fascinated in equal measures. Something rolls and turns within her chest. She wants to hurl the book across the room, yet is unable to. The chronometer ticks. The dinner bells chime. She doesn't hear them. She turns the page instead. The next etching depicts a scene of a sturdy gibbet from which thirteen people are hung by their necks, one for each of the Apostles and the thirteenth for the Redeemer himself.

And this in His name? she thinks. How could you?

A fire roars under those poor souls, too. Nearby, a soldier holds a baby by its feet, arching back in preparation to smash its head open on a large rock.

She turns the pages with excitement at what might appear next, horrified and yet still looking, a light prickly sweat sweeping through her undergarments. The rotation inside her slows. She feels one of her little gardens begin to open near her soul, but this is not one she had known before. There is something different. The glass sphere that holds it is dark and dusky. A pleasant quickening swells within her.

Horrible, horrible people, she thinks. How could you do this?

She turns away, then looks back, flips some more pages and finds the next drawing, studying the details of each and every one as if compelled.

The library is filled with thousands of books. There are volumes of poetry, books of maps depicting places both known and exotic, in color and exquisite detail. Others on physics and mathematics filled with precise drawings of angles and quadrants and sections and formulae. There are books with nothing but prayers. The library is a universe unto itself, a sampling of all knowledge known to man and here she finds, among all those lighted stars, a blackness that threatens to consume them all. She goes back to the shelves and finds another book. Her finger drags along the spines, thock thock thock.

This time she finds Actes and Monuments of these Latter and Perillous Days by John Foxe. She sits with it and spends the next hour in the company of untold miseries.

A man being drawn and quartered by four sturdy horses, a crowd of onlookers pressed in tightly around him in a circle to enjoy the spectacle.

A shirtless woman, baby at her breast, being sewn up into a heavy cloth sack. She has been condemned to be thrown in a river and drowned. Her eyes turn heavenward, one hand thrown up in a gesture of exhortation.

People are being torn asunder by wild beasts. Sawn in half. Whipped. Racked. Hung by their hair. Each calling to their maker amid their tortures. Everywhere she looks, people are praying or murdering, or both. She goes back to the beginning and starts again.

Faith can feel the sphere that holds that dusky garden open wider inside her. The essence that flows from it thrills and horrifies. Her breath quickens, her cheeks flush. She knows now the garden it holds. It is filled with brambles and tall grasses, luxuriant thick-leaved vines. A strange, wide-eyed creature peers up from the leaves. Snakes wind tubular paths through the moss, their tongues licking at the air. Vines snap and twist, now sentient, muscular, pushing open the lid of the sphere and winding their way out, tickling across her heart, along the aorta to wrap greedy fingers around her hollow lungs. They squeeze, tightening her breath.

Amid the brambles there is an old house with a battered thatch roof and next to it a barn buckled at the knees. Kneeling on the moss-slicked ground between them is a young girl in black. Her dress is ripped and pulled down to her waist. Across her back are many ragged, bleeding welts. She is motionless, staring at the house. The small crooked windows on the second floor are oddly bright. Her nostrils flare at the smell of burning wood. Of lamp oil on her hands. The old thatch roof begins to lift and sag in waves of heat. Streams of thick smoke pour out and rise, black columns disappearing into a blacker sky. The shapes of two people appear in a window, silhouetted by the incandescent light that fills the room behind them. She knows them. Her mother and father in white bedclothes already aflame, hands raking at the air, terrified, wailing piteously. The ridge-beam cracks, a sound louder than a musket shot, and the great pile of thatch that was the roof sighs and caves in on itself. Her parents disappear, sucked suddenly downward through a volcanic eruption of sparks. The whole pile ignites into a tower of flames, the popping and hissing almost drowning out the screams of the people buried within.

The girl watches all this without moving, her face glowing in the firelight as if lit from within. Rapturous. Her eyes widen with glee. Something like a smile bends her lips. The moon rises from behind the billowing smoke and pours its silver lacquer over everything. She yanks her hair from the binding ribbons and it leaps out like freed snakes. Staggering to her feet, she throws her arms up in herald and begins to sway, acting out an ancient dance, feet stamping circles into the muddy ground. Her rotations grow faster, entranced, out of control, madly spinning until she drops to her knees. She lingers there on all fours, panting. Her face lifts to scan the house for movements, the fire dancing across her wet eyes. There are no more screams, only the pop and sizzle of the raging fire.

She stands and throws her head back. From her open mouth comes a laugh so corrupt, so distorted by years of disuse, that it sounds like nothing human. A howl, but like no animal. Only a rasped moaning like the winter wind in the trees.

The sound rises up and out of that dusky sphere, and echoes into Faith's chest. The vines that twist around her lungs grip harder, painfully, forcing the howl up through her trachea, out across her extended tongue, flinging into the library of Ashford Hall, across shelf after shelf of leather-bound volumes with all their calculated pretensions. A gale tearing off the moors to rid the world of its illusions.

ICARUS
RISING

Icarus Rising

What price, perfection? called the woman across a roomful of wrecked and burning equipment to a scientist who was hopping madly amid the shattered machines to avoid the fire. His clawed fingers raked at the hot air as he screamed, AAAAGGGHHHH. The woman was beautiful, exaggeratedly so. Aquiline nose, full lips rouged, muscular body unclothed, her skin covered with fine white feathers that rustled with each blast of heat. The scientist wore a torn lab coat. His hair was filled with a wild, electric wind.

What price? MWAHAHA, he cackled insanely.

Anything! Anythingggg…

His eyes widened in horror as the floor gave way and he was swallowed by great tongues of fire. Below the woman's feathered feet, the floor began to splinter, CRRRACK. She sensed the danger, spun about, took three long strides, and jumped gracefully out an open window, WWHISK. She was twenty stories above the street. It didn't matter. As she began to fall, a pair of wings that had clung invisibly to her back opened like sails and stopped her descent. Huge, white, with long finger-like feathers spreading at the ends, the wings stroked the air as taut muscles rippled along her back. WHOOSH. Up and away she raced from the burning factory, climbing high above the city as the building behind her exploded into a ball of searing white light. KAH-BOOM. An angry, dark cloud boiled upward to fill the sky behind her. Her wings spread wide, white feathers showing brightly against the charcoal background. TO BE CONTINUED, screamed across the bottom of the page in bold 3D letters.

Darrin grinned a trainwreck of teeth, whistled his approval at this last scene and flipped back a few pages to go through it once more. KAH-BOOM, he mimicked. On the final page, he stroked a calloused fingertip over those gorgeous wings and closed the comic book. The title, Icarus Rising, sailed over an illustration of two hands opening to release a small white bird. It made sense once you read the story – the freeing of the bird being part of a ceremony to commemorate the triumph of the bird-people on planet Icarus against their archenemies, the humans.

He folded the comic in two and looked around at a suddenly colorless world. Nothing had changed. The barren kitchen, sink piled with dishes, Hoosier cabinet with one door missing and a phonebook for a leg, icebox with its untouchable contents. A buckled linoleum floor a testament to that one failed attempt at respectability. There, in the middle of nowhere, where no one could possibly notice. Or care.

ZZITT ZZITT. A fly buzzed drunkenly against the yellowing ceiling lamp, trying to bang its way through the plastic cover, then fell to the table, stunned. ZZITT. In Darrin's mind, the word appeared next to the fly in capital letters. It was the way he saw things. The fly flipped back onto its feet, spun left and right. Tongued the gummy surface where it sensed the sugared coffee someone had spilled that morning. Darrin raised the comic book slowly, suddenly intent, crooked teeth biting lethally into the tip of his tongue. He swung down hard on the table. THWAACK! The fly transported itself out of the way and hummed out an open window.

Dag blam it. Darrin pointed the comic book at the window and said in his best heroic Captain America voice, Come back here winged creature and I will not be responsible for what happens next.

He stood up, shoulders rolling into a desultory slump, and stuffed the comic book in his back pocket. Outside the window, across a dusty yard, was a broken-down shed, a pile of old crates tilting sickly, and a rusty flatbed truck. Beyond that, the prairie, rolling hills of dry grass after which were only more hills of dry grass. Everything muted by a fine haze of wind-blown silt. The prairie the truck the shed the crates, all a soft drawing done with the same piece of beige chalk. There was no KAH-BOOM. No PHOOMPH or TAKA TAKA TAKA. Just the endless dry grassland. Darrin's face creased with disappointment.

Small drifts of dust gathered on the windowsill. He flicked a pile, lifting a small cloud that drifted outside. It would be back. The dust was everywhere, touching everything. Darrin looked deep into the landscape hoping to see something, some bright glint, a movement, a spot of color, but found only what he already knew. He reached his hand out, looking through his curled his fingers, and squeezed them in an attempt to reshape the very world before him with his hidden powers, but stopped at the sound of heavy dragging feet above him. THUNK SHRRESH THUNK.

The Gods were awake.

Darrin lived in that desolate place with Phthonus and Nemesis, whom he called Gran'pa and Granny, and their adopted daughter, Atë, who he politely referred to as Mom. It was not easy for him having the God of Jealousy and the Goddess of Revenge as grandparents, and the Spirit of Recklessness and Ruin for a mother, but he had realized who they were after reading a Marvel circular about the minor Greek deities and had come to see that this was simply his fate. In fact, it had made things easier once he understood why they were the way they were.

Darrin trudged out to the hall and stopped at the mirror to comb his hair. Again. The comb left neat, freshly oiled streaks. He cocked his head, flipped his collar up then back down, let his tongue prowl the ruins of his teeth, ran the back of the comb down a field of acne on his cheek and slipped it back in his shirt pocket. His face creased.

From the upper floor came the sound of drawers being opened and shut, a door slamming, WHAM, then opening then slamming again, SHHHSSH-WHAM. Muffled shouts hurled from room to room. The boy looked up the stairs. A drift of fine prairie dust filled the corners of each step. He picked at a piece of peeling wallpaper, flicking it impatiently. He could see it all. Nemesis sitting on the edge of her bed, wrapping her bad leg in old Ace bandages just to get through the day. Cursing her bad luck. Atë raking through a box of costume jewelry, comparing one earring to another on either side of a face too old for both of them. Cussing and throwing them back in the box. Pulling out some more all over again. Phthonus sneaking sips from a flask he kept in the sock drawer. Dragging a dirty sleeve across his lips to catch the drips.

On the wall next to Darrin was a gun rack with a shotgun and an old repeater Winchester. A leather gun belt hung on the end. Darrin drew the revolver, a matte-black Colt his father had given him on his eighth birthday. His dad had taken him out behind the shed, set a few coke bottles on crates, and shown him how to shoot. The sound and kickback had frightened Darrin. He missed every time. His father looked disgusted. As things turned out, that was the last look he got. Early the next morning, while Darrin was still asleep, his father had driven off in his old Buick and never come back. Darrin figured it was his fault. Like his mom always said. Little Mr. Fuckup.

Darrin's father had left before he had read that Marvel circular, before he had figured out who his family really were, but when he thought about it afterward, he figured his Dad must have been Momus, the God of Mockery and Criticism.

Darrin popped the cylinder to see if it was loaded. Four outta six, he noted. The gun was cool and heavy in his hand. More shouts and banging doors upstairs. SHHHSSH-WHAM, hung in the air for a moment. In a quick, fluid motion, Darrin raised the gun and sighted at the middle of a pale green door on the second floor. The door handle turned. He cocked the gun. The door cracked open. He aimed at the slit of light. The person inside screamed something through the thin walls and the door closed again with a bang as if kicked closed. SMMACK!

Think I wouldn't? he murmured to no one, then straightened up and spoke in a voice suddenly clear and strong.

These are dark and desperate times. With some conviction, we can change the world.

He slipped the gun back in its holster and scuffled his way out the screen door, down the front steps, and into the hot afternoon sun. He squinted and chewed his tongue to get some spit. Out across the prairie there wasn't another house in sight. Not a house or a road or a horse or a person. Not even a hint of one. Just the grass and scrub trees, the dust and endless empty sky. Darrin resigned himself to lean against the wall and wait. The buckled clapboards clicked behind him as they swelled in the late afternoon heat. He picked at one of the few remaining patches of paint, a crinkled lichen clinging to the bare wood. KRUNK, KRUNK, came the heavy sound of boots down the stairs inside, then cabinet doors banging in the kitchen. Hollered voices echoed from room to room.

Darrin kicked a stone across the yard toward the shed. It skittered along the ground raising plumes of fine powder and banged the shed. THUNK, the letters getting dusty before they disappeared. He spat and kicked another. More plumes rose, drifted in the breeze, and fell quickly back to the ground in an active demonstration of the gravity of the place. Nothing ever leaves. Heavy boots thumped on the porch and the screen door smacked open, WHACK, ejecting an unsteady Phthonus. The door slammed behind him and he pounded down the three porch steps, walking hard for the old truck, head down, dragging the scent of liniment and gin behind him.

Git them crates set away boy, he blurted as he passed without so much as a look back. His right arm was stiff and swung awkwardly by his side, the hand curled into a permanent claw, a twisted shape of which matched exactly that of a bruise on Darrin's arm. And those on the back of his neck.

Darrin kicked another stone and mouthed, Yessir. The dust rose and drifted after Phthonus who popped the hood of the truck and began to rummage around inside, prodding with his good hand. He was still dressed in his filthy work overalls even though he was on his way to town. The boy looked at him with contempt.

Corrupt earthling, he said under his breath. Thou art truly a master of… 'crepitude.

He had tried to sound like Thor but was not certain about the last word.

There was a bustling on the porch and Atë slapped her way out the screen door.

Com'own Granny, she hollered back into the house as she minced across the yard to the truck, wrestling with her tight flower-print dress.

Jus' let them dishes sit. We don' hurry we'll be late for meetin' agin.

If she noticed her son by the steps, she didn't let it show.

Well I'm not like to hurra on this here leg, Sueann.

You know how Preacha feels bout startin on time, retorted Atë, pulling the truck door open with a rusty screech.

Preacha or no Preacha, I ain't goan nowhere fast on this here leg.

The screen door swung open again and an old woman stepped out using a stick as a cane, one leg twice the size of the other. The boy offered his hand to Nemesis as she navigated the steps down from the porch. She leaned into him and whispered, There's a plate a limin pie in the ice box. She paused. Don' you even thinka touchin' it, y'hear?

Yessem, he said without a hint of the disappointment he felt.

She chucked his hand away at the bottom of the steps and hobbled across the yard. Atë sat in the truck with one arm out the window, slapping the door in an attempt to speed up the world. Phthonus slammed the hood shut, climbed in and started the truck to a loud eruption of black smoke. PATA PATA KAH-VROOM. The gears ground like a metal shop, KREE-UNCHH, and they lurched out of the yard. Darrin watched them jolt down the narrow track, PITTA PITTA CHRRICK BOOM, pulling a cloud of dust behind them, a veil to cloak their dispersal into the world. Every Saturday afternoon when they left for town – Atë and Nemesis for the revival and Phthonus for the bar – the boy scrubbed himself, put on a clean shirt, combed his hair and waited by the door. They had yet to ask him along.

As the truck disappeared, the boy shrugged and slouched up the steps to the kitchen, kicking the floor as he went. He opened the ice box and wiped a finger lightly over the edge of the lemon pie. He looked out the window, licking his finger. Far off in the distance, he thought he saw a flash of white light. Briefly, like a glint of metal or glass. He reached out again, thinking he could use his inner powers to draw that glint into the world, his finger curling as if he could squeeze what he had seen into existence by sheer will. His fingers closed slowly, his face crushed with exertion. MRRRGGHHH. A minute passed, but there was nothing but the grass and scrub.

He grabbed his gunbelt from the rack, strapped it around his waist and walked out across the yard into the withered grass, heading up a nearby hill to his lookout. As he worked his way up the path, he drew the pistol and spun it on his finger: forward, back, then forward again, WISHH WISHH, then slipped it back into the holster, THWAKK. High on the rise above the house was a place from which he could look across the whole valley. When he got there, he could just make out the plume of Phthonus' truck already a mile away, where the dirt track fanned into the county road. He watched them drive down the asphalt until they disappeared over a rise. He spat as if to say good riddance.

Fifty yards off, a coyote loped through the grass. Darrin drew his pistol, squinting down the barrel with one eye, left hand steadying his right. He tracked the loping animal, pulled the hammer back with his thumb. Sensing something, the coyote froze in mid-stride and turned to look at the boy with the gun. Darrin stared back. He fingered the trigger.

Think I wouldn't? he murmured, then louder, Get thee hence furry creature, lest I unleash my terrible power on thee.

As if commanded, the coyote loped off into the tall grass. Darrin holstered his gun and spat again. Wind rustled his collar, ran through the grasses, turning the valley into a restless brown ocean. Amber light from the evening sun cast sideways across the land, giving a certain clarity and three-dimensionality to things that had just minutes before seemed flat. A red-tailed hawk circled high above in long, lazy circles, casting down its raspy cry. SKREEE KREEE. Darrin sat down and propped his back up against a boulder. The sun felt warm on his cheek. He let it make him drowsy. He looked down at his battered home. Out to the county road empty of cars. He glanced around once to see if anyone might be out riding.

Satisfied that there was no one around to see, he extended his arm and sighted down the length of his index finger until the tip seemed to touch the top of a distant rise. He lifted his hand slowly and as he did, a huge white pipe rose out of the ground, soil and stones splitting from the base as it rose. GAGAGRRRR. It rose as if the very motion of the boy's hand were pulling it from the ground, and by the time his finger stopped, the tower was three-stories tall. Darrin took a moment to admire his work, then slowly swung his fingers sideways. The top of the tower opened revealing a metallic armature. ERRRRHH. The armature opened like a Japanese fan, becoming a set of propellers that began to turn slowly in the wind. WHUMP WHUMP WHUMP. As the blades turned, the whole tower began to glow with a cool light, lit by the turbines inside. Darrin repeated the same thing a dozen times until every hillock and rise along the valley had its own windmill.

Darrin watched this for a while, thinking and stroking lines into his oiled hair. He pointed down the valley with both hands and spread his fingers out slowly. As he did, streams of gleaming liquid metal flowed out from the base of each tower and spread across the valley. GLUBB GLUBB GLUBB. They snaked in irregular botanical patterns, beginning thick near the windmills and attenuating further out until the whole valley was covered with a web of silvery roots. Even as the towers pulsed with cool light, so too did the metallic roots, the light running through them in cyclical waves. HMMMN. HMMMN. The boy considered this. He pointed to several places in the valley where the metallic branching was finest, tapped at the air, and watched as pods swelled up from the ground in those places like huge, domed fruits. Each of the pods glowed rhythmically with the same cool light as the roots and the tower. Pulsing at the same beat. The boy took his pistol out, spun it a few times idly while studying his work, and slipped it back into the holster. His fingers raked the air as if he were drawing many lines at once and as they did, the areas left open between the silver roots began to infill with furrowed rows of multi-colored crops.

He felt a movement above him, another hawk he thought, and looked up to see not a bird, but a winged woman descending from the clouds, turning slow circles as she approached. This did not seem strange to him. Build it and they will come. He watched her make one pass overhead, as if examining the village he had made. Of course she would want to see it, he thought. Then she swooped low and landed near where he sat. WHOOOSH. She touched down with exquisite grace, her wings expanding and filling with air as her feathered feet fell lightly on the ground. Her wings folded along her back as she walked over to Darrin. He stood to greet her. She was tall, beautiful, her unclothed body covered in fine white feathers. When she smiled, her teeth glowed, a cool bioluminescence like that of a firefly. Like the energized windmills and metallic roots. Her eyes were entirely white, no pupils at all, and they too pulsed with the same inner light.

Greetings earthling, she said formally, one hand raised in salutation.

Her stiff use of English would have been comical if she were not real. If she were not a head taller than he was and powerfully muscular. If her posture had not exuded extreme self-assurance, her neck so straight and face calmly reserved. Darrin was certain that, wherever she was from, she must have been royalty.

Howdy, he said, and then thinking that wasn't quite right for royalty, added, Greetings. We welcome you to our world.

This place, she asked, gracefully waving a feathered arm at the newly created village. What name is it known by?

Name?

Yes. The name. This place, she said again, pointing to the windmill towers and silvery roots that lay like a web across the valley.

Prai…rie, I guess? he answered hesitantly, eyebrows knitting in confusion.

Village of Pray Rie, she said, seeming to be satisfied with that. And you made it?

Yep, he answered, trying not to smile, lips mumming to cover his bad teeth.

Impressive, she intoned with a certain solemnity, and Darrin felt his chest swell, the edges of his ears burning.

The winged woman continued with her questions, specific questions about things Darrin knew. What were the towers for? Why were the roots silver? Why did everything glow with a synchronous pulse? What was in the domes and what grew in the fields?

He answered each of these slowly and carefully, giving thought to each one before speaking so as not to seem too smart or proud. She was, he thought, stunning. He couldn't even look her in the eye for fear of blushing, so he faced the village as he spoke and pointed at the things and places he was describing. She told him her name was Isis. He repeated it and let the word linger in his mouth, willingly. He could feel her eyes on him, those impossibly empty eyes. Her attention was radiant. Just being there with her. Talking. Having her listen to him. Exquisite.

The sun began to set in a glory of ignited clouds, tempering to green and purple before extinguishing. Night swept over the valley and the cool lights of the town glowed brighter for it – the towers, the roots, the dome-like pods all softly pulsing their synchronous light. The moon rose above the distant hills, a massive pale orb pocked with its own history of violent collisions. Silver grasses flowed in waves across the prairie. And still they talked.

Isis looked up to the dark sky and Darrin, following her gaze, saw yet another winged person spiraling down out of the darkness. This time it was a man. He landed with a great flapping and lifting of dust, his wings folding behind him with a flourish. WHHHOOOSSHH. He was taller than Isis, enormously powerful in build, also covered in fine feathers, but his were black. His eyes, too, were entirely black, like two shards of polished obsidian. He strode forward with purpose and utter confidence. The woman turned to him and introduced Darrin by name. She began to explain about the village and the power source, and how it was all Darrin's creation, but the bird-man appeared to have little interest.

There was a distant sound across the prairie. PITTA PITTA CHRRICK BOOM. They all turned to see the headlights of a truck turning off the county road. The lights rattled as the truck made its way up the washboard track to the house, weaving side to side the way a boat might sway in rolling surf.

Phthonus, you is dag blam full as a tick, mumbled Darrin to himself.

The truck careened into the dusty yard by the house and plowed to a stop. The engine fell silent and was replaced by the muffled sound of people screaming at each other. The headlights stayed on, twin beams raking across the ground. The passenger door creaked open and two figures spilled out. One began to hobble slowly toward the house, dragging a leg. The other pushed past the first, taking long angry strides and disappearing through the porch door, hollering unintelligibly all the while. The hobbling figure made it to the steps, struggled to the top, and went in. The door on the driver's side opened and a disheveled figure staggered out, walked a few steps to the front of the truck, turned and began thrashing in the headlights, hollering, #$^%@! He lifted one arm to shield his eyes against the blinding light, twisting back and forth, batting at the air until he grew wobbly and fell to the ground

Thus! the birdman said in a commanding voice, pointing accusingly at the man lying motionless in the headlights.

Thus is it revealed. The truth of what these humans are. Come Isis. We are not of this world. We do not belong here. Why can you not see this?

He looked at the boy skeptically.

What potion has this Darrin deceived you with?

Potion? Hey I ain't got no potion buddy. I don't even drink beer.

Horus, calm thyself, Isis pleaded. You are mistaken. This Darrin is a great creator. Look, she said sweeping her arm at the glowing village. Look at what he has accomplished.

Hah, the birdman answered derisively. That? Nothing but dreams. Who doesn't have dreams? This Darrin is just like them, he said, a black finger extending toward the rundown clapboard house in the valley.

I am not like them, Darrin said defensively. They're not even human!

Horus didn't seem to hear this last. He swept the boy out of his way with a powerful smack across his face, THWACK! He grabbed Isis and pulled her toward him.

We are leaving, Isis. Home to Icarus. Now!

Darrin stood, wiped a sleeve across a bloody lip and drew his gun. He cocked it and leveled it at Horus.

Let… her… go.

Horus sneered. What would you do with that toy, human?

You don't think I would? I mean it mister. Take your grubby hands off of her.

Then regaining his poise, he added Captain America style, I don't want to kill you. I just don't like bullies.

Horus laughed and pulled Isis with him, his wings beginning to unfold. Darrin fired. BANG! The bullet hissed past Horus' head and out into the dark prairie. ZZZITTT. He turned to face the boy, glaring. Time stood still.

Then the birdman's face softened.

MWAHAHA. I'm impressed. This Earthling is brave. He has spirit. He should come with us.

Horus turned to Isis and commanded.

Isis, goddess of magic. You have the power within you. Do it! he said, pointing at Darrin.

Isis hesitated, studying Darrin. She walked over, and gently pulled his shirt up over his head. She asked him to turn around and softly laid her hands on his back, above the shoulder blades. His skin began to tingle. Then to burn.

Be strong Darrin of Pray Rie, she whispered.

It felt as if fine roots of fire were growing into his body, wrapping themselves around his shoulder blades, then down his spine, up through the muscles of his neck, around his collar bones. Nodules began to grow from his skin above his shoulder blades, hardening and expanding outward into a set of magnificent wings. White wings like hers. Darrin flapped them. It came to him as naturally as walking. He flapped them harder and the stroke lifted him off the ground. A huge smile pulled back to show his wrecked teeth. He puffed his chest.

God almighty. This is better than fried chicken.

He flapped his new wings as hard as he could and lifted into the air. Horus and Isis followed him as he made a long circuit above the village, the lights glowing beneath them, beating like a botanical heart. They made one full circle and then Horus called, Time to leave. Isis. Darrin. Come.

With hard clean strokes of his dark wings, WUMP WUMP WUMP, he rose into the night sky. Isis made one slow turn around Darrin, nodded her assurance and followed after Horus.

Wait for me, called Darrin, and began to struggle after them, flapping as hard as he could to catch up. He could see the glowing village below. His little rickety house, the headlights of the truck still lighting the yard. As he got higher, he saw the nightlights of Beauford and then, on the horizon, three soft domes of light marking distant cities he had only heard about.

His back began to hurt. The wings were strong, magically so, but he was just flesh and bone. He could feel the connections to his body beginning to weaken, the muscle and tendons beginning to tear, the fine tendrils that rooted the wings inside him beginning to shred apart.

He looked down into the darkness, suddenly terrified at the height.

Isis, I can't, he called after her, his voice tinged with fear.

Isis. It hurts. I can't go on any more.

Isis looked back him, her blank eyes somehow full of pity. Shame. Disappointment. She looked at Horus who hovered nearby.

I told you humans were weak. This is none of my doing, he said, and flew off.

At the same moment, one of Darrin's wings tore out of his back, RRRIPP, leaving a bloody hole. He screamed, eyes pleading to Isis, hands outstretched. She looked disgusted and flew off after Horus. Darrin flapped his remaining wing uselessly, THWAP THWAP, spinning himself in crazy circles as he fell. Glimpses of Isis' white wings appeared above him as she disappeared into the night clouds. Darrin screamed something that blurred incomprehensibly in the rushing air. The black earth flew up to wallop him. SPPLATT!

It was after dawn when he woke. His face was numb, plowed into the ground, bits of grass jammed in between his teeth. He lifted his head slowly and blinked at the sun. Spat out the grass and wiped his arm across his face. There was no sign of the village, only the endless, empty prairie.

Down below, a screen door slammed. Atë pounded down the three steps and hollered at Phthonus, still lying in front of the truck. The headlights were off. Dead battery.

Ya'll never get it started now, Darrin thought.

Nemesis came to the screen door and started haranguing Atë about getting breakfast ready. Atë was still screaming at Phthonos to get his lazy, no good, filthy butt up out of the driveway. Phthonos stirred, stood up with great difficulty, and began throwing wild punches with his good arm at the voices echoing around him. Darrin watched their curses and blasphemies appear as bold letters in the air above them.

For several minutes Darrin sat on the top of the hill just watching the absurd spectacle playing out before him, absorbing the whole crashing disillusion of his life until he couldn't stand it any more. He stood and drew his Colt. Flicking open the cylinder, he counted three bullets left.

Perfect, he said, eyes narrowed in determination.

He flipped the cylinder closed, stretched his arm out straight, and fired at the raging gods.

BLAM!

BLAM!

BLAM!

The sound of the gunfire echoed out across the empty prairie and disappeared. Phthonos, Nemesis, and Atë, now suddenly stilled, turned as one and looked up at the hill where Darrin stood. They stared for a moment, seeming somewhat confused, then one by one shuffled quietly inside.

Darrin turned away. He looked at the sky, at the clouds where Isis and Horus had left him so coldly. At the prairie like a restless brown ocean. He kicked a divot of dirt, took a long breath and let it hiss out, then sat down and started crying.

The comic book, having fallen out of his pocket, lay forgotten behind him. A breeze rustled the pages, opening them to a picture of a burning laboratory and the words, What price, perfection?

THE
ISLAND

The Island

Paul stretched out on the sandy beach of a small cove overlooking the Pacific. Relaxed and happy, he mused to no one, Well you can't help bad luck bro. He wore nothing but white boxers. His uniform was folded up under the banyan tree. He hadn't put it on in months. He curled his toes and pushed his hand through the warm sand, lifted some and let it trail in fine streams through his fingers. It was a windless day, the water in the cove calm enough to hold the sky. Beyond the reef were whitecaps, thin white lines that arose from nowhere, drifted sideways and dissolved into nothing. Paul watched the lines appearing and disappearing. A minute passed. Then an hour.

Inside the reef the water was so clear, schools of fish could be seen swimming among the coral twenty feet down, appearing as sudden fluorescent blooms each time they changed direction in a single sweeping motion. In a few places there were deeper pockets where the water changed color from aquamarine to azure, and far down within those pools something glinted like sunken gold.

Paul picked up another handful of sand and watched it drain out from the bottom of his fist, letting it trail from his hand onto his chest, forming little drifts among the tufts of curly blonde hair. Handful by handful, he made piles of sand on his body, warm dollops that followed the line of hair from his chest down his stomach to where a narrow stripe of blonde fuzz disappeared into his boxers. He rolled to his side, brushed the sand off, lay back and started again. He was a friendly looking man, slim and muscular, hair and skin sun-bleached to the color of the sand, eyes the same pale blue as the water. As if the god of creation had squeezed a handful of the beach into a man-shaped effigy and filled it with those pacific waters.

He smiled broadly and exclaimed, Wang-man did say private island, but wow! Not in my wildest dreams.

He ate bits of fruit from a coconut shell and listened to the quiet lapping of the surf. Slipping a piece of pandan into his mouth, he caught Charu's scent on his fingers. His nostrils flared and he looked around to see if she was nearby, but he was the only one on that long curve of white sand: a beach as empty and pale and perfectly-shaped as a crescent moon. He yawned pleasurably as his body lengthened in a long stretch and then rolled onto his belly, looking back into the dense pandan grove that grew along the edge of the beach. The trunk of each tree sat high off the ground, held aloft by a conical buttress of its own roots. In the broken light of the grove, half-hidden amid the maze of the standing roots, he saw Charu collecting fruit. She looked as if she had just stepped off the wall of a Khajuraho temple, a stone carving morphed into warm flesh: wide hips, impossibly narrow waist, spherical breasts high on her chest, broad shoulders, luxurious black hair piled in cumulus plumes on her head. Paul liked the way her hips swelled each time she bent down to pick up a fallen fruit and how the shadows of the pandans flowed over her like water as she walked from tree to tree. He dug his toes into the sand and arched his back a little, lifting his head up to get a better look, smiling. He watched her and smelled her on his fingers, chewing on a piece of pandan, a fine trail of juice dribbling from the corner of his mouth. When she walked out of sight to the back of the grove, he rolled over again and went back to playing with the warm sand.

Sweet-as bro, sweet-as.

-- ..- -- -... .- .. .-.. .- -.. -.--

The Mumbai Lady was docked in the port of Kuala Lumpur, the pastel colors of the dawn sky shimmering in the calm water like an oil slick between the anchored yachts. She was tied up at the end of a long concrete pier, as she was far too big to fit any further into the private harbor. The lines of the ship were unabashedly hydrodynamic. Her hull was covered in a polymer that made it shimmer an iridescent white, a kind of mother-of-pearl color that blushed peach and mango wherever it curved. The crew was lined up along the starboard gunwale in dress uniforms, hands behind their backs, awaiting the arrival of the owner. The first mate had received an urgent call from the owner's personal assistant not five minutes before and had sent the crew flying to their posts. It was the kind of touch that the owner most appreciated. Punctilious formality. Grandiose ceremony. That sort of thing. At the top of the gangway stood

Paul Scobie. The first mate leaned into him and ribbed, Don't let any of these babes fall in the bay this time, Pauly, eh what? Paul chuckled back, Aye, she'll be right, Danny. No worries.

He ran a hand through his sandy hair nonchalantly, but moved to block the corner of the titanium ramp just in case. It had happened once before, not so long ago, on a different ship, right where the gangway reached the deck. Some supermodel, long legs black miniskirt stiletto heels too much wine. A sudden headrush sent her tumbling backward over the rope, and down she had gone to cold waters of Boston Harbor, an emergency room, and a lawyer's office, in that order.

A flock of seagulls rose squawking in the distance, and Paul looked up to see eight stretch limos glide between the still-quiet warehouses, pull up to the pier and park side by side in neat diagonal rows. Their black doors opened like beetle wings and out tripped thirty people in evening dress – men in black, women in floor-length silk gowns – their conversation spilling out with them, an animated bubbling, pierced by the occasional squeal, the nonsensical high-energy buzz that follows an all-night party. They stumbled to the end of the pier, wine glasses still glued to giddy hands, and began working their way up the gangway, grasping the rails and pulling themselves up with the same aggressive vigor they used to climb the social ladder. Leading them was Wang Yungfa, billionaire scrap metal magnate and owner of the yacht. He circled his glass in the air to rally the troops, guiding them confidently to what he had assured them would be the ride of their lives. They followed unquestioningly, willingly, greedily, iron filings to the magnet of undeniable success, hoping to get a little of the charge themselves just by rubbing around him a bit. On the wrist of Wang's left arm was a platinum Sky Moon Tourbillon wristwatch, with sapphire crystal and a black crocodile leather band.

Set me back about a million three, he was happy to tell anyone who glanced in its direction.

On the other arm was a woman who had cost him far more. Standing a head taller than him and draped in a gossamer gold sari that floated around her as if levitated, was Charusheela Kamasamudram, would-be goddess of the silver screen and doyen of Wang's court. He called her by her stage name, Kitty Kumar. She preferred something else. It's Charusheela, but you can call me Charu, she would purr through expensively whitened teeth. Call her Kitty, Wang would retort. He liked the name. You know, Kitty Kumar, the actress, he would say blithely then turn to her and ask for the umpteenth time, What was that movie you were in again? He knew full well that her longest appearance was a three-minute screen test, the one he'd seen by chance, the one that led him to scoop her up and slip her into his Kuala Lumpur apartment, but he asked her anyway. Their private little joke. What was that movie? She would smile back through eyes as deep and full of sorrow as the sea, let his dig make another small, invisible wound and politely change the subject. If those wounds had been visible – the thousand little nicks she'd acquired from years spent appeasing men of power, back stabs from rivals, virtual scratches down the eyes from jealous wives – she would look like some horrid crash victim who had just managed to walk away. Instead, one saw six feet of luxurious café au lait skin that begged to be touched.

Paul saluted as Wang and Charu passed him, regaling them

with a chipper, Welcome 'board Sir, in a pacific accent that surfed between Hawai'i and New Zealand. A friendly accent that meant no harm to anyone. They did not notice, pushing past him to lead their guests across the teak upper deck, past the outdoor pool and the bocce court (with real grass), down one deck to where the Japanese tearoom was (with its own Zen meditation garden), and back to the bar where they all gathered for a little more liquid inspiration. The steward uncorked flowery bottles of Perrier-Jouet.

50 grand a pop, Wang shouted. 50 grand!

Outside, anchor lines were cast off and the Mumbai Lady eased away from the pier. Twenty minutes later, when they passed the outer breakwater, the decks shivered as the captain ordered the triplet of diesel engines to all ahead full, 40,000 horses urging them toward open water. To the guests, the feeling coming up through their supple leather shoes was just another part of the big tingle they had hoped to find.

-- ..- -- -... .- ..   .-.. .- -.. -.--

Jean-Pierre looked down from the banyan tree at the pools of water next to the spring, three teardrop shapes reflecting the flowering trees. He had fitted a bamboo pipe into a crevice in the cliff to catch the water at the source and guide it out to the first pool. It fell with a bright, burbling sound. That pool was small but had the cleanest water, which they used for drinking. The water that overflowed from there ran into to the second pool, which was the biggest and deepest, and was used for bathing. The third pool was the one they used for cleaning things. Scraping dirt off purslane roots or scrubbing out gutted fish. Jean-Pierre had designed them and built them with Paul's help, lining the edges with rocks so they wouldn't cave in. He lay on a platform in the banyan tree with one arm stretched out in front of him, using his spread fingers to measure the size of the pools the way a painter measures his subjects. He was debating whether to rework the third pool into a pure circle or leave it ovate.

Directly beneath the banyan was the fire pit they used for cooking, with three stone seats set around it. A flat stone was set in the center of the pit to be used as a grill. A set of bamboo spears leaned against the trunk.

Bamboo! C'est incroyable, non? he had bubbled to Paul as he felled the culms. You can do anything with it. Eat shoots, make the tools, build, yes? Why did I never know this before?

Paul had shrugged, Dunno, bro.

After finishing the fire pit and the spears, Jean-Pierre had made a basket of woven pandan leaves for Charu to gather fruit in, threading a twisted vine through it as a handle. Now he was working on building a tree-house in the banyan, a huge spreading tree that may have been over two hundred years old. Watered by the same underground stream that fed the spring, it had grown to immense proportions, thick branches snaking out horizontally in all directions, aerial roots dripping down alongside the trunk and fusing over time to form one massive bundle. He had split a pile of bamboo slats earlier that morning and was bending them into arcs, lacing them together to make spheres that were caught within the branches of the banyan. Each sphere was a room, and each room was connected to one or more of the others with ladders or vine bridges, forming a sprawling inter-connected structure within which they could live. He was working on a large central room, which had a flat bamboo and pandan leaf-mat floor so they could spread out comfortably. A large opening in the wall looked down on the pools of spring water. He took a last look and made a decision. Ovate, definitely. With a spry youthfulness he climbed up a bamboo ladder, through a nest-like sphere where Charu often slept, and out above that to the viewing platform in the highest branches of the banyan.

Jean-Pierre looked out at the mountain that rose at the center of the island, hand over his eyes against the sun. A cloud trail streamed off its sharp peak like a wind sock. In the other direction was the pandan grove, the crescent of sand at the lagoon, and beyond that the ocean spreading out to all the places in the world he never wanted to see again. He caught sight of Paul diving for fish, watched him surface with a big parrotfish flapping on the end of a spear and swim back to shore with powerful side-strokes. Even from so far away, Jean-Pierre could sense the muscular ease with which he moved. Charu must have been waiting for him because as he walked out of the surf, she appeared from out of the pandans, skipping down the beach to meet him. They put his catch in the satchel she was carrying, tugged and tussled for a bit like kids, then stripped and made love right there on the beach. Jean-Pierre smiled, gave them a double thumbs up and went back to work. He liked building things, making things with his own hands. He'd rarely done it this way before, always working his designs out on CAD and having someone else manufacture them. The flexibility and strength of bamboo could be understood through touch as he bent it into shape. The pandan leaves had a fresh, spiced smell when he wove them into mats. It was such a pleasure to touch and feel – finally really feel the world. He picked a long bamboo slat out of the pile, flexed it into an arc to test its strength, bowing it back and forth a few times, and then began weaving it into the half-built wall of the main room.

-- ..- -- -... .- ..   .-.. .- -.. -.--

Ten miles outside the Singapore Straights, the captain of the Mumbai Lady set a course east-northeast to take them past Pulau-pulau and engaged the rigid sails – 80-foot-long wing-shaped panels that were attached by titanium knuckles to the upper deck. He stroked his finger lightly up a touch pad on the console of the bridge. The sails swiveled up from their prone position to a 60 degree angle, cutting into the ocean wind like three swords. He felt the ship rise lightly in the surf and ordered the engines to full-stop. As the ship fell silent, it continued to glide through the slapping waves at the same speed on wind power alone. The decks no longer shivered with the mechanical vibrations of the diesels, but each time the wind shifted direction and the computer adjusted the shape and position of the flaps on the sails to compensate, a small shudder would run through them. The sails made a low, tuning fork hum that could be heard by all but the oldest passengers, and the captain swore he could trim the sails simply by listening to their pitch.

As the captain raised the wingsails, he also engaged the lubrication system. The mother-of-pearl skin of the Mumbai Lady's hull was made of a semi-porous material that could be used to extrude a microscopic layer of organic gel, the way fish skin does, reducing the friction and drag of the water. The crew called it KY-ing. Within a minute of having deployed the gel, the ship gained 5 knots. The captain didn't keep it on all the time because there was no need for it at lower speeds, and he couldn't run it in port because of the pale slick it left in the ship's wake. Wang would moan, It's organic. It's like fish food. What's the problem? But the harbor master at Kuala Lumpur had threatened to bar them if they, in his words, Came back into port oozing whale pus, so the captain only turned it on in open water. The lubricant was constantly replenished from a large vat nestled in the bow of the ship that was fed a mixture of plankton and water every day. A network of tubes ran from the vat along the inside of the hull to distribute the lubricant, like some kind of metallic vine growing on the inside of the ship. Pumps cyclically increased the air pressure in the vat to push the lubricant back through the tubes and, late at night, when the ship was empty of guests and utterly quiet, it could be heard chug-chugging like a mechanical heart.

The captain checked the output of the electrostatic induction panels that were installed in all the floors and ceilings. They allowed specially-designed devices to be used on board without the need for power cords. Lights, computers, TVs, electric razors, all of them cord free. An unplanned side effect of the panels was that, under particularly dry weather conditions, a static charge built up in certain materials: silk, nylon, polyester, skin. On the first night at sea, the rabbit fur trim of a young woman's jacket had begun to glow, her cuffs and collar flaming with Saint Elmo's fire.

Many of the crew members believed that the Mumbai Lady was more than just a ship, more than a clever compilation of carbon fiber and titanium. Between the little shudders that she made in response to changes in her environment, the daily meals of plankton that kept her skin moist, and the mysterious aerial energy that filled her cabins, they came to feel that she was, in a very real sense, alive. Jean-Pierre Arceneaux never saw her that way. To him the ship was a machine. Non! he would spit, rebuffing gossip at the dinner table with a flip of his hand.

Ce est ma création. I design it, I should know. Juste a machine. Oui?

Jean-Pierre stood on the foredeck looking up at the wingsails cutting through the ocean air. Almost everyone else was still asleep (it was before noon and the passengers were distinctly nocturnal), but when he heard that the sails were being raised, he came onto deck. He was an architect, heavy on theory, given to writing moody epistles on radical design. Normally he designed buildings. The Mumbai Lady was his first foray into marine architecture. The buildings he created were known for their extreme fragmentation of space and manipulation of surfaces, and they were all finished in the same polymer that gave the Mumbai Lady her mother-of-pearl sheen. Without the gel. Because of their striking individuality, his buildings had become instrumental in initiating the architectural movement known as d_pearl_s, short for deconstructivist pearl-surfaced structures. Often composed of layer upon layer of shell-like forms, their detractors referred to them pejoratively as d_clam_bakes. Jean-Pierre had been born in Paris to a French father and Spanish mother, raised for most of his childhood in a different major metropolis every few years (he liked to say his nursery had been the VIP lounge at the airport), went to an architectural school in the US, and trained at several of the hottest design firms in Europe before winning the competition to design Wang's first office building. With that feather in his cap, he had opened his own firm in Hong Kong and continued to design all of Wang's buildings throughout Asia, fifteen in all and six more on the drawing board. Jean-Pierre was the kind of person who couldn't keep his mind off things and how they were made. While eating he would rethink the basic elements of the fork. A simple bicycle ride became a contemplation of drag versus inertia schemes. When making love, he considered the shape of his partner's muscles from an ergonomic point of view. He looked at the Mumbai Lady's rising sails and calculated the stress load on the knuckles.

-- ..- -- -... .- ..   .-.. .- -.. -.--

Charu stood in the middle of the pandan grove, eyes closed, breathing the sweetrose scent of its flowers. Jasmine, she thought, thinking of the garden at the house near Mumbai where she was born. But no. Not jasmine. Gardenia? and she recalled Kuala Lumpur where she had lived as a 'kept woman.' A vile phrase that, she thought, frowning then posing and delivering her line, But it is ten times true, for truth is truth to the end of reckoning.

Ylang-ylang? No, that's not it either. The smell was wilder, something born of the island's virgin soil and its infinite loneliness.

And its freedom.

How different things are here, she said to no one, breathing deeply. Even their scents. Even mine, and she nosed the skin of her arms.

She moved lithely through the shadows of the trees, dancing an odissi of her own invention, her arms and hands flowing slowly through angular postures, hips and chest and head moving independently of each other like a lizard. She danced languidly, stopping from time to time to put some fruit in Jean-Pierre's frond basket, then returning to her dance, shadows pouring over her in long stripes.

Leaves fluttered overhead. The sound of the surf came from the outer reef. A low moaning of wind in the heights of the mountain. In a well-practiced voice, as if she intended to be heard by an audience somewhere beyond the grove, she spoke,

This isle is full of noises, sounds and sweet airs, that give delight and hurt not. Sometimes a thousand twangling instruments will hum about mine ears, and sometime voices.

She could almost hear her mother say, Pro-ject, Charu. Pro-ject! Let them hear you in the back row.

She strolled through the grove, resting for hours at a time in one spot, doing nothing, reciting lines, stretching, talking to herself, walking again, acting out all the parts of whatever play came to mind. When the sun began to lower in the sky and the day lost its heat to ocean breezes, she started her daily walk to the mountaintop. First, she removed her gold sari, folding it carefully and setting it on a flat-topped rock. Next her shirt and petticoat, each slipped off slowly, ceremonially, folded and placed on top of the sari. Above those went the many gold bangles that decorated her arms, set on the cloth as weights against the breeze. In the middle of the hollow tower of bangles she dropped her diamond-studded nose ring and the ivory hair pin, peeling off all signs of wealth and status in an act of regeneration no less complete than that of a new-born lacewing fly shedding its juvenile skin to reveal its teneral self, pale and soft-bodied. Released of all those old trappings, no longer rich or poor, Northern or Southern, movie star or wannabe, Brahmin or Shudra, she stepped naked out of the banyan grove under an immense sky that held all possibilities.

She followed the narrow path up the mountain, moving cautiously, each step her first and her last, each breath the beginning and the end, noticing all the small things that would have passed unknown to the person she was before. The bend of a blade of grass where she had stepped the previous day. A spider weaving its web between ferns growing on a mossy boulder. The low hum of wind cutting across the cliffs. She made her way to the summit from where she could look out at the ocean in all directions, a dented sheet of gunmetal with flashes of rust following the sun to the west. On other days it had been silver, teal and black, as moody as she had been not so long ago.

She stood on top of that mountain, on top of the highest spot she could find, and spread her arms wide, thrilling in the heady place, and let the cool fingers of the trade winds tease quick fields of goosebumps from her skin. Her long hair blew around her like black fire as she turned to the four corners of the world and announced in no uncertain terms the revelations of her rebirth.

-- ..- -- -... .- .. .-.. .- -.. -.--

Dinner was resplendent, as always. Charu sat at the captain's table with Wang and eight others, unable to stay in the present, the fine edge of life aboard the Mumbai Lady already becoming thin and brittle. Over beluga caviar she chatted unaware with a man from the Ministry of Construction, remembering the lotus flowers that had bloomed along the canal near her house when she was a girl, jumping and splashing through them in the brown water. Sipping shark fin soup she wondered what had become of Damini, the girl with skin the color of cloves and a gold nose ring, who lived in the small house across the lane. A year older than Charu, Damini had always been testing the world and getting them both in trouble. Just at that moment, on the horizon where sea and sky fused, Charu saw a long strike of lightning quiver and disappear without a sound. She mouthed the name, Damini.

What's that Kitty? asked Wang.

She wanted to say, I was just thinking about my old friend, Damini, you know the skinny girl from Mumbai and then there was a strike of lightning on the horizon and you know I told you what Damini means, right? Isn't that weird?

Instead she settled for, Oh, nothing darling.

As she nibbled her Kobe beef, idly knocking the matsutake mushrooms to the side with her gold fork, she thought of the corner room in her old house where she would sit to read, the way the light came slanting in the window, colored by long, yellow panicles of the bendra lathi tree outside. A simple house, a bare room. A piece of stiff cardboard with an advertisement for hair coloring her father had used as a patch over a broken pane of glass. The woman in the ad was upside down.

Kitty?

Mmm? I'm sorry, what's that?

Davide was asking you about Switzerland.

Oh I'm sorry. Yes. Lovely. It was lovely there this time of year, so cool. Snow on the tips of the mountains.

Halfway through her Tahitian vanilla bean ice cream sprinkled with gold leaf, Charu thought about a day when she was thirteen, at home alone which was rare. Normally, her mother or an auntie was there with her but they had all gone out for one thing or another. She had been looking through some old copies of Filmfare, pining over the Bollywood scene, dreaming herself into the pictures. She stood in front of the mirror in her parents' room, looked around once to make sure no one was there, and opened her shirt. She pressed on the sides of her budding breasts trying to build some cleavage, massaging them and wondering if she would ever look like the women in the magazine. She squeezed them to puff out the nipples mumbling some kind of childish incantation, a prayer to Parvati pleading that they grow. Years later she began praying they would stop.

Had that really worked, she wondered?

You all right Kitty babe? asked Wang. Charu looked up startled and fussed with her sari.

Maybe just a little off, darling, and whispered in his ear, It's that time! even though it wasn't.

Coffee and brandy were served and people began migrating to the bar and aft deck to enjoy the sunset with music and more wine. Charu stood, straightening her back with a deep breath, and reminded herself of who she was and why she was there. Someone was playing the piano and she thought of a line from an old song. What was it? Don't go looking for loneliness, it'll be there waiting when you get home, or something like that?

She adjusted her sari on her shoulder and strode out among the crowd, high priestess among the faithful. This wouldn't go on forever, she reminded herself. There had been others before her, and she knew there would be others after. Wang wasn't the marrying type and he was nothing if not restless. Keeping his attention was a full-time job, and when that attention fell onto someone else she would be sent back to Mumbai with a satchel full of pricey accessories and a stack of useless memories. The Mumbai Lady would get renamed Shanghai Missy or The Balinese Princess in honor of whomever had arrived to fill her shoes. The ship wouldn't even have to go into dry dock. Easy. For the moment, though, Charu was Wang's muse and his idol, and because he loved her everyone in the room loved her, casting their affections at her like rose petals. She had rubbed against him long enough and hard enough that she too had become magnetic and could feel her pull on people as she passed through the room. Conversations subsided, heads swiveled, eyes narrowed above orthodontic smiles blossoming like night flowers. People were drawn to her, their well manicured hands reaching out to touch her soft skin lightly, their lips shaping her name.

She worked her way through the crowd, making sure everyone was happy, fighting off the constant desire to be somewhere else, then slipped out onto the foredeck and found a place out of the wind to escape for a while. Charu had been born into a family that was always on the edge of ruin. Her mother had seen Charu's beauty as a ticket out and capitalized on it at every opportunity, dressing her in the flashiest clothes she could manage to buy and pushing her shamelessly in front of the eyes of men. It was she who cooked up the Kitty Kumar persona, but she didn't need to coax the thespian out of her daughter. That must have been genetic. Or God-sent. When Charu was three she had already begun to mimic the odissi dancers she had seen. At eight she would come home reciting commercials she had seen on the TV in the window of a local shop.

Laaa, la la la la laaaa. Come alive with the Liril freshness, she would urge her friends, splashing in an imaginary waterfall. Tingling with the exciting freshness of lime. Then, soaping herself in an imaginary shower. Liril, the Freshness Soap. To make a fresh… new… woman of you. Finger points toward an imaginary camera. Wink.

At twelve she began performing short skits of Shakespeare's famous scenes in the weedy lot behind the house, playing all the parts herself. Her family and friends teased her that she'd be the next Madhuri Dixit, but when her afternoon prayer by the mirror was answered with immoderate excess and her mother had to let out her blouse another inch every few months, it became apparent to all involved that her route to success lay somewhat south of the classics.

She played along. She read the 'great books' only when she was alone. Instead, she watched the women around her with sharp, quiet eyes. She looked at the TV in the shop window, and films when they could afford to go to them. She rifled through old issues of Filmfare and taught herself how to walk with poise and stand with presence, how to push her lips forward and sway the small of her back, how to smile with her eyes, and giggle with her nose, how to use her arms and hands to say yes, or no, or yes yes yes! The way it worked out, she never made it onto the silver screen. Wang plucked her before she had a chance. And yet she'd been an actress all her life, performing anytime there was an audience, and often when there wasn't. A hard habit to kick, she came to realize.

Across the deck she saw Jean-Pierre leaning against the gunwale, staring up at the wingsails. She glanced up to see what he was looking at. The translucent membrane stretched over the sails was filled with moonlight. She could hear the trade wind moaning across their cambered surfaces, like something calling from far away. She thought it sounded terribly sad and felt herself falling into the sound, compelled to listen. She wondered if that was what the Sirens really sounded like. Not the pert, harp-strumming maidens of the movies with their high, warbling voices, but instead some low, irresistible, far-off moan that drives men mad.

What potions have I drunk of siren tears, Distilled from limbecks foul as hell, she called up to the sky, in a good strong stage voice. Jean-Pierre couldn't hear the words with the wind cutting across his ears, but Charu had caught his attention. He nodded at the sails, gave her the thumbs up, and crowed, She's nice, no? Charu glanced back at the sails uncertain of what he had said, and gave him a weak thumbs up to play along. She put her back against the cool metal wall behind her, dropped her sari off her shoulder and let the dangling gold pin in her bellybutton glitter in the moonlight. Jean-Pierre gave her a winning smile and returned to watching the sails.

-- ..- -- -... .- ..   .-.. .- -.. -.--

Paul walked along the long crescent curve of the beach to a rocky promontory. He carried a long spear in one hand and a leaf satchel in the other. Fishin' time, he called out to the lagoon, as if to give it fair warning. He looked out to the reef to gauge the strength of the surf and saw it was still calm. Paul had always known the sea. He'd been born on a trimaran running the

Canaries to Lisbon. His mother had gone into labor two weeks early and they were making 30 knots in a desperate attempt to get her to a hospital. They didn't make it in time, and Paul was christened with salt water, the whole Atlantic his baptismal font. He'd been bouncing around the world ever since then, working crew from one port to the next, jumping on anything that had a sail. He had turned his nose up at the Mumbai Lady when Danny first brought him to look at her.

Diesels Danny? You must be kidding bro.

But when he had seen the massive wingsails going up for a test, he'd signed right on. The way he planned things, it was going to be his last ride. After so many years banging around he'd gotten tired of the constant motion. Crewing was a great adventure, but the life was scattered and tenuous. Work. Friendship. Love. Nothing ever lasted very long. Too much rum and weed, not enough substance. He'd been planning for some time to give his sea legs a rest. Head down to New Zealand, which was as much a home as he had anywhere. Some family here and there that he knew of. Leaning over the gunwale with Danny one evening, looking out over the endless expanse of rolling sea, he'd voiced it for the first time.

I tell ya' Danny, all I want to do is settle down and breed. A house. Sprogs in the yard. The whole thing. Feel what it's like to look at the same horizon for more than a day.

Danny just looked at him speechless.

You must be daft, mate. You'll go stir crazy in a week.

Think so?

Know so, mate. I've done it a dozen times meself. Trust me. It never lasts, Pauly.

Paul walked along the lagoon, the sand warm between his toes, spear slung over his shoulder. He climbed up on the promontory rocks, looked around at the calm water and back to the pandan forest. The old banyan tree could be seen billowing above the smaller trees around it, the bamboo spheres Jean-Pierre was building visible among the leaves like the nests of some giant, mythical birds. He couldn't see Charu and thought she must be deep in the pandan grove or off on one of her strange walks up the mountain. He'd followed her once, ducking behind trees like a little boy so as not to be seen, but he need not have gone to the trouble. She was in a trance, alternating between her odissi and a slow parade, stopping and noting all the minutiae of the world. Naked as Eve in Eden, her skin burnt and peeled in places. He followed her only that once, realizing that there were some things people should be left alone to do.

Off the end of the promontory there was a deep pool Paul hadn't explored yet. He slipped into the water and swam out to it, floating his spear ahead of him like a water snake. When he reached the pool he stopped to take a few deep breaths, then pointed the spear down into the water and dove after it. The pressure built in his ears, the salt water burned his eyes. He was looking for something to catch, but found instead a rush of images flowing into him from the dark water. Stories only the ocean knew. A broken picnic basket filled with sand caught under the barnacle-encrusted piers on the Strand near Sligo. A child's skinny fingers searching for a red plastic bracelet she had dropped in the shallows of the Saddlebunch Keys. The skeleton of an old wooden fishing boat sticking out of the mud under a hundred feet of water in the Mozambique Channel. Arctic light rippling through ice floes over the back of the HMS Vengeance as she slipped quietly through the Bering Sea, her pump jet noticed only by a lone bowhead whale. These and a thousand other images scurried into his mind. Places he'd been to, places he hadn't, all connected by the great continuum of the ocean and all suddenly one within him. The boot of a sailor bitten clean through by a reef shark near Chandanpur. A family of five from Minnesota splashing on the Jersey shore, their thin white skin baked red as lobsters. The twisted hulk of the battleship Yamashiro lying shrouded in murky waters at the bottom of the Surigao Strait with all its unspent munitions and the remnants of 1400 souls, letters from home folded neatly in their breast pockets.

Paul surfaced with a fish flapping on the end of the spear, and took a gulp of air. He didn't even remember spearing it. It was like that sometimes when he dove, as if he had plunged into some ancient amniotic fluid, his skin dissolving as he coalesced with the entire living ocean. The visions would stagger through his mind wildly until he surfaced, leaving him gasping, looking around at the endless water, stunned, wondering what had hit him. That was the second reason he wanted off ships, the one that he never mentioned to Danny or anyone else. He swam for shore, the fish in tow at the end of his spear.

-- ..- -- -... .- ..   ..-. .- -.. -.--

It was one of those glorious Pacific sunsets that lights the sky on fire and flashes green as it sinks into an endless and all-consuming sea. Charu and Jean-Pierre strolled back to the aft deck, where they found the other guests chattering excitedly about a gathering darkness on the horizon, a line of black clouds that seemed to rise out of nowhere, stretching as far as the eye could see east to west and boiling like bad chemistry. Lightning sparked cloud to cloud, sending delayed cannonades of thunder across the water, echoes of a distant battle. People in their evening dress watched the spectacle, calmly, oddly thrilled at the performance. They went back to their conversations, indifferent to the gathering storm, a sign not so much of their hubris as their faith. It was, after all, the Mumbai Lady they were riding. Their confident ease turned to nervous laughter as the storm front came hurtling across the ocean, clouds rising furiously into a smoldering sky. Conversations paused as heads turned anxiously to look. When the wind started snatching napkins and loose clothing, Charu and Jean-Pierre led everyone back into the bar. Only the crew remained out in the weather, working quickly to secure any loose gear or still-opened hatches.

Within a half hour the storm front had descended on the ship, bringing gale-force winds that slammed waves against her, washing green over the decks. Charu stood at the window of the bar looking out at the tempest, holding onto the rail with white knuckles as the ship heaved and lurched. Her face reflected dimly in the dark glass and with each bolt of lightning she could see herself flinching, the gold of her sari glimmering momentarily like it was lit from within. She pulled it a little tighter around her shoulders. Behind her everyone else was huddled together around Wang, who was laughing too loudly and waving his champagne glass around like a flag. Two couples walked away and stumbled over towards where Charu was, collapsing into chairs at a nearby table, one of the women pawing through her purse to find her dramamine. Through the leaves of the ficus tree that separated them, Charu could hear their muttering.

I told you. I hate cruises.

God, I know what you mean. I think I'm going to puke.

Wang is such a jerk. Why did we come anyway?

It's not Wang's fault. It's the captain. They've got more radar than NORAD on this thing. Couldn't they see a storm coming and, like, get out of the way or something?

Yeah, that's right.

I want to get off this thing, Charlie.

Get off? Kelly, babe, the next stop is Hawai'i, sweety.

Oh Christ. I think I'm going to puke.

Charu listened and watched the lightning flash through the storm. She imagined herself stepping out onto the deck to the gunwale, one hand clasped on the railing, the other flung into the wind, her hair whipping behind her, and in a baritone that would tremble the hearts of those watching, she proclaimed, Blow, blow thou wild wind. Thou art not so unkind, as man's ingratitude.

Paul was lashing down the teak chairs on the pool deck, when the first mate howled through the wind from the bridge.

Cap'n says to stand by at the lounge. Case we need to abandon ship.

Paul looked at him in disbelief.

Get off the grass, bro!

Just in case, Pauly. Ain't happening but get down there anyway. Cap'n's orders.

Paul gave a mock-salute, finished tying down the furniture and made his way back along the rails, his uniform flapping angrily as he pushed against the wind. He passed outside the window where Charu was standing. She was surprised that someone would still be, could still be, out in that weather, and she gripped the railing tighter. Paul made his way to the aft door of the bar and waited for instructions. Inside he could see the passengers still whooping it up. Wang was in the middle of the crowd, waving his arms like a band leader, keeping the flame alive, laughing the whole thing off.

Waves? What waves? snickering loudly above the moaning wind, fluted glass raised high as he called for more champagne. Then he went on with his story about the island they were headed for.

You're gonna love the Great House. Picture this… heavy mahogany beams, teak furniture, dark and cool in the day, all lit up with candles at night. It's gorgeous. Amazing views of the ocean. And each of you has your own private cabana. You saw the pictures, bamboo ceilings and gauzy drapes flowing in the sea breezes. You know. Real romantic! and he nudged the young couple next to him.

Who likes swimming? he raised his hand like a school teacher. Well there's the cove and two pools, one salt-water and one fresh… and jacuzzis all over the place. Tennis? We got any budding Nadals or Sharapovas on board? There's six courts. No waiting in line. He looked around to judge the effect of his pitch and added, And the bar's opened twenty-four seven, hands thrown in the air for effect, luxuriating in the rousing chorus of hoots and applause that followed.

Jean-Pierre stood nearby, looking calm and collected in his immaculately-cut suit. He knew the game as well as anyone.

Nothing got done without a healthy dose of bravado. Putting up a skyscraper is no small undertaking and he had learned the number one rule of being a high profile architect: exude confidence even when you haven't got a clue. He saw Wang glance at him and when their eyes met he gave him the double thumbs-up and flashed a winning smile.

-- ..- -- -... .- ..   .-.. .- -.. -.--

Jean-Pierre watched Paul walk up the trail from the cove with a brace of fish over his shoulder, strung on a wire he'd stripped out of the base of the wingsail. How'd it work? Jean-Pierre asked about the spear. The spear had worked beautifully, splitting the water unerringly to find its target. Remembering how it had pierced clean through the mahi mahi, a little cloud of blood puffing from the wound into the crystal water, Paul had to admit that Jean-Pierre had done a fantastic job of making the spear.

You're a wanker but a right clever wanker, he said.

Jean-Pierre grinned and popped a thumb. That evening, he would wrap the fish in bundles of pandan leaves and bury them in the coals to bake. Somehow he had ended up as cook. Paul only knew how to make burgers and Mac'n'Cheese. Charu struggled to boil water.

Jean-Pierre was sitting in the shade of the banyan tree, carving out a large pumice bowl with a piece of obsidian. Across from him, lying on its back on a bed of ferns, was a sea turtle Paul had caught a few days before. When the bowl was done, they would slaughter the turtle and make a stew. For the time being, it lay there slowly paddling its feet in the air and mouthing silently. One eye seemed to look straight at Jean-Pierre.

Merde. Don't look at me like that. What can I do about it anyway?

He dug away at the bowl a little more.

Oui, oui, oui, I know. I could do something about it. But I'm not going to, so stop looking at me!

The turtle continued to roll its flippers.

You talking to me, bro? Paul called from where he was washing in the spring pool.

No no. It's nothing.

Next to the turtle sat a basket of clams that Charu had collected from a tidepool. She liked gathering things and there was so much to gather. Clams, shrimp, seaslugs. Seaweed along the rocks, snails on the windward side of the mountain where the trees were mossy from the ocean dew. Eggs from doves and gulls along the mountain ridges. Pandan and coconuts. Food was not a problem.

Once they tried eating a mash of nuts Charu had collected. It turned their mouths red, then black, then numb. An hour later a burning sensation started in the front of their heads, their eyes bulging with amazement at their own illumination, the skin along the edges of their lips crackling like electric nets. It slowly melted their brains into boiling sweet molasses that dripped down their spinal cords, seeping into their hearts and lungs, turning their breath to sweet fire. When it reached the base of their spines, it began to pool and spread an aching, endless desire through their groins. Their eyes twitched as they stripped in front of each other and in the morning they found themselves at the base of the banyan, tangled in a coital pile, exhausted, sticky with coconut oil and fruit juices, flecks of nut mash and blood dotting their matted hair. Then came the blowback, slamming them down with gut wrenching shivers and a searing thirst, their eyes shrinking into pinholes, the day growing dark and filled with horrid, ghostly shapes, the branches of the old banyan morphing into bony, twisted necromancers who moaned long tales of death at sea and the shame of humanity in voices that sounded like the wind. They never touched those nuts again.

-- ..- -- -... .- ..   .-.. .- -.. -.--

Wang was up on his chair, regaling his guests with a description of the perfect white sand cove on the south side of the island, when a rogue wave rose off the port beam. Through the window, Charu watched it lift and curl, bent by the gale into a claw-shaped arc that towered over the Mumbai Lady. Lightning burst in triple succession and the wave turned momentarily transparent, a frozen curl of deep-green glass. For just the instant it was lit, Charu saw something huge within the wave. It appeared for only an instant – a mashup of metal cylinders, grilles and pipes pressed into a huge block like some gargantuan hammer. She couldn't have known that it was a 75-ton industrial gas analyzer that had been washed off the deck of a cargo freighter in a similar storm years before. That it had been bobbing around the central Pacific ever since, its empty air tanks keeping it afloat, traveling the circular currents with a billion other pieces of wreckage, discarded plastic, and packing foam. She saw it just briefly, just a flash in the lightning strike, tumbling ominously inside the wave as it hurtled toward the ship, and she whispered, Mjölnir, as if she knew its name. The last thought that passed through her brain was, It's Thursday.

When the analyzer struck the Mumbai Lady the shock

punched out every piece of glass on the port side and buckled the hull. Above the shattering glass and screaming passengers an audible gasp could be heard followed by a long, drawn-out metallic groan, an anguished cry that sounded more sentient than just bending titanium. Hairline fissures shot out across the hull like thin ice cracking under a heavy boot. The once semi-porous skin of the Mumbai Lady became fully porous, spraying seawater into the cabins and passageways and down the stairwells to the engine room. A minute and a half later the order to abandon ship was given, sending the passengers scrambling for the life pods. They ran and pushed, their sweat rich with the odor of fear, having finally arrived at a reasonable mental attitude for people floating somewhere 1,000 miles from the nearest land. There weren't enough places for all the passengers and crew in the pods – no one had ever expected to use them – but in the end, they never had to hash that out.

Charu had been thrown to the floor of the bar by the impact of the hammer wave. She struggled to her feet, wind lashing through the missing windows. The room was dark. What little light the emergency lamps threw showed a bent and broken world, pitching sickeningly. Seawater flooded across the deck. By the time she found her footing, everyone was already out of the room struggling desperately aft toward the life-pods. She saw them moving down the lurching deck and tried to follow. Jean-Pierre was with them. He got halfway aft, then looked quickly back to the bar. Merde! he spat, slapping the wall next to him. In his mind was his computer sitting on the bar in its leather case. Months of work. All his ideas for several revolutionarily new buildings. He hesitated, then ran back to get it. Charu saw him coming up the deck as she struggled to stay upright. Paul staggered by with an armful of life preservers. The wind howled, the deck lurched, sending the three careening into each other, slamming up against the central wingsail. The ship heaved, the gale caught the underside of the sail, and tore it free of its moorings. Eighty feet of carbon-fiber ripped from the deck like a cardboard box top. As the knuckle-joint tore from the deck it stripped out 50 yards of control and structural cabling from below, a wild mane of wires that sparked and shrieked as they slipped from their sheathings. Charu clutched onto the two men at the sound. The sail tumbled upward in the wind, the wires attached to its base spinning and snatching at everything in sight. Caught in the whirling mess, Charu, Paul and Jean-Pierre were reeled in against the wingsail and flew off the ship as one. In that same instant, the hull tore in half and the Mumbai Lady disappeared into the waves with all hands. The wingsail looped up through the air a hundred yards, whump whump whumping like a helicopter blade, before it landed with a dull smack on the water. For the three unintentional passengers, there was the cutting pain of the cables, the brain-stunning whirl through the air, and the sudden impact on the sea. Then nothing.

-- ..- -- -... .- .. .-.. .- -.. -.--

Charu found Jean-Pierre and Paul down at the cove, looking at the wingsail where it lay by the pandans. The shadows of the leaves on the white sail were filled with the hollow blue of the sky. From one end of the sail, multi-colored cables spilled out onto the sand. She could tell that Jean-Pierre wasn't looking at the colors, he was measuring the sail in his mind, making a mental list of available materials. He pulled up on one end.

She's so light, he noted with interest. He pushed on the sail with his hand to test the resiliency, poked it, tapped it. It resonated with a low drum beat. He started looking around at the knuckle, sorting through the cables, pulling off the loose ones, handing them to Paul to be coiled individually and stacked for future use. He bent down and peered into the knuckle. The metal brackets that had held it to the deck of the Mumbai Lady stuck out at odd angles, some still holding the bolts that had been stripped out of the ship. He tapped on a bracket.

Aluminum? asked Charu.

Titanium, said Jean-Pierre spinning around on his knees. Where did you come from, eh? I thought you were walking?

I am walking. Here. On the beach. What're you doing, anyway?

Jean-Pierre tapped on the brackets, If we can get these off, maybe, I dunno, maybe I make machetes.

Sweet-as, bro, said Paul.

Paul nodded at Charu, Pretty awesome, what?

Then turned back to Jean-Pierre, But how the hell we going to do that, bro?

First we got to get these off. Then I'll show you.

Paul slipped his Gerber out of the leather holster on his belt, and kneeled down to help.

I am so friggin' happy Danny made us wear these, he said to Jean-Pierre, waving the tool in front of him. I was like, no way man, I'm not wearing no lame multi-tool, but Danny-boy said, wear it or walk, so – he waved the tool again – here it is.

He crouched next to Jean-Pierre and the two got to work loosening the bolts. Charu stood there, arms crossed over her chest, biting her lip, watching the backs of the men as they worked. They were beating on the end of the sail, trying to get the brackets off, and the sail rumbled like a war drum. Her face slowly dissolved from concern to panic as she realized that Cain and Able were weaponizing.

Alternately pulling and pounding, they managed to muscle off the brackets. A few days later Jean-Pierre led them to the end of the cove where he had fashioned a forge out of stones. Next to it sat a large pile of driftwood and forest brush. Using sticks and vines and leaves, he had also made a large funnel, the small end of which pointed into the forge with the wide end open toward the ocean. Jean-Pierre wet his finger and held it into the air.

What do you think Paul. Wind coming?

Sun's low, maybe five six o'clock. Another hour there'll be a land breeze, but – he swiveled his head to look – wrong direction. It won't go in your funnel. Tomorrow morning, though. Sea breeze'll be up, all right. Six, seven in the morning.

Magnifique. OK. Tomorrow.

Paul lifted his palm and Charu watched them slap a high-five, giddy as frat boys at a party. She followed them back up to camp and watched them out of the corner of her eye all that evening as they worked on making a heavy hammer out of a potato-shaped rock, splitting the end of a pandan branch and lashing it to the rock with wet vines, then drying it over the fire to tighten the grip. They were joking with each other and butting shoulders. Charu wasn't amused.

She slept badly, dreaming they were on the beach, a steady wind rushing across the lagoon down the funnel into the fire which glowed white hot in the forge with a constant sucking sound. Paul was feeding sticks in from the side, that burst into flames as he put them in. His shirt was off and he was sweating heavily. The brackets in the fire were already glowing pale orange with the heat. Jean-Pierre held onto one with a set of over-sized pliers made of sticks. Leaning into their work, their faces were hard with the intensity of soldiers, the fires of imminent destruction crackling in their eyes. Paul was pounding on the metal bar with the stone hammer to shape its edge, sending a shower of sparks scattering into the night each time he struck. Charu had something to say, a line from one of the tragedies, but she couldn't get it out. She was digging her feet in the sand getting ready to deliver her soliloquy, but she just couldn't remember it. How does it start? she thought, increasingly frustrated. Jean-Pierre turned the still glowing blade over, studying the shape. He hefted it a few times to feel its weight, Paul looked up at him from where he squatted near the anvil stone. Charu was getting more agitated. She had to say her line but just couldn't remember it. Jean-Pierre looked down at Paul. Charu saw the disdain in his face. She had to speak her line. This was her part, the moment she should step in to save them from themselves. It was all falling apart. Why can't I remember the words, damn it, dogs, havoc, what is it? She had to stop them. Jean-Pierre rolled his shoulders and swung the blade over his head in a long circle like he was going to split wood. Charu remembered and screamed, her arms thrust out wide. Cry Havoc! and let slip the dogs of war… but it was spoken too late. The blade whistled, sparking as it arced through the night air, and cleaved straight down through the back of Paul's head, sinking to his eyes. He jerked once, his mouth gaping, and fell forward onto the sand, the hot blade hissing and spitting boiled blood. Jean-Pierre whirled around to stare at Charu, a long, hard look that spiraled far back into antiquity, speaking of pillage and possession, then turned back and started butchering the body. Charu woke, wet with sweat, seasick, the echo of her own terrified voice still in her ears.

-- ..- -- -... .- .. .-.. .- -.. -.--

The sun rose on the morning after the annihilation of the Mumbai Lady. It found the wingsail floating on calm seas, an eighty-foot mother-of-pearl surfboard, with hundreds of colored cables wound around one end. Inside the tangle, Charu, Jean-Pierre and Paul were lashed down like Ahab to Moby Dick. They lay perfectly still, battered and in shock, their minds emptied of all thought and filled with the immensity of the sea. All they could see was the nearby surface. If a large wave passed beneath them, the sail rose to the point where they could see the horizon, briefly. Frightened by the sudden motion, they would grab at the cables that held them and make quick sideways glances at each other for reassurance. Then the sail would slide back to where there was nothing but the close, restless contours of the sea. This repeated, endlessly, through the day. Occasionally something would scrape hungrily against the bottom of the sail and they would pull their hands and feet in reflexively, breaths held while they listened. The sun beat down on them and by noon an ugly thirst had begun to curl inside their throats. They licked at it and bit on their cheeks to draw some spit but it would not be appeased. The first day passed that way, heaving on the surface of eternity, the sea threatening to swallow them at any moment. They spoke little if at all, each one's mind reaching out to some distant place or distant person they wished were closer, revolving around the repeated mantra, Is this how it ends?

Jeanne-Pierre had lost one of his shoes and most of his bravado. He seemed on the verge of crying, his face turned away from the others. Everything was so distant. His office in Singapore, the half-built projects he was supposed to be visiting, those on the drawing boards his staff was working on, an upcoming lecture tour, a meeting with Japan's minister of culture about a new museum scheduled for the following week. It all seemed so tinny and far away, like a toy model of his life he had played with once, long ago when he was a child. His ear pressed against the sail, he listened to the sound of his finger tapping on the surface and, despite himself, being fully aware of how ridiculous the thought was given the circumstances, he mused about redesigning the camber struts. Charu had her sari pulled over her head to protect herself from the beating sun. She thought of home in Mumbai, of where Damini might be and what she'd think when she heard of Charu's tragic end, of her mother who would be so disappointed at the sudden end to her monthly stipend. She thought only for a moment about her apartment in Kuala Lumpur with its marble foyer, walk-in closet, 360 degree view of the city, and staff quarters. That was all behind her now. She let it go. Through a gap in the cloth, she looked surreptitiously at the men on either side of her, debating to herself, which was the better bet. In the end she decided neither. She was on her own at last. She stretched her head up to look out over the expanse of ocean that surrounded them and said as firmly as she could, speaking to the very back of the crowd, Now would I give a thousand furlongs of sea for an acre of barren ground

She laid her head back down, laughing at her own pretensions. Her shallow need to quote the classics. Paul twisted around inside the cables until he faced up to the sky. He had always known he might die at sea and snickered because he had just made up his mind to give up sailing. In a month, he thought, he should have been hanging on the Bay of Plenty, eating kiwifruits and getting laid. That ain't gonna happen, he thought.

The sheer size of the sail gave it stability in the water. Smaller waves would lap against its sides like surf against a dock, splashing over the surface but not moving it. With larger swells, the end of the sail would lift and the surface would warp and twist as the wave passed underneath, one end falling as the other rose. This repeated all day, in endless yogic undulations. It could be comforting. It could be terrifying. In time the rolling and slapping became so commonplace as to be unnoticed. They lived within the motion, becoming flexible and sinuous, hollowed out and filled with nothing but waves.

Lost in that wave-induced trance, their minds would skip across the immensity of the ocean, flying over the hammered surface in all directions at once, or spiraling outward from the center like a blind man searching for a dropped coin in an endless field of grass, probing further and further outward as if, by doing so, they might stumble across some imaginary place and, just by thinking it, make it be. At other times, there was nothing but the sky. Empty, empty sky. Even when it held a rack of clouds, or the infinite colors of the sunset, or so many stars that counting them led only to hysterical laughter and bewilderment, the sky was empty. Not a bird, not a bug, not a single petal from a windblown flower. Not a scent other than salt. They would lie on their backs, the cables stretched across their chests their only bed sheets, and fall upwards into the void. At night, they would stare at the star-stippled blackness and be crushed by their own insignificance and the certainty of their abandonment.

And then there were times when their minds filled with the depth of the sea. If they let themselves wander there, they were soon lost, their souls sliced from them, sinking helplessly down to where the water first lost its light, then its heat, then further still into the lifeless gloom, unable to stop their descent, until they reached the silt-coated mountains that lay at the bottom, deep valleys layered with the alluvium of millions of years. In the place of vegetation, those dark mountains were covered with the remnants of what once had lived and moved through the world. Plankton and krill. The bones of fishes and whales. Fragmented hulls of countless ships and all the hapless sailors who had walked their decks on their final journeys.

-- ..- -- -... .- ..   .-.. .- -.. -.--

Their evening meal of roast mahi-mahi and turtle soup finished, the carefree islanders washed up in the third pool, cleaning themselves of the grease and ash from the fire. Then they slipped into the middle pool to wash the salt from their bodies and their clothes, splashing water over each other like children. Jean-Pierre brought over a shell filled with coconut oil and dabbed it on Charu's burnt skin, her shoulders and the places around her lips and eyes that were split and dry. Then she took the shell and did the same for him, and he for Paul, until they were all tended, each wincing at the touches but happy for the attention. They lay down around the firepit under the banyan and watched the light ripple on the bottoms of the heavy branches. After a while Charu got up, half-squatted into a pose to begin her odissi, and cupped her hands in front of her in supplication. She tapped the ball of her right foot hard against the ground and slowly took one step forward, then again with the other foot, her hips swaying gently with the motion, head and shoulders rolling, eyes closing and popping open to look at Paul and Jean-Pierre every few steps. This was the bhumi pranam by which she begged forgiveness of mother earth for stamping on her, and she wondered if there was such a prayer for the father of the oceans for stamping in his waters. Her hands extended outward and swung slowly in front of her to press into prayer as her eyes rolled heavenward. The firelight shimmered through the banyan leaves, illuminating Jean-Pierre's nests. Hands pressed in prayer, her eyes fell slowly back to look at the ground as she sank in a low squat, opened her palms and touched the earth lightly, passing them over the sandy surface in a light caress. Then she lifted her hands to her head as if scooping water from a pool, pouring that invisible liquid over her face and hair in blessing. As she rose, facing the men where they lay by the fire, she curved one leg backward, pelvis spreading, spine bending, eyes smiling, little peeks of her body showing through her torn sari.

Paul rose first; Jean-Pierre followed just behind. They began in imitation, touching lightly to the ground, palms gliding over it caressingly, and lifting their cupped hands to their faces to cleanse themselves. Then they began to dance in slow contortions around each other, weaving in and out of the firelight and the forest shadows, disappearing behind the massive trunk of the banyan and reappearing from the ferns on the other side, coming into the light and heading back into darkness, holding close to the ground, then lifting their arms lightly to heaven. Pressing their bodies close together as one, then peeling off to wander the circle alone. The ground felt like it was swaying, waves rolling beneath it to lift and bend the surface. They danced until they grew tired and the fire burned down to coals, then ash, and they were surrounded by a darkness without measure in which there was no more banyan, and no more island, and no ocean or distant lands or stars above. Only each other's closefelt heartbeats as they drifted off to sleep.

-- ..- -- -... .- .. .-.. .- -.. -.--

The sun rose from a liquid horizon, twinning itself in the mirror surface of the sea. Just dawn and already searing. Paul worked his way out of the cables and stood up cautiously on the sail. Legs spread for balance, hands out touching the air, he turned around in a circle scanning the horizon in all directions. There was nothing. His shoulders rolled as his head sank. He blinked shyly at Charu who he saw was watching him. His tongue dragged across split lips. He started turning once more then stopped, staring at one spot on the horizon. Jean-Pierre and Charu watched him blearily, heads still resting on the sail, unable to muster the energy to ask what he was doing. Paul raised his hand to shield his eyes, crimped them shut and open again, and looked back at the horizon. He coughed and sputtered dryly, words failing to leave his throat.

Take a… look a'… this mates.

He looked back at Jean-Pierre and Charu still tangled in

their cable webs and pointed at them weakly then out toward the horizon. Jean-Pierre wriggled out of the cables and crawled over to help Charu. They locked arms and helped each other stand, unsteady on the shifting sail. Holding on to each other, they shuffled over to where Paul was and looked in the direction he was pointing. They stared and stared, desperately wanting to see something, but there was nothing but water.

Right there! Paul said jabbing his finger at the horizon, but no amount of squinting and shadowing their eyes with their hands could make them see what he saw.

Land, guys. Right there. Can't you see it?

Land? came the joint reply.

An island. There's an island for chris'sake.

Jean-Pierre had his arm around Charu's waist. She had her arm around his neck. They held each other as steadily as they could and looked out into the great expanse of their new world but there was nothing there for them.

Trust me, Paul said softly. Just trust me, OK? He pointed upward and breathed. I saw frigate birds, then jabbed his finger again at the horizon. Look. Right there. An island!

Charu and Jean-Pierre sat down and tucked their feet under the cabling. They spent the rest of the day standing and sitting in turns, trying to see what Paul had seen. Jean-Pierre smiled thinking he knew a good bluff when he saw one. Exude confidence even when you haven't got a clue. People love that. They need it. Charu stood next to Paul and followed the muscular line of his arm to the spot on the horizon it pointed toward, thinking, Yeah, yeah, OK. A little speck of green. Yeah, maybe I see it.

Evening fell and a heavy mist lowered over the ocean. The next day, all the world was white.

-- ..- -- -... .- ..   .-.. .- -.. -.--

The dawn was oddly cool, shrouded in a heavy seaborn mist. Paul, Charu and Jean-Pierre woke in their separate niches in the banyan tree, curled into the spherical rooms like mice in their nests. They climbed down from the great tree slowly, walking as if still asleep to the spring pool. They were naked, their clothes having fallen to rags or been salvaged for some other purpose, even Charu's bangles had been scavenged to be hammered into hinges and clasps. They slipped into the water to rouse themselves. It was warmer than the air and they floated next to each other, each feeling that they were drifting on an endless ocean. They looked at each other across the water.

Are you hungry?

No, not really. Not anymore. Are you?

No.

There's plenty of food.

They all chuckled at this, dryly.

Then come with me. I have something to show you.

Charu led them out of the pool, beneath the overhanging branches of the banyan tree and through the grove of pandans, away from the cove, up along the path that she took to the mountain. They followed in single file, walking quietly and slowly, in no hurry to get anywhere, looking at all the little things she pointed out along the way. She showed them where a spider had built a webbed nest on a mossy rock. A flower the size of a plate growing low to the ground, and another smaller than a fingernail that sprouted from among the ferns on the side of an old tree. A snail tracking across a leaf as flat and broad as an elephant's ear. They leaned in to look at the snail, a tiny white squeeze of spiraled shell with two brown antenna probing the air in front of it, as it slipped across the dewy surface of its world. They watched the snail like children, their heads bowed in close to the leaf, foreheads almost touching, eyes wide with wonder.

They drifted for some time separately, moving up the mountain on paths of their own choosing, each lost in their memories and revelations. If their paths brought them close enough, they would stare at each other through the leaves, amazed, as if seeing another person for the first time. Unimpressed by their nakedness, with no shame or urgency, they would circle each other, walking through the dappled leaf-light, appearing and disappearing behind clumps of tall grasses.

Somewhere along the steep path up the mountain, they gathered and moved together, rising upwards as one, feeling the rock and soil beneath their feet, the sea breeze pushing at their backs, urging them on. The going was slow, but not uncomfortable, somehow freeing. Almost euphoric. Just as they reached the summit, the mist was swept away by a fresh ocean wind and the world was revealed once more. The ocean was calm, suggesting a quiet nobility. Broad shouldered, compassionate, limitless in understanding. To the east, the sun sent flashes of pale fire glinting across the surface to greet them. To the west the water was still dark, still waiting to be woken. They stood at the summit, on top of the highest perch and looked out into the distance turning slowly, backs to one another. They saw everything they knew, and everything they had forgotten. All the things they longed for, and those they would no longer need. All the places they had been to, and those to which they would never go again.

A
SIMPLER
LIFE

A Simpler Life

The search began with two young people, a man and a woman, who worked at the headquarters of an international software development firm. She in strategic planning and he in human resources. The company was based in a major coastal city, and cities are by nature complex places. Human nature, human complexity – architecture, machines, products, information, food, art, music, religion, and all the rest. For these two people, the city was nothing short of intoxicating. Limitless. Never were they bored.

The headquarters was in a sleek new building on the waterfront, a collocation of brushed-metal sine waves that looked like some kind of interstellar spaceship had inexplicably docked among the brick warehouses of a past era. The entry lobby of the building was an open, three-story atrium. In the center sat a model of the Earth, a large globe, somewhat taller than even a tall person. The surface of the globe was made out of a flexible LED matrix, like a spherical TV screen, that displayed real-time information from an array of geo-stationary satellites monitoring the surface of the planet. Looking at the globe was like seeing the Earth from the international space station in real time. The side that faced the sun was bright, the other side dark. As lights came on in the evening in cities around the world, tiny points glowed on the dark side of the globe. In winter the northern hemisphere turned white, shifting to green again in the spring. When real clouds moved across real continents and oceans, their images moved across the model globe identically. Only smaller. Without the rain. Standing next to the globe, a person could reach out and touch the earth like Zeus reaching down from Olympus.

The couple bumped into each other for the first time right there, in front of the globe. The sun was rising over France, the Atlantic still an endless dark sea. He tripped, she caught him. He blushed, she joked. He found her stunning, she thought the same. Trying to sound casual, to say something, anything, she pointed at the globe and chirped, If you look closely you can see the lights of super-tankers. They leaned in to look, their heads close enough to smell each other's hair. They breathed and smiled, shyly, searching for invisible ships in between furtive sideways glances. Meeting by the globe became "their thing."

Two days later, they said good morning in front of a polar storm whitening Tierra del Fuego. He offered her his hot coffee when she shivered. The next week, they chatted as a Category 5 typhoon blotted out the Pacific from the Philippines to Japan, spiraling behind them like a huge swirl of cotton-candy, the beautiful white cloud obscuring the utter devastation beneath it. They made plans for dinner and a movie over the weekend. He pointed to the crisp black dot in the eye of the storm and blurted, People fly into those things. On purpose! Can you believe it?

On the following Monday, they met on the dark side of the Earth, the shape of Africa defined subtly by a stippling of lights marking coastal cities. A soft halo of sunlight pushed around the horizon from the opposite side. She gave him a peck on the cheek and whispered, My place again tonight? Lightning flashed silently across the Serengeti.

They took their jobs seriously, rushing all day to stay on schedule, then playing hard at night, clubbing or going to concerts or the latest gallery openings. This went on for a year, the two of them pushing themselves, enjoying life to the fullest, unaware that the pace of their wired lives was taking its toll. One day while sitting in a cafe with their iPads on the table, simultaneously finishing spreadsheets for the office, updating Facebook pages, texting friends and chatting on their cell phones, they caught each other's eyes. In one of those sudden epiphanies that changes one's life forever, they knew that this could not go on. They unplugged, shut down, and spent the rest of the day talking it over.

What on earth are we doing? Why am I jonesing for the newest iPhone, I mean who the fuck cares?

Yeah, I know. I know. Like, we're going crazy staying in touch with people just so we won't be left out.

In the end, they realized they were just skimming the surface. That nothing they did seemed to have any deeper meaning or inherent value. Within the month, they had sold their apartment and moved to the country in search of a simpler life.

They were thrilled with their decision. They still commuted to work at the same company in the city, but the evenings were theirs to enjoy. They sat in the dark by candlelight on the stone terrace in their backyard. On weekends they went for long walks in the woods, stopped in at the local farmer's market, baked their own bread. Copper pots hung in clusters from racks over their huge stove. They cooked up storms. When it grew cold outside, they sat by the fireplace with hot toddies. They read books. Did absolutely nothing for hours at a time. The slower life allowed them to recharge, to recenter themselves, and they found they went to work refreshed and more focused. Life at work in the city still tended to burn them out by the end of the week, but they felt they'd struck a balance between the two worlds. This went on for a year until one day, while at their local CSA picking up their share of late summer greens, they happened to see a couple from the farm unloading bushels of corn from their truck. They knew then and there what they were missing. Working in the city each day, only spending evenings and weekends in the country, they were not really part of the rural community. It was like they were guests at a feast, snarking only the best stuff from the table but doing nothing to contribute to the meal itself. They quit their jobs at the software company, sold their lovely home, and bought a share of a communal farm further upstate. They moved in with a group of young, energetic people who were raising produce for the same CSA that they had once been members of.

The change was not easy. Their hands blistered, the skin on their arms and face burnt until it cracked. For the first few months, at the end of each day, their muscles were so sore that they just sat on the edge of their bed and cried, wondering if they would be able to go back out to the fields the next day. There was more than one moment when they felt like packing it all in and heading back to the city. But, as the seeds they had planted sprouted and grew, as they harvested the crops that they had tended, as they delivered that food to customers who reveled at the beautiful arrangements of peppers, squash, spinach, and chard, they found in themselves a new energy. An energy unaided by the copious mugs of java that had fueled them in the city. Every full-moon, when the CSA members gathered for grand parties in the big barn, they would dance until drenched, watching each other, slim and strong, suntanned and wind-burnt, and break into smiles. They would walk outside for some fresh air, stand side by side in the fields, moonlight falling over the crops, the deep pungent smell of compost and soil mixing with their own sweat, and feel more alive than they had imagined possible.

Living this way, they thought more about their place in the world, as humans, as individuals, about what a miracle life is. Had they never had time to think about those things before? Or the inclination? It seemed like in the city, despite being massively interconnected, tapped into databases and information networks, they had never concerned themselves with this most basic of thoughts – contemplating the wonder of the world. The long talks they had about this brought them to a conclusion that surprised even themselves. Despite the idyllic quality of life on the farm and the joy of being part of a tight community, when it came right down to it they felt that they were still a part the global economy. A very small part but just as dependent as everyone else on petroleum and cars and cell phones and every other piece of modern technology and, through those things, to the resource wars and rampant pollution that plagued the world. In a quick, bold decision, they gave away their shares in the farm and moved deep into the country.

They lived completely off the grid. Zero footprint. Nothing coming in. Nothing going out. They raised what they needed, traded some things with a few other homesteading families who lived in the hills near their camp. Their house was part log, part cob – a simple structure made of materials that had been gathered within a hundred yards of where it stood. Wood from the forest, grass from the meadow, mud from the river. They had a small vegetable patch, just big enough for what they needed. They hunted game and fished. Gathered acorns, mushrooms, and berries from the woods.

If life on the farm had seemed hard at first, it was luxurious compared to what they had chosen this time. Anything they wanted they had to make themselves. Anything that needed doing they had to do themselves. The smallest project might take a day or a week to accomplish. Life was simple all right. No machines, no power, no communication beyond themselves, no change of clothes, no sugar, no salt, no butter, no oil, no caffeine, no alcohol. Over the first few months, the unmitigated frugality of their chosen life bore down on them and there were many times when they dreamed of the little comforts they had back on the farm. Some hot, buttered bread. A soft place to lie down.

In time, though, they found their stride. They figured out how to take care of the basic things like food and shelter, and they found themselves awash in the beauty of the world with nothing but time to enjoy it. At night they would listen to the music of the river, the quiet rustling of wind in the pines, and watch the moon trace slowly across a night sky so heavy with stars it looked solid. A fox might trot across the meadow, silverbacked in the moonlight, or a herd of deer would appear hesitantly from the woods, walking silently, their heads rising and falling in constant vigilance. The couple would see this and feel deep within themselves an immediate connection to the world they lived in, and know they were where they were supposed to be.

They lived that way for two years and then one spring, as they began to lay in their crops for the year, just as they were spading the ground and building up the furrows, a thought occurred to them. Agriculture. That simple and most basic thing that was the mainstay of their existence was in fact not a basic and simple thing at all, not original to the human condition but a recent development. In fact, nothing had reshaped the planet more, for better or worse, than agriculture. Forests obliterated, grasslands plowed under, entire ecosystems erased so that humans could grow their food. In its total impact on the planet, agriculture was a technology far more aggressive than, and as singularly human as, nuclear energy. They decided to leave behind agriculture entirely and go back to the forest. Hunting and gathering is all they would need.

They left the cabin and the half-tilled vegetable patch just like that, and walked into the forest with only a knife, a hatchet, a home-made bow and some arrows, some rope and a cloth bag for collecting things. Over the course of the spring and the following summer they made a shelter in a cave, closing off the entrance with a wall of woven branches. They made a few simple bowls and cups from clay dug in the stream that they baked in the coals of their fire. They killed and field-dressed their game – deer, fox, possum, rabbits – and from the pelts made rudimentary clothes: a cape and a loincloth for each of them, and moccasins for when it got cold. They developed in their minds mental maps of the landscape. A pool along the river where fish were known to linger. A spring of fresh water running between grey boulders on the side of a hill. A patch of blackberries in a grove of paper-birch. Burdock, dandelion and sorrel in the upper meadow. A stand of oaks for acorns below that. Jerusalem artichoke on the river banks. Forest trails along which they could reliably hunt or trap game. They roamed in long, irregular circuits through these and hundreds of other places, their lives spent in constant motion. Their senses on constant alert. Not in fear. Certainly, there were coyotes and bears, the occasional cougar, but that was not the reason for their alertness. It was because the secrets of the land were revealed in its minutia, and staying alive meant being sensitive to even the slightest thing. Forced to be hyper-aware, in time they found themselves conscious of the voice and moods of the place where they lived as if it were there own bodies.

It was a meager life. If they had had little in their log cabin, now they had even less. Their hair was matted into thick dreadlocks. When it got too long they simply chopped it off with the knife. Without a razor, they both grew hairy. Their skin, sunburnt and coarse, was covered with hundreds of small scratches from crashing through brush and bramble in pursuit of game. The thorns and twigs that slid off the fur of the animals they chased left bloody cuts on them. Soon, they no longer looked human, and they no longer thought of themselves that way. Not the human of the city, at least, or the human of the town, or of the farm. They had transformed back into the human of the forest, which was not so different from any other animal that lived out there. They felt themselves returning to the very roots of human existence, utterly purged of the trappings of their former lives.

One day as they hunted, the man was struck by the thought that the steel in the knife and hatchet he carried was a crystallization of thousands of years of technological development. In the million-year arc of human existence, those tools were almost as recent as an iPad. Feeling that they were the last remnants of their 'civilized' past, he threw them off a cliff, an impulsive act they both admired, then regretted in the months to follow. The blades had been infinitely more useful than an iPad. With those gone, there was nothing in their lives that did not come from the land and had not been taken by their own hands. In the summer they shed their fur cloaks and roamed the forest naked. In the winter they half-hibernated, sleeping under piles of dry leaves and living off stored nuts and smoked fish.

The next spring, as they were roaming the edges of the meadows in search of new shoots, discussing where they should go next to forage, they realized together, as if their minds were now one, that they had missed something. A part of their former civilized life they had not eliminated. Something that was so pervasive they hadn't even noticed it. Language. It was, after all, the advent of language in ancient times that had allowed for the avalanche of technologies to develop that would separate humans from the natural world. If they were to find their way back to a place within nature, as a truly integral part of the world around them, they would need to shed language, too. They looked each other hard, eye to eye, wondering if they could do it. They spent two days speaking about anything they could think of, veritable torrents of words, some of deep meaning, others just wild ramblings, and then on the morning of the third day, they fell silent, never to speak again. There were times when they regretted it, when they ached to say something. They would look at each other, straining not to speak, tears welling in their eyes. It took a year, but over that time they fell into a pattern of simple gestures, grunts and whistles. What they could not express that way they knew was not worth expressing.

It was late spring and they were smoking fish over a fire in their cave. They caught each other looking at the smoke and, without a word spoken, they knew they had found yet another thing they had forgotten to shed. Fire. The most powerful of the ancient tools. They agreed through hand signs to do without. No cooking or smoking food. No heat for the cave. With that single act they purged themselves absolutely and totally of all remnants of humanity, and thus began their summer of bliss.

Naked, there was nothing between their bodies and the world they lived in. Nothing between themselves. They knew each other as they wished, in mutual comfort and desire.

Wordless, the many other sounds of the world around them flowed into their minds, filling the vast regions of thought that had previously been occupied with their own voices.

Without tools or technology, they found themselves at one with the world, touching it and being touched by it, taking from it only what they needed, leaving no more trace of their passage than a fox or an eagle.

Each day was pure rapture, their minds, their very souls alive with all things great and small around them. The sweep of cloud fronts across the sky. The gentle rising of fish to the surface of still water. A fingernail-sized mushroom growing beneath the trunk of a fallen tree. Each of these clear and present in their minds. As autumn set in, however, they found it harder and harder to find enough food. The nights grew cold and they buried themselves in huge piles of fallen leaves that they had stashed in their cave like squirrels. When the first snows fell, their stores of food exhausted and the insulation of the leaves insufficient, they began to freeze. Shivering, they decided to backtrack the process of shedding civilization. They looked for the buckskin clothes they had made but found that, over the summer, small animals and insects had gotten into them and eaten so many holes through them that they fell apart when they tried to lift them. They tried to light a fire but their hands were too stiff and clumsy from the cold. They could not spin the fire-sticks fast enough to make a flame. Weak and numb, as a last ditch effort, they decided to walk through the forest to their old log cabin where they thought they might still have a few matches left. They set out in a heavy snowstorm but they never made it. A day later, they were found by a group of snowmobilers – naked, hip deep in a drift, arms locked around each other, motionless.

Half a year later, released from the hospital and back in the city, they wrote their story down and it became an instant bestseller. They spent a year touring on the lecture circuit. The film adaptation is scheduled for release this summer. They are in discussions with a major toy company about a pair of action figures designed in their image, part of a whole line of survivalist products that are in the planning. Money grows on trees. They bought one of the brick warehouses on the waterfront near their old company, gutted it and put in huge plate-glass windows overlooking the river. If you're in that part of the city, you may chance upon them in one of the local coffee shops. You'll know them when you see them. A well-dressed couple, always in black, with shaved heads, their skin completely covered with hatch-marked scars, a finger or two missing from frostbite. They'll be grunting and whistling to each other in their own language over lattes as they gnaw on baguette sandwiches like raw bones, their eyes bright and alive with ancient songs.

Only after having come back to the city did they realize that there was one last thing that they had not shed. After having given up everything in their pursuit of a true, natural state of being, they had, in the end, not parted with one thing. The absolute, final remnant of their human condition. Each other.

It is said that one room in the attic of their warehouse is filled with dry leaves that they have shipped in from a place deep in the country where the air is clear and the forlorn cries of owls and coyotes still pierce the quiet of the night, and that they sleep each night cocooned within those leaves, naked, nestled together, entwined in fetal positions like yet-to-be-born twins.

41718770R00160

Made in the USA
Charleston, SC
06 May 2015